My Sprig of Lilacs

a novel

Greta Sharkey

Lamberson Corona Press

DEDICATION

This book is dedicated to firefighters and other first responders, and to all the healers who put the people and lives of others back together in times of trauma and disaster.

CHAPTER 1

The rabbi stood on the altar, just to the right of the crucifix. His silvery-white beard framed his tan and aging face. He wore a black suit, a whiter-than-white shirt, and a plain black tie fitting the occasion. His expression was somber, but dignified, despite the past painful days. A Catholic priest from this parish stood beside him at the center of the altar. Chosen to officiate at the service, he too, bore a countenance of solemnity as he looked down the center aisle of the large church over his small silver-rimmed glasses. Dressed in white vestments, he appeared to be a few years younger than the rabbi, though both were regarded as father figures in the small community. The pastor of the Methodist church stood to the left of the priest. A younger man, with salt and pepper hair that was cut a bit longer, he wore black clerical attire with the customary white collar. He joined the others in mournful dignity, hoping no one would notice the small tear slowly expanding in his right eye. All three clergymen had been chaplains in the fire department, which made this both a professional, yet very personal duty.

Other members of the clergy were present too, some on the sides of the altar and others mixed in with the congregation in the side pews. They were there to represent the many denominations of Waterview, this saddened community that had come together this day to mourn, to comfort and to be comforted.

The sunlight seeped in through the stained glass windows, with scenes depicting suffering and triumph, as it met the subdued lighting inside the church, creating strange shapes on the dark wood, while nearby statues of The Blessed Virgin and St. Joseph offered their condolences with sad and all-too-knowing smiles. The candles on both sides of the church between the altar and the two side exits flickered inside their dark red containers, giving off a warm, musty smell.

The organ played and a soprano with a sweet velvety voice sang, *Come back to me with all your heart. Don't let fear keep us apart...* while everyone's eyes were fixed on the steady and slow movement of the long line of men filing down the center aisle in their dark uniforms, their white hats held at just the right position by their sides. Strong and brave men with tears in their eyes moved forward as the music reverberated inside the church. It was heard in a slightly different way through the outside speakers that carried it where more people had gathered to watch the procession of firemen, as they marched to the slow, relentless drumbeats that cut through the otherwise silent air. It was cool and damp. A mother reached down to button her toddler's jacket while trying ot to miss a second of the procession. The sky was strewn with smoke-like clouds that seemed to move with the same mournful cadence coming from the drums below. The flags drooped at half-staff as far as the eye could see.

The funeral procession was made up of firefighters who had come from all over the state to pay their respects, realizing all too well that when one fireman dies in the line of duty, they all die a little, maybe more than a little. In this case it was two. Two fire engines slowly rolled toward the church, each bearing the coffin of a hero, each a husband, a son, a brother, and a neighbor. One was a father-to-be, or rather, a father-never-to-be. The other had recently married. Those who knew them well wept. Those who didn't know them well wept too. That's the way people were in Waterview. When the smothering blanket of grief fell over the town, few remained outside. All came to pay their respects. Even the children, who usually spent their Saturdays running and playing, stood watching but not fully comprehending what they saw. Slowly and unconsciously, the people in the crowd moved closer together.

This was the funeral service for the two who had died in the fire when the temple roof caved in. It was also a prayer service for those who had gotten out in time, but not without severe burns. Some were in the burn unit at the local hospital. They would survive, but they would carry scars with them forever on the outside and on the inside as well, never quite coming to terms with their own survival while two of their brothers died. There was nothing else they could have done.

Inside the church, Father Kelly moved forward. The music stopped abruptly.

"We are gathered here today to honor two of our most beloved brothers and to comfort each other. Let us begin with a silent prayer. Let each of us offer up our own thoughts and prayers according to our own beliefs."

As the church fell silent, a young woman in a long gray skirt with an over-sized gray sweater sat looking up cautiously at the woman in black in the first center pew. Paulie's wife, no, widow now. She looked so frail. The woman in gray looked down quickly afraid to meet her eyes, a lump growing cruelly in her slender throat. She plunged her hands into the deep pockets of her sweater instinctively, feeling cold, forlorn and confused.

"Dear God," she whispered silently. "Dear God, help her. Dear God, help me."

The young woman in gray continued to look down, pretending to pray, for there were no words, nothing to ask for or to promise God. It was all a blank now. Her light brown hair tied back from her pale face, she wore no make-up. When she felt that she had pretended long enough to look respectable, she looked up again, this time at the other woman in black on the other side of the front pew. The woman, dressed in a black and visibly pregnant, appeared to be near her due date. What a shame! What a terrible shame! Briefly she glanced around at the hugeness of the grief and then let her thoughts return to her old friend.

"I'm sorry Paulie," she whispered to herself as the lump exploded in her throat releasing a deluge of tears. Terrified, she looked quickly around her. She was not the only one crying, of course not. As she searched frantically through her pockets for a tissue, a hand, slightly wrinkled with a gold wedding band, reached out to her with one.

"It's sad. We all feel so bad," the woman whispered. "My name is Angie Bookman. My family lived next door to Larry 's family since he was a baby."

"Thank you," the young woman mumbled as she wiped her face, sensing that Mrs. Bookman was waiting for something. "My name's Dora. I went to school with them."

"Oh," the older woman said sympathetically.

"But I didn't know either of them, not very well," Dora stammered defensively, suddenly feeling that this blur who had identified herself as Mrs. Bookman was about to make her cross a line she didn't want to cross.

Father Kelly came forward again, this time to begin the service and the funeral rites. He made the sign of the cross as the first coffin was moved to the altar. It was Paul's.

Dora focused her eyes on the crucifix and let her mind wander. Her mother had wanted to come to the service, but was recovering from the flu so she decided to stay home. Dora was alone, so alone today.

... a fine young man, an honor student in both high school and college, but most of all, a good neighbor who served in the volunteer fire department for ten years...

Dora tried to shut out the words. It was too much to handle all at once. Her mother had offered comfort by telling her that she knew how it felt when someone who was once a close friend died because didn't she lose her childhood friend Leo in Korea? Dora was sure that her mother meant well but had no idea what it was like. No one would!

... married right here in this church less than a year ago, many of us were here, making this so painful...his young widow...

Dora blinked back more tears, hoping Mrs. Bookman wouldn't notice. She didn't. She was caught up in the priest's words. Dora squirmed in her seat, suddenly aware of all the discomforts of sitting in one place for a prolonged time. Her mind slipped away from what was happening on the altar as she listened to the soft, anxious beats of her heart. She felt too warm now. She needed air. The smell of incense was filling the church and making her queasy. From time to time, she felt the rippled softness of Mrs. Bookman's thigh bump against hers. Room, she needed room. She felt trapped between these people, Mrs. Bookman and some unknown man next to her on the other side. Church never had been a place that made her feel comfortable and funerals were the worst. Still, there had never been any question in Dora's mind as to whether or not she should be at this funeral. She had to be here. She knew that morning when she heard the news, the morning after the loud sirens had awakened her in the middle of the night. She would be here and it wouldn't be easy.

The other coffin was moved to the altar now. It was the minister's turn to offer the eulogy. Dora looked around, the rest of the congregation coming into clearer focus now. She'd only known Larry as someone who graduated a year before them, a face on the bulletin board outside the gym, always the star athlete, but she doubted she ever had exchanged any words at all with him. He had become a close friend of Paul's later, of course, when they both had joined the fire department. Geez, what must it be like to lose your husband when you are about to give birth? It made Dora think of her own husband, overseas now, keeping the world safe for democracy. No, no make that mending the men and women who were trying to keep the world safe for democracy, or something like that. Her husband was always reminding people that he didn't create war and that he was there to pick up the pieces. If he had been anything other than a doctor, he would have been an outright pacifist, but being a doctor, he was on the other side of the war coin, the mender, the fixer, the first-do-no-harmer. Yes, he'd rather be taking out some kid's tonsils or fixing a broken ankle, but as long as there was war, he had to be where he was needed most. She was proud of him, but she was scared, too. But then, Paulie had proven that one didn't have to be in a war zone to die suddenly and way too young. Many things about life make it dangerous. It was a wonder so many people did make it through to old age.

After the minister talked about Larry, the rabbi gave an inspiring thank you to everyone who had tried to save the chapel of the temple. He thanked all the churches that had offered their own chapels for the temple services, declining graciously, saying that enough of the temple building remained so that they could have their services there. He closed his tribute by saying that we needed to be sure we didn't take anyone for granted, not our immediate family, our loved ones, or our neighbors.

Whenever we go out into the world, we should do so without having regrets because regrets are just a waste of time. We do our best and when we reach out in love to those around us with our minds and hearts, there is nothing to regret.

"No regrets," Dora thought. 'Well, that's more easily said then done."

Dora's discomfort was turning into an aching longing mixed with hopelessness. She felt a gnawing inside her, deep down where life begins and ends. The sounds around her faded and then grew louder as her thoughts, confused but ever-present, wandered about.

Dora looked up and watched as the priest gently moved the burning incense over the coffins. The service was ending now. The final hymn, the audible cries of inconsolable grief from the pregnant widow, the cold and blank silence of the other, and the slow movement of the coffins back toward the daylight, all signaled the end. Dora was crying again, now uncontrollably, mopping her face with the tissues she had finally found in her pocket. Mrs. Bookman turned to her and handed her a small card with words printed on it. She looked as if she were going to say something but then turned away, wiping her own eyes and hurrying out the side door. Dora put the card in her pocket and moved toward the same door, slowly, turning briefly to catch a last glimpse of Paulie's coffin. She watched for no more than a few seconds as the last two pallbearers carried it from view, and then she left, inhaling the fresh air deeply into her lungs and turning for home.

CHAPTER 2

Dora was glad to be home, away from the crowd, the incense, the outpouring grief and Mrs. Bookman's thigh. But there was one thing she couldn't leave behind. There are some things you can't hide forever, things you put carefully away in a secure place, a place known only to you, but then the day comes to take it out and face the truth. She took off her sweater, thinking it smelled too much of a funeral, and hung it in the back of her closet. She began to climb the long stairway that led up to the second floor and then on to the attic. Moving slowly, tentatively, she felt as if there were a ghost up there and she was about to confront it. In a way, that's what it was now with Paulie gone. Dora felt a chill as she started up to the attic.

They'd been friends since kindergarten, Dora and Paul, pals, buddies, almost like brother and sister. Well, no, not exactly. They'd made mud pies and sand castles together and gotten yelled at together when they dragged dirty footprints into the house, Dora's or his. They'd played baseball in Dora's backyard with the clothesline post as first base, the old pear tree as second and the bumper of Dora's dad's car as third (when he was home, otherwise it was the lilac bush, but that made the run to third a little short) and the old shed was home. There were other kids, too, but the lineup changed from day to day and only Dora and Paul were the regulars. Sometimes they'd draw lines in the dirt for the bases, but they always got worn away too soon. Then, they'd ceremoniously stop the game and redraw the lines in the dirt after arguing about where they had been and taking it all so seriously. Silly kids! Other times they used articles of clothing for the bases, a cap, a sweater, a jacket, but their mothers always got mad about that. They never did understand why. After all there was Tide and Dash and all those other things. What was the big deal?

Sometimes they'd play all day in the hot sun so that when they finally got tired and went to their respective homes, the sweat would mix with the dirt kicked up from their games and they'd come in with their arms and legs all streaked with muddy sweat. "Don't sit on the couch until you've had a bath."

"Now?"

"Yes, now."

"But I'm hungry."

"Shower now!"

Dora continued up the stairs to the attic slowly. She was halfway there now, feeling a little tired (out of shape at thirty two?) and thinking maybe she should leave it for another day. She sat down on the middle step and listened to the silence of the house. She wondered if Paulie would come back to see her if he could. Sometimes, when they were about eleven or twelve, they would talk about things like that and she would come home and have nightmares while he went home and slept soundly.

In recent years they had seen each other around town but never spent more than a few minutes talking when they met. They had separate lives, had grown apart by necessity and who expected Paulie to die so suddenly? Sure, everyone knew that being a fireman was dangerous and now and then you would hear about it on the news, and sometimes Dora had dreams about fires, deadly fires, but …well, who really expected it to happen like this?

Whenever someone close to Dora died, it brought up questions about things she didn't normally discuss. Visitations they called them. She would dismiss the thought of them but never completely. There had been stories in her family, like that time her father claimed to have seen his mother after she died. It had made her an insomniac for a whole summer. But her dad was the farthest thing from superstitious and he never believed anything he didn't see with his own eyes. He didn't drink and was the last person anyone would expect to hallucinate. Every time he told the story, every detail was the same, even the last words his mother said to him. "I'm independent now."

Dora shook as another chill ran through her body just thinking about it. A chill, why? Why would it be so bad to see someone who you had loved dearly? Didn't the love go on like the words of that Titanic song? Her father felt comforted and enlightened by it, although it never made him religious. She looked up the stairs at the attic. It was probably dusty up there. Maybe there were bugs and who knew what else. She'd been meaning to clean up there but had never gotten around to it. Why had she saved it anyway? In the wrong hands it could incriminate her, open a whole can of worms, a Pandora's box and it wouldn't be worth it. It was way past the time she should have thrown it away. How foolish she was to have kept it this long.

Dora pulled herself up and was about to continue up to the attic when she heard the phone ring. She paused to listen. The answer machine was on as usual and she had no intention of answering if it turned out to be a telemarketer or someone like that. She strained to hear the voice.

"Dora, are you there? I'm not trying to sell you anything today. No really, dear, I wanted to know how you were and how the funeral was …"

Dora ran down the stairs, almost losing her balance as her mother's childhood warning echoed in her mind.

"Never run down the stairs dear."

"Yes, Mom. I'm here. I was just in the other room."

"Oh, I thought so," the soft and aging voice said. "I wanted to know how the funeral was."

"How the funeral was?"

"No, I didn't mean that exactly. That is not what I meant to say. I wanted to know how it was for you! How you are. I am sorry I wasn't well enough to go."

"Well, you know Ma, I tried not to get all emotional but I started crying and I felt like a fool, but then everyone else was crying so…"

"It was a funeral sweetheart. People cry at funerals, especially when it is for someone so young. I was worried about you, being all alone there and all."

"I wasn't alone. I had Mrs. Bookman," she said more to herself than to her mother.

"Who?"

"I'm sorry, it was this lady I don't even know. Some woman introduced herself to me and started talking when I was sniffling and leaking all over myself and just wanted to be left alone."

"I'm sure she meant well. Mrs. Bookman? I don't think I know her."

"Probably not. Well anyway, it was an impressive ceremony I guess, lots of firemen. They really do give a person a respectable and impressive ceremony with the procession and everything."

"I guess it will be on the evening news. I'll have to watch. I remember when my friend Leo was killed in Vietnam."

"Yes, I know, Mom. I really feel bad for his wife though. They didn't have much time together did they?"

"As a married couple, no, but they went together for three years I think."

"Maybe. But I feel bad for her, and all that Paulie missed out on, his future, kids…" she was rambling now.

"Well, you never know, but Paul had a good life, a meaningful life, and you two were such good friends."

"That was so long ago, Ma."

"Honey, I know we can't live in the past, but memories can sometimes lessen the pain. I know it isn't easy but it is the quality of life that matters, not the number of years.. That's what I have learned over all these years and Paul and Lawrence were two people who really made a difference. Remember that time they saved that little boy in that house fire? Paul carried him out? The kid looked so scared and Paul looked so loving. Those are things that most people don't get to do in life, to save a life like that. He would have made a great dad, but life happens the way it happens, I guess."

"Yes, the little boy," Dora took a deep breath and swallowed hard. Paul was so moved by him. He once told me that when you save someone's life like that, you form a kind of bond. He used to visit the family from time to time. We were all proud of him, then. I was so proud to say he was my friend." Dora swallowed hard almost loud enough for her mother to hear through the phone, she thought.

"You were a good friend. He could always count on you."

"He always wanted to be a father. He used to talk all the time of what he would do when he had kids. Of course that was when we were about thirteen." Dora gave a little laugh.

"That's good, dear. Remember the times that made you laugh. And in time, his widow will find happiness again. She is young and she has a good support system. Her family and the fire department won't ever let her down if she needs them."

"I suppose." Dora slid into a chair at the kitchen table.

"So, Dora, have you heard from Bill? Is he staying out of harms way?"

"He's in a war zone. He's always in harms way."

"Well, at least he's not on the front lines."

"Mom, this isn't that kind of war. There are no front lines, just lines all over the place and bombs going off…" Her voice trailed off. "I did get a letter from him and he said it was tough going, as far as the kind of wounds he had to treat, but he's hanging in there."

"Your husband is a real human being and a good doctor. You should be proud of him."

"I am, but I'd be a lot happier being proud of him right here."

"Pray, honey. That's about all you can do. That and keep yourself busy."

"Like that was ever a problem."

"Maybe for you I should say, 'take a little time for

yourself.' How is the teaching going?"

"You know, days of frustration and days of triumph."

Well, that's how life is and no one can say that you are not also making a difference."

"Yeah, one of my students said that he couldn't see why I was concerned that he wasn't doing the work. Told me that I get paid anyway, so why should I care?"

"Oh my, these young people today."

"So, Mom, when do you think you will be up and around?"

"Maybe in a day or two. I am feeling better, just don't want to risk a relapse. Had that once. Being sick is such a waste of time."

"Yeah, well, getting better isn't, so take it easy. Are you sure you don't want me to come over?"

"No, no. I have everything I need here. We'll get together later in the week if you want. Stop over after school and we'll have afternoon tea."

"Sure, Mom. Love that."

"Okay honey, take care and call me if you are feeling down."

"I will. I'm fine though. Don't worry."

When Dora hung up the phone, she looked up the stairs and decided to leave this part of grieving for another day. What had she been thinking? This wasn't the time. There would be plenty of time. Her husband wouldn't be showing up to clean out the attic anytime soon.

CHAPTER 3

Elizabeth Brennan Black was in her early seventies and remained an active member of the community. She had lived in Waterview all her life, having been born when there still was both water and a view in this small but growing hamlet. She was well read and kept up with political and social issues. Baptized Catholic, she didn't attend church regularly but lived by the basic rules of decency and fairness and had raised her children, with the same values. She was proud of her daughter Dolores and her son Taylor. They were both good people. She wrote poetry when the spirit moved her, mostly about motherhood, friendship and her relationship with God. She kept a neat home and since her husband's death, lived "simply but purposefully," as she liked to put it. She had dabbled in photography and had photos hanging on one wall in her living room. There were pictures of her family, of course, at all ages, photos of community groups. and close-ups of birds and flowers. On the burgundy sofa, there were two needlepoint pillows, one that she had done when she was younger, before she gave it up because the close work strained her eyes, and the other done by Dolores when she was sixteen. It had been a Mother's Day gift. Elizabeth's work had a single large rose intricately decorated with stitches that were perfectly aligned, creating shadows in all the right places, the placement of colored threads against the oatmeal fabric yielding the impression of sunlight coming through the sheer white curtains on the nearby bay window. The other pillow was simpler, the outline of a mother and child made with just enough lines of stitches to provide the form, but not one in excess.

Next to the couch, on one end, there was a table with a crystal lamp topped with a plain off-white shade. The table on the other end was almost identical, but the grain in the wood was a bit lighter and there was an empty green depression-glass vase next to it. In the May it would always have lilacs from the bush outside the kitchen window, but at this time of year, it rarely had flowers in it unless Dolores brought them from the local florist or Taylor sent them to Elizabeth on her birthday. Taylor usually did that because he lived by the Ohio border and didn't get home to see his mother as often as he wished, or as often as she would have liked.

Elizabeth tried to remember if she had ever met a woman named Mrs. Bookman, the one Dolores said talked to her in the church, but she couldn't place her. Must be new in town. Bookman, Bookman, no, not someone she knew at all. She had known a Brookstone once, Leo's aunt. She met her at Leo's funeral. Vietnam. A horrible war. Armies fought and people died and then someone would come to the door and …well, bad news. Leo had been her childhood friend just as Paul was Dolores'. Elizabeth was still feeling weak from the flu, but she was getting better and knew that she would feel better about everything when Dolores came over for tea in a few days. Maybe Dolores would feel better, too. It was bad enough that she had to worry about her husband over there in a war zone. This funeral couldn't have helped. Dolores reacted more emotionally at funerals than most people who were not actually in the family of the deceased, probably because it reminded her of her father's funeral, her first. It is better when your first funeral is a distant relative, not a parent. Elizabeth had been so involved in her own grief at the time that she didn't give enough attention to Dolores. Taylor, being older, handled it a little better, at least outwardly, but Dolores was only fourteen when her father died suddenly in an accident. It was Taylor, though, who wanted to go after that drunk driver, tell him what he had done to their family.

She could still remember vividly how the police came to the house to tell her, how they didn't tell her at all. How cruel it had been that they told her Joe had been injured and was in the hospital when, in fact, he had never even made it to the hospital alive. A neighbor outside the door had told the policeman that Mrs. Black had high blood pressure and that he would call Taylor who was in the area on business and was planning on surprising his parents. They had agreed that Taylor would break the news to her, but in the meantime, she was frantically trying to get someone to take her to the hospital. And when Taylor came, she knew. He didn't have to say a word.

Dolores stood there dumbfounded. Elizabeth

remembered the look on her daughter's face as if it had been burned into her memory. No sudden grief, no tears, just a look of confusion and disbelief as she repeated over and over, "I can't believe this." Only later, after the funeral was over and all the relatives went home did Dolores tell her mother that she had dreamed it all six months before, every detail right down to where her brother was standing when he told them and where her mother was sitting as she burst out in tears and cries of grief. Now some people might think Dolores was making this up, for what, attention? But it had happened before and while they both dismissed it when it happened, over time, it seemed very odd.

Deciding to make herself some tea, Elizabeth went into the kitchen, and took a small teapot and cup from the shelf. The pot was just the right size for two cups of tea and it nested in the cup that came with it. They both were white with a tiny spray of lilacs that extended from the cup up to the pot. It had been a Mother's Day gift from Dolores. Dolores was the one that always remembered that her mother loved everything lilac. She even got lucky once and found some Red Lilac cologne by Lentheric, a gift she had always bought for her mother for Christmas at Gladden's drug store when she was a child. When they stopped selling it, Dolores had gone on to buy other things, but on that one occasion when she found it, she had to buy it. It was at a Christmas gift fair at the Methodist church and it was old, but unopened and more of a sentimental gift than anything else.

Elizabeth reached for the kettle, once-silver-colored but now spotted with burn marks and dents, filled it slowly with water and set it on the gas stove, turning the heat on low. She pulled a dishtowel away from the flame. "Wouldn't want that to catch fire!" Reaching up into the cabinet above the sink, she took out the small box of Lipton's and dropped one bag into the cup, setting it carefully on the counter top. She headed through the open archway into the living room to the couch where she lowered herself, raising her legs as Dr. Woodruff had advised, propped a pillow under her neck and waited for the kettle to whistle. She closed her eyes, for a moment, just a short nod, knowing she could hear the teakettle and that it would wake her if she dozed off. She felt oh so relaxed. Elizabeth started to fall asleep until the whistle on the kettle began with a slow moan and then rose gradually to a high-pitched blast.

"Thank God for the teakettle," Elizabeth said to herself as she pulled herself up and hurried into the kitchen

CHAPTER 4

Angela Bookman moved into her sister's old house when her sister, Thelma passed away. It was the end of February when it happened. Thelma had been ill only a short time, or maybe it would be more accurate to say that she knew she was ill for only a short time before she died. In truth, the cancer that had spread throughout her body had been there for quite some time, but it went unnoticed or perhaps, denied. Thelma had been a busy woman, too busy to take care of herself, too busy to ask for help when she needed it. Angela should have known, having a bond with her twin that crossed the miles in the form of premonitions and familiar sensations. Angela should have recognized the aching in her own body that mimicked Thelma's pain, but she didn't. She, too, was caught up in a busy life, full of community meetings and classes and social activities. When the phone call came alerting Angela to her sister's illness, she immediately boarded a plane and made her way to her Thelma's side, jolted out of her routine and into a reality that forced her to reexamine her priorities and to wonder when she lost track of her relationship with her mirror image.

Thelma's appearance in the hospital shocked Angela. It wasn't fair that Thelma, who did everything right, should die of lung cancer. Not fair at all. Angela was there with her when she passed, and for weeks after, she coughed and went pale and suffered in ways she would never have expected. Then she suddenly pulled herself together and took up residence in her sister's house. Where else did she have to go, now that her daughter Rachel had moved away. There was nothing left for her in Kansas. Here in New York, Angela could make a new life for herself. She knew that some people would continue to mistake her for her sister, people who hadn't heard, or that she might even shock some of those who had, but with her husband gone, three years now, it was time to make a new life and she wanted to be where Thelma had been. It was all she had left and it brought her closer to Rachel, in case her daughter had time to get away from her busy life in New York City. Yes, it would be easier for Rachel to visit if she were so inclined. It was just a few hours by car, and even less by train. Angela thought the time would come when her daughter would realize that she missed her mom and would want to visit. When the glitter of the Big Apple started to wear off, perhaps then she would want her mother in her life again.

Angela had often visited Thelma and she felt like she knew her sister's neighbors. That's why she had gone to Lawrence's funeral. He was the neighbor who was always there when Thelma needed anything fixed or needed yard work done. She had never married.

Angela looked in the mirror and pretended that the reflection she saw was Thelma. Thelma, when she was still fresh and vibrant and full of laughter. She drew her fingers up over her cheeks, trying to lift her skin and to be young again. Her once smooth porcelain skin was now covered with a soft layer of down and there were tiny crevices lining the top of her lip. Still, she was good looking, a more mature version of her younger self with dark, almost black hair that cast reddish highlights when the light hit it the right way and thin penciled eyebrows that arched above her brown eyes in such a way that she always looked a little surprised. Life, however, seemed no longer to hold any surprises for her. Not good ones anyway. Below her chin there were little signs of weight, gained and lost and gained over and over again. Now, Angela was thin except for her hips and thighs, which stubbornly held onto the cellulite that had been the bane of her existence since she was twelve. She had been so very conscious of them and their intrusion into the space of that young woman at the funeral. What was her name again? Dorothy? Doreen? Oh yes, Dora. That poor girl had looked so forlorn, so alone, and something about her troubled Angela. She seemed to be about the same age as Rachel, about thirty-two or three, she thought. Moving into Thelma's house and Thelma's life was the only way Angela could find a reason to be these days. Once she overcame the strange reactions from people who had known her sister, she blended in more. She felt that she was really home. What she left behind in Kansas was no more than a few trinkets and a few inconsequential acquaintances, none of whom would ever really know she was gone unless someone mentioned her name and she doubted that anyone would.

Her life had been defined these last years as Rachel Bookman's mother and Sol Bookman's widow. With them gone, she had pretty much become a nobody. Now, here, she could become Angela Bookman, a person in her own right. Even though she started out as the mere refection of her late sister, something about Waterview opened itself up to her and granted her permission to become whole again. It would take time, but as far as she knew, there was no lack of that now.

Five blocks away, Dolores Victor had decided to make it a short day and turn into bed early. The funeral, the conversation with her mother, and the inner ghosts of deeply guarded secrets exhausted her. She put on the thin gray sweatpants and the "I Believe In Angels" tee shirt that she used as pajamas, wrapped herself in her old worn out rose-colored chenille robe, and drank a cup of unsweetened tea as she stared through the blank beige wall between the living room and the hall. She had tried watching some TV, even got brave enough to turn on CNN and hope they wouldn't be talking about the war. It was one of those things you couldn't not look at sometimes. The more you tried not to look, the more your morbid curiosity got the best of you, like a rubbernecker on the highway or a child trying not to look at the road kill that was unavoidably stuck in the middle of the street you had to cross to get to school. But it was there, the number one story on all the news channels. She turned it off. The house was quiet now, the TV silent, and Dora was as alone.

Dolores loved being alone as much as she hated it. She worried every day and night about Bill, wondered where he was and prayed unconsciously that he'd make it home soon. But she also felt a calm in the house when she was alone, a calm that allowed her to charm the old inner demons so that they would rest a while longer until the inevitable day when she would have to confront them. She knew that they had to be exorcised, but did not know when or how. She knew she would never be whole until the story played itself out. It was as if pieces of a puzzle danced in her head begging to be assembled and promising to reveal some secret and important message. Tomorrow, she'd have to go up to the attic and pull out the old box that she'd hidden up there years ago. If she waited and Bill came home, it would be too late. As she sipped her tea, her mind wandered. She knew she was still awake, she could see everything in the room, but the dream fragments intruded anyway. Visual horrors and internal turmoil, didn't everyone have them? Was that why her mother named her Dolores? Dolores Black. Did her mother even think of what her name meant? Darkness and suffering, why not Joy or Merry? Maybe that was why she married William Victor, for his name. Dolores Victor had a sound of triumph. Sure, why was she even thinking of this? Must be getting sleepy. Time to turn in. She placed her teacup on the table and headed for bed. As she dragged herself into the bedroom, pulling back the heavy blankets, she began to cry uncontrollably. Where was the predictability, the reasonable expectation that day would follow night and night would always lead to another day? Why did Paulie have to die? Why did some die before they even got a chance to live while others seemed to waste their lives and yet live absurdly long, accomplishing nothing of value? Why hadn't she told him? He should have known. It was his business! Maybe things would have been different if he had known. Maybe, somehow, it would have made a difference even though reason told her it would not have mattered as much as she imagined. You never really know, do you?

CHAPTER 5

He stared at the hard gray floor for a few moments as if time had stood still, like when the film got stuck sometimes when he went to the movies with his friends for a Saturday matinee when he was a kid. Back in Warrensville where there was this one dirt road that was still unpaved and dust blew all over the place during the dry spells of summer. Like this place, dusty and dry most of the time. If he kept looking at the floor and let his eyes go out of focus, he could imagine that he was back there. Home. Back where he grew up, where the whole town was so small that everyone knew everyone else and if he so much as spat on the ground in front Mr. Brewster's grocery store, some nosy neighbor or Nell Brewster herself would phone up his mother and say something like, "Mrs. Victor, I saw your son Billy expectorating on the walkway right outside my husband's store on his way home from school again and I really thought you were a respectable woman who brought your son up better than that…" and his mother would warn him all over again beginning with, "How many times do I have to tell you that spitting on the ground, especially where people walk, is unacceptable behavior…" and he would think that if all the women in Warrensville would tell their husbands and brothers what she was always telling him, maybe he would have better role models and wouldn't have to resort to such "unacceptable" behavior to look like he too, was one of them and the walkways in town would be a whole lot cleaner. Anyway he had "expectorated" in the dirt, not on the "walkway," but what was the use of trying to reason with anyone in Warrensville? Pretty in its own way with its old-fashioned white picket wooden fences, it seemed to be stuck in time, something he noticed on those few occasions when he went to visit for nostalgia's sake since he had no family left there. He always wondered how and why the little village had maintained itself into the twenty first century, obviously needing so much upkeep, a waste of time in a world that had turned to more practical things than painting and repainting old houses and whitewashing fences like something out of Tom Sawyer. Small town! It seemed to be the last to get computers and cell phones. It was resistant to change, both in technology and thinking. And yet, that was why they called it "Historic Warrensville" and charged tourists too much to get into the local museum that consisted of some old tools, furniture and letters and even a grocery list written with fountain pens and other odds and ends. He had always wanted to get out someday and see the world, the real world. Be careful what you wish for!

Yes, if he let his eyes lose the focus on this melancholy floor and thought only of these words and images stored up in his head from decades ago, maybe he could make it through another day. Even the sounds of explosions that he knew all too well, could be transformed into memories and images from so many

Fourth of July celebrations in Vets Memorial Park where he had eaten hundreds of badly boiled hot dogs accompanied by the best-tasting but very unhealthy potato salad, homemade by the women of the VFW auxiliary. But then, someone always managed to fix the film and the movie went on. The screams from the soldier, heroically wounded and waiting to be taken to a field hospital, and his Saturday matinee companion would always lean over and say something like, " Man, this is a great movie. Someday, I want to be a Marine!" Yeah right, a Marine. That kid ended up as far away from the military as his skinny legs could take him. They both had at least once referred to their hometown as "this hell hole." Yeah right, like they knew anything at all about hell holes. Foolish kids. Like they say, you don't know what you've got till it's gone. He probably would have felt the same way about Waterview if he had not met Dolly Black who had made that place all the more inviting.

A moan, a real one, from a real soldier, not an actor, brought him back to reality. He had had enough. He had seen so much blood, blood he had not had any part in spilling, but blood of many mothers' children who once had spent Saturdays at movie matinees eating popcorn and dreaming of adventures they would have someday, adventures that would end with each and every one of them a hero at the end and going home as if nothing had happened, except now they had all these cool war stories to tell their children just like their great grandparents had told their parents. Those were heroes who came home in glory and lived happily ever after. Men who were greeted by their waiting girl-next-door girlfriends who would provide joy and comfort and never be confused about why there weren't quite the same. But now, the girls-next-door were here as well and they all went home "different." Sometimes, he wondered what it would have been like to have been a small town doctor like Doc Larabee, a man who never got sick himself and who was always ready to make a house call when needed and who got to play golf up in Aimsley on Wednesdays. But that had never been an option for Bill, not in those early years and not now that his country had called him to duty again.

The time went slow when he thought of Dolly, his wife. Oh how she had frowned at him the first called her that. Dora, Dory, Doreen even, but not Dolly and never Dolores. But after a while, "Dolly" grew on her and he longed to call her that again as he held her and made up for lost time. Maybe they would even have children while there was still time. He'd settle down and have an office and make rounds at a hospital near home and then retire and spend some well-earned time fishing in the quiet of the river just a few miles north of town. He wasn't getting any younger and although he and Dolly had talked about having kids, there was something in her response that made him wonder if she really wanted any. She said she did, but there was something in her eyes that made it seem as if she was afraid it would never happen. Dolly! So organized, so understanding and yet a bit sad sometimes. What could she be going through now? She probably read right through his greatest efforts to reassure her that he would be safe, as if anyone can be sure of that. Here, so near to the fighting and the snipers and the insurgents who you couldn't tell from the innocent civilians until it was too late, he worried about her safety in quiet little Waterview where one took security for granted. He was not there to protect her and he felt he should be. Life throws odd curves at you and they explode before you recognize that they are what they are and not some innocuous plaything. Doors needed to be locked and women shouldn't go out walking in the park at dusk even in the places with the best reputations. Things happened in schools, those sanctuaries that were once considered safe and secure, when the worst thing a kid had to deal with was ridicule from peers and an occasional black eye from the schoolyard bully. Those days were gone and Dolly's being a teacher did not automatically mean the worst she would ever have to deal with would be a spitball from some class clown who couldn't shoot straight. Unfortunately, he thought, whether you were a surgeon in a the military working at a hospital in a war zone or a teacher with a two masters degrees working in a small close-knit town, you never could predict what might happen. Here these dusty and miserable streets, amid the remnants of buildings and gardens that showed evidence that it had once been a more beautiful place, the unexpected might fall from the sky or from a car or even from a woman walking through a market. The world wasn't safe anymore, not even Waterview.

Whenever he imagined what Dolly was up to at home, he would squint his eyes down and try to picture her in her office talking to a student and smiling in that reassuring way she had. She had a way of making people, not just young people, but everyone who came into contact with her, believe that things could be accomplished, that "impossible" was just a made up word for people without imagination. Even though he'd seen arms and legs blown off and wounds that were deeper than the physical, he carried with him, that idealism that Dolly had given him, wrapped up in hope like a Christmas present. She believed in win-win solutions in a world of no-win attempts at everything. They had had long discussions about such things. She believed that peace was almost always possible but he had his doubts.

The longer he stayed in this place, the more he saw it. Dolly saw it in little ways every day of her life even though she was not in a place where people were killing each other on a regular basis and dismissing it because you could name it. WAR! We are at war! But why? We don't have to be. Not really. People would tell her that war and people enemies and even allies were not that simple and that she was not a realist. Nice ideas but far from reality. Still she insisted that we get what we expect and we create our own reality. Bill would look at them and nod but as time went on, he saw it more and more. The political is personal and war is as personal as you can get when you finally get to look at the faces under the helmets or whatever people wore on their heads to show who they were. It was all the more personal when what was inside was ripped or blown open. That's when you saw it the things Dolly believed.

How he missed those long and warm discussions with her and how she always said that the righteous indignation we carry with us when a perceived injustice is committed against us is the result of a wound that is deeper and harder to heal than those that bleed out in the open. But then, there were people who seemed to be pure evil. You could look into their eyes and see the emptiness where a soul should be. Sweet Dolly. Hopefully she would never see such darkness. How he missed her. How he hoped she missed him but not enough to hurt too much.

Bill stood up and walked into the hallway. He stopped briefly at a handmade plaque with a poem. It was new. Someone had added it to the decor of the blank green wall and the peeling paint.

Bearing the bandages, water and sponge,
Straight and swift to my wounded I go,
Where they lie on the ground after the battle brought
in,
Where their priceless blood reddens the grass the
ground,
Or to the rows of the hospital tent, or under the
roof'd hospital,

To the long rows of cots up and down each side I
return,
To each and all one after another I draw near, not
one do I miss,
An attendant follows holding a tray, he carries a
refuse pail,
Soon to be fill'd with clotted rags and blood, emptied,
and fill'd
again.

I onward go, I stop,
With hinged knees and steady hand to dress wounds,
I am firm with each, the pangs are sharp yet
unavoidable,

One turns to me his appealing eyes- poor boy! I
never knew you,
Yet I think I could not refuse this moment to die for
you, if that
would save you.

----- Walt Whitman

CHAPTER 6

"I am glad to see you looking so much better now, Mom," Dora said casually, as she carried the teapot into the dining room from the kitchen.

"Well, you know, I get a bout of the flu every year, but I get over it and my immune system is still strong."

"Well, I still think you should get a flu shot. No use being sick when you don't have to be." Dora set the pot down on the table right in the middle of the white lace tablecloth next to the fresh cranberry scones she had baked and brought over fresh from the oven. They were still warm.

"I don't trust those shots. I got sick the last time I had one and I think there is something meditative about being forced to rest and take care of yourself."

Dora shook her head in frustration. Her mother was not getting younger and she still refused to admit that natural cures were not always sufficient. Sometimes she picked the wrong times to be brave. And yet it was she who always said it…

"Well you know what you always taught me…"

"I know dear, an ounce of prevention, but for me that does not come in the form of a flu shot. Believe me, Dolores, I will not die from the flu. It will take something a lot more dramatic to kill me. I survived cancer twice and I'm not going to die from some silly virus."

"Well, I am not in the mood to speculate on how you or anyone else is going to die. I have enough to worry about. I heard from Bill yesterday. He tries to be upbeat, but he sounds worn and tired and I think he can't wait to come home now."

"Sit down, dear." Elizabeth pulled the chair out for her daughter and Dora sat down. "I miss him too. I always liked Bill and I am glad you married him, but it is hard not to have a husband home with you. Your dad was always home right up till the day he died, but then, you get used to being alone. It is different when it is so unpredictable and I know you worry. When he finally comes home, you will have so much to do to get ready, all the loneliness will be gone and forgotten."

Dora thought her mother had a way of oversimplifying things sometimes. She had learned that it was her way of covering up her concern and making herself feel better as well.

"Of course, its nice having you so nearby," her mother continued. "I miss Taylor, but last time I talked to him, he said he was thinking of coming down. Knowing Taylor and how he gets busy with so many things, I think it will be a while before he actually does. And I miss Lucy and Ellie. I haven't see my granddaughter in what, seven years? She was nine, yes, seven years! She doesn't even know who I am. And Troy, he moved to London. I probably won';t ever see him again. Maybe when Bill comes home we can all get together and celebrate. Maybe next spring, when the lilacs are still in bloom we could have a picnic or something. Taylor always mentions how he misses the lilacs by the kitchen window."

"That would be nice, all of us together again." She sipped her tea and broke a piece off the scone. "When I think of family, I don't usually think of everyone scattered so far apart, but that is what family is these days. I never had the urge to leave Waterview. I've seen enough of the world to appreciate it but most places I've been, well they are nice to visit…"

"But you wouldn't want to live there. I know, but when I was a young girl, I used to dream of escaping the hum drum world and going to Paris and living there. Getting an apartment in some artsy part of the city and painting, but I never did paint and never learned any French. How have you been sleeping?"

" Mom, I sleep pretty well, but I had this awful dream the other night."

"About Bill?"

"No, you'd think I would dream about him, but I figure that I worry enough about him while I'm awake that I don't need to dream about him at night, at least not often. No, this was really upsetting. I was driving down the street by the elementary school and suddenly this kid on a bicycle came out right in front of me and I heard this thud and then everything went black. It took me a few minutes to realize that I was awake and that it had been a dream. It was awful."

"Oh what a terrible thing to dream about. It's every driver's nightmare."

"It felt so real that I couldn't get back to sleep. So that's why I look so terrible. Thanks for asking," she laughed.

"I couldn't imagine what it would be like to hit a child. My friend, Thelma, once told me she hit a child and even though the girl was fine, she never felt quite as secure when she drove. You knew Thelma, didn't you?
"

"Thelma?" Dora thought for a moment, but she couldn't quite find a face to fit the name.

"Well, maybe not. She lived here a long time, but maybe you forgot her. We were friends when you were little, but then our paths just parted. Odd, how that happens sometimes. She's in the photo over there on the wall, the one of my high school reunion. She died of cancer a few months ago. Gee, maybe it was a year ago."

Dora got up to look as her mother pointed to the photo. It took a few moments for her eyes to focus on the one that was Thelma.

"That's Mrs. Bookman!"

"Who?"

"You know, the lady I sat next to in church at the funeral, said her name was something like Bookman! I forgot her first name."

"No, that's Thelma Cooper." She paused and thought a moment. "You mean her sister, Angela? Did she say her name was Angela?"

"Angela Bookman, yes, but this is her face. You said she died? The woman I saw looked just like her."

"They were twins.

"They sure were."

"Thelma got left back so she was in my class. She was really smart but not in the way the teachers wanted her to be. Angela graduated a year before us and moved away soon after."

So she lives here in Waterview?"

"She lived in Kansas, but when Thelma was ill, Angela came here and I guess she stayed. Funny you should sit next to her in church. Kind of like seeing a ghost!"

"Guess it would have been if I had known Thelma. She gave me something, but I don't remember what I did with it. Probably a Bible verse or something. I guess I lost it. Well, it doesn't really matter."

Dora felt herself tuning out as her mother talked about politics, current events and the chores she had written down on her to-do list. Her mind wandered back and forth between Bill and his last email about the war and the box in the attic. She was counting the months now until Bill was supposed to come home and it seemed that there were only five if nothing changed and she knew that she really should clean the attic and part of that would be getting rid of the box. She had managed to keep it hidden up until now, but now with Paulie gone, it was time to get it out, confront it and destroy its contents once and for all. Why had she kept it in the first place? There was nothing it could do for her but make her feel bad and even though Bill was not the kind of person to go looking through her old memorabilia, she decided that tomorrow was the day to begin the process of cleansing.

"…and so I think I'll have to get the garage painted and the bushes pruned before next summer." Her mother's voice interrupted her thoughts.

"Um, think I'll get some work done around the house this weekend myself."

"I called the man who cleaned out the gutters for me last fall and he said he'd come and do it again. I should have had that done last month, but he was busy and…"

Maybe she should have told her mother all about the things that happened after her father died and before she went back to college that fall, but it would have only complicated things and who knew how it would have turned out anyway. What could her mother have done to help her when she, herself, was grieving. It had been a difficult time and nothing she could have said or explained to her mother could have made it any easier for either of them. In many ways she envied her mother's ability to bring everything out in the open, to keep no secrets that would come back to haunt her. She had always admired that about her mother. Dora was different. She felt she had to be. She never wanted to hurt anyone but then, sometimes she did just by trying too hard.

"If you ever need a handyman, I found a good one. You don't have to do everything yourself."

"I know, Mom. But I am a pretty handy woman myself, you know."

"True. You always had a knack for fixing things. But just let me know if you ever need one. His wife works in the library and she went to school in the Bronx when she was a kid and they met in high school…"

The whistle on the teakettle in the kitchen began to rise in pitch signaling that there would be more tea. Tea had always been the vehicle for conversation and renewed bonding between Dora and her mother. When Dora had been away at college, even though college was not that far away, she sometimes missed the chats with her mom while other girls had conflicts with their mothers that she never understood. And still, Dora had kept many things to herself, not because she didn't feel she could go to her mother, but because she felt that she shouldn't burden her with things she could fix herself or at least try to. As close as they had always been, there was a space, an undiscovered territory of privacy that each kept from the other. While Elizabeth suspected that her daughter sometimes slipped into this space, she never imagined what she did there. As for Dora, she had no idea that her mother also had secrets, things that went far beyond her daughter's ability to even imagine. So they drank more tea and bonded in that permissible space they had made for themselves. They drank tea until the afternoon turned into dusk and then they watched Jeopardy together before Dora went home. The evening turned into night and both women confronted the silence that haunted and soothed them until the dawn of another day.

On the other side of the dried up stream, across from the elementary school, in the darkness of Thelma's unchanged living room, Angela Bookman was leafing through a book she had picked up at the library, her new fresh library card having been used for the first time. The small lamp provided just enough light as she ran her fingers over the title page, *Surviving Survival.* Then the dedication: *"To all those who have lost a loved one and find survival both a blessing and a curse. This book was written for you so that you may find hope and renewal to move on to a higher plane of living."* Angela closed her eyes as they welled up with tears about to overflow. She had lost her husband and her sister and in a way, she had lost part of her daughter, who, in seeking adventure and her "own life," had distanced herself from her mother. Angela felt so very alone. She let the tears overflow, turned off the light and stared into the darkness.

She could see the moonlight in the corner of the living room window. The moon was full, just as it had been on the nights Sol died and Thelma died. Five years and two months apart, but so similar in how she remembered them. Some moments she was so overtaken with grief that she felt hopeless, and wanted to run away, get out of a cage, but was unable to escape because, no matter how far she ran, the cage just grew bigger. Maybe that was why she had come here, to seek comfort that the empty house on the Kansas prairie could not give her. After Sol died, she had opened the door of that house and had run as far away as her strength and energy could take her before she fell to the ground sobbing. Soon after, Rachael left and then there was the call from Thelma telling her about the cancer. In that last year, Angela traveled back and forth between Kansas and Waterview, each time staying longer with her sister until it ended and she sold her house and stayed where her sister's memory was still warm. She held the book to her bosom and let her mind empty. It was then she thought about the young woman at the funeral, Dora. She let her mind's eye call back the image of that sad girl who seemed to have a burden so heavy that Angela could feel it almost the same way she had always felt her sister's emotions. But why this girl, someone she didn't even know? Angela exhaled a long sigh and heard her sister's voice as if it were coming from Angela herself.

"Help her."

CHAPTER 7

The time had come. Dora packed up a small cleaning basket with some rags and Endust and made her way up to the attic, this time with determination instead of trepidation. It wasn't just about the box with the memories now. It was about cleansing and starting fresh and getting ready for Bill's return. She had to believe he would return and that nothing would come between him and home again. She had allowed herself to feel down in the doldrums long enough. Having just finished teaching "Invictus" to her students, the words had followed her home from school. *I am the master of my fate. I am the captain of my soul. I am the master of my fate…"*

The stairs to the attic were narrow and steep and the door at the top needed more than a little push to open. Dora leaned against it with her shoulder and although it resisted at first, it finally gave way. The attic was lit by the sunlight coming through a small window, and there was no need to turn on the light which Dora recalled, didn't work anyway. There were boxes piled high on all sides, some containing wedding presents she had never used and some she hadn't even opened after the wrapping was discarded. Behind one stack of boxes filled with file folders, was an old white toy chest with Peter Pan and Tinker Bell on it, from her childhood bedroom. Her mother had always called it Pan-Dora's Box, and laughed at the double meaning. But now as

Dora looked at it, she thought, "Mom, you have no idea." Inside that chest, she knew she would find the small pink box..

Where to begin. Okay, begin with the box. Get that over and done with. She knew that once she opened the box, she would not be likely to finish anything else. She stood for a moment and resisted taking a deep breath and looked around for something to sit on. Oh, what the heck, sit on the floor. After all she was wearing old worn out jeans and a tee shirt that had stains from the last paint job, so why not sit right on the dusty old floor? She sat next to the toy chest. After spraying it and wiping it with a rag, she opened it carefully, hoping not to see any spiders or ugly bugs. There were none. There was an old scrapbook on the top, from her dancing school days. She opened it briefly, smiling at a photo where she was wearing a purple tutu with a sequined top and posing in a very "graceful" pose. It had been taken when she was six years old and thought she would one day be a famous ballerina. Trouble was, she wasn't really graceful and had very bad balance when she tried to perform an arabesque or anything requiring her to stand on one foot. She closed the book carefully. This was not why she had come up to the attic. She moved a few other items aside, including an old wallet, a small mirror and a mismatched pair or winter mittens her mother had made her wear to school to keep her hands warm, even though they were not a pair. She'd been embarrassed to be seen in them. Then she saw it. The box. It was a pink satin quilted box that was meant for storing nylon stockings or fine lingerie, out of date even when her elderly aunt had given it to her as a teenager. She picked it up and put it in her lap as she sat with her legs twisted around her like a pretzel. She slowly traced the stitches that made little diamond shapes in the satin before opening it. Everything inside looked the same as she remembered it, even though she had left it undisturbed for the last 6 or 7 years. She had checked it once after her mother sent it over, when Elizabeth was cleaning out her own attic. Her mother told her that she had not looked inside and it was still; covered in dust, but she never could be sure. Carefully, she lifted the paper on the top.

It was a newspaper clipping. She unfolded it. "Local Heroes Save Five-Year-Old Boy." She looked at the date. Eight years ago. There he was, Paulie, holding the little boy in his arms. Larry stood next to him. Paulie! Wow. She must have slipped it in before she shoved the box into the back corner. Paulie loved kids. He had once told her he wanted to have a dozen and she had laughed at him hysterically and told him he should marry a cat. She had saved the clipping because she could hardly believe that this was the same Paulie she used to chase around the backyard and throw balls at and here he saved this kid's life. And now he was gone. She wondered for a moment, whatever happened to the kid? As she stared at the picture, she started to feel her throat getting tight. She put the clipping on the floor next to her and wiped a tear that unexpectedly fell from her right eye with the back of her hand.

Next, she opened an envelope with an invitation to Paulie's high school graduation party. He had been accepted to Kenyon College in Ohio and she was going to SUNY Purchase, less than 100 miles from home. There were theater ticket stubs from a local performance of Guys and Dolls and an old empty box of spearmint gum, and then she saw it, the unmarked manila envelope. She could just destroy it without looking at the contents. Just take it and burn it or bury it or shred it piece by piece without another thought. That would make it quick and easy. But, no. As much as she knew it would be painful, she needed to examine the contents once more to make sure what she thought was real had not been a dream, a really bad dream. She wasn't done mourning, even after all these years. It would take one more look and then she would be done and have to move on. It was time to bring things to a final close.

She had forgotten which piece of paper was which, but she knew it was all there, the whole story after her father's death. She opened one paper carefully and saw Paulie's handwriting. *"I am so sorry to hear about your father. I will be home next week and maybe we can get together. You talk. I listen. I don't know what to say anyway, but I want to be there for you. You've always been a great friend to me and I want to be there for you.*

She stared at his handwriting and ran her hand over it and then held it close to her heart. Paulie, um Paul had come home and he had been there for her and she loved him for it, maybe she loved him more than she had realized. He had comforted her as no one else would or could. The depth of her grief was equaled only by the depth of her affection for her childhood friend, an affection that turned into something more, if only for one brief shining moment in time. But then, he had to go back to school and so did she. He said all that needed to be said when he left. "If you ever need me for anything, to talk or to help you in any way, please call me. For anything, you hear?" She had reassured him that she would and she intended to. He had called her the week after they were both back at college, but for some odd reason that she couldn't remember, she had brushed him off. That was a mistake.

Next she pulled out the box from the pregnancy test. Why had she saved it, of all things? She had written on it in bright red ink, "Oh no! Now what?" What stupid choices she had made from that point on. And yet, even if she had made better ones, why would it have made any difference in the end? Paulie should have known. She should have told him. When she found out, she tried to call him a few times, but she kept getting his roommate. Finally his roommate told her that Paul had gone to his girlfriend's house to visit her family for the weekend and did she want to leave a message? That was the end of that. How was Dora to know that that relationship would last only a few months, something she didn't find out for years. Dora leafed through the papers, the medical papers with the words, *spontaneous abortion*, and the one other letter from Paul saying he was still there for her if she ever needed anything. Apparently, his roommate never said anything about her calls and so when he came back to Waterview to live, Dora kept her distance even though her mother kept insisting that Paul was unmarried because he was waiting for her. Dora never believed that at all. Then she started dating Bill, a medical student at her college. They married and he went off to one war after another. But now she was sure he would be coming home once and for all. She scooped up all the papers and headed down to living room closet to get the shredder. It was way past the time to close that chapter of her life. She plugged the shredder in and slowly fed it and as it devoured that part of her past leaving nothing to keep the sorrow alive. The only paper she kept intact was the newspaper clipping. After all, Paulie had saved a kid's life! That was one thing she didn't want to forget. Paulie would live inside her for that alone. Nothing would take that away. That was how she wanted to remember him, always. She placed the clipping in the top drawer of her desk.

CHAPTER 8

Jim Kelly got up early on Sunday mornings, especially on days like this one, when the forecast was for an unseasonably warm day for November, and perhaps, a dazzling sunrise. He pulled on his light gray slacks, a black watch plaid shirt over his plain gray T-shirt, and tiptoed out of the rectory so as not to wake his fellow priests. The coffee pot that had been programmed the night before was now producing hot aromatic coffee. Jim walked down the long hall to the open kitchen and poured himself a black coffee and headed out the door and down the steps, closing the door gently behind him. The garden outside was full of bright chrysanthemums and a few remaining daises needing deadheading. Where he grew up, down on Long Island, they called them Montauk daisies and when they bloomed, it was his family's cue to take their annual off-season trip out to the end of the island. Or was that the beginning? It depended on which bumper sticker you read or which way you were facing at the time. For Jim and the rest of the Kellys, it was a new beginning, a time the family came together to talk, to bond again, and to feel the glorious refreshing mist of the fall beach as it washed all cares away. This morning felt a lot like that even though his parents were long gone and his brothers and sisters were scattered about the country.

He'd start the morning with a prayer, nothing formal, just his own words asking for inspiration, as he would be putting the finishing touches on his homily for the ten o'clock mass, this one specially dedicated to the veterans of the parish.

The sun was slowly rising now, just above the eastern trees. He couldn't see it, but he could see its light and the colors it cast across the base of the sky. Streaks of yellows and oranges announced the approach of the sun in all its glory.

His mind turned to Lawrence Marshall and Paul Hicks and their impressive, but deeply sad, funeral. They were the same age as one of his nephews, Michael's boy. Michael Jr. was a fireman up in Ramsay, a tiny town in northern New York by the Canadian border that had been settled by a small group of Australian immigrants years ago.

It was exactly three weeks since the funeral of the two firefighters and the loss in town was still palpable. Jim needed to address that in the homily. Most of it was written and had been for almost a week, but Jim was still looking for a way to personalize it to the town and add a bit more in the grieving process without taking anything away from the veterans who were being honored at today's mass. As pastor of Blessed Sacrament Church, Jim Kelly had suggested that the other two priests tie it in as well in whatever way they could at their masses.

Now he could see three quarters of the sun above the horizon and its splendor didn't disappoint. He sipped the coffee, which had cooled enough now, and sat down on the bench opposite the statue of the Virgin Mary. He closed his eyes and experienced a moment of gentle peace.

Mark 12:38-44 *Beware of the scribes, who like to go about in long robes…*

The story of the widow's mite, the meaning of giving from the little we have… Father Kelly thought. He had the text of his not-to- exceed-eight-minutes homily and all his practice readings had brought him only to six and a half, so now he had a full ninety seconds (should he choose to use them) to tie it all together. He always left that for Sunday mornings at sunrise. That way he could add or alter the message enough to include any sudden event that might need to be addressed. Now it was just about linking service to monetary giving and honoring the memories of Lawrence and Paul along with the men and women who served and were serving in our armed forces. He slowly drank his coffee and let the rays of the rising sun shine on him. He never took the responsibility of delivering a truly inspirational and healing message to the people of his parish lightly. His mind drifted back to the fire department and the men and women who served Waterview. Then the link came to him, almost miraculously, although Jim Kelly never took that word lightly either.

***

By 8 a.m., Elizabeth Black was up and had decided to go to the 10 o'clock mass. After all, she hadn't been at the funeral and she wanted to pray for Paul and Lawrence and light candles in their memory. She wanted to attend the veteran's mass because she also wanted to honor and pray for them and their families and light a candle for Leo, something she had been doing since he died in Vietnam so many years ago.

She started her day with a bowl of oatmeal and a cup of herb tea. Maybe a piece of raisin toast as well. After all, it was Sunday. She could splurge a little. She took her time getting ready, not so much because she wanted to, but because it seemed that the older she got, the longer things took. She didn't waste time putting on a lot of makeup as she had done when she was young, when it seemed to glide onto her face and make her look…well, stunning! Yes, there had been a time when she looked stunning with her makeup and hair done just so, but now she knew too much makeup would make her look pasty, or worse, like a dried prune that had been dropped in cake batter! Just some color for the eyebrow, she didn't use pencil because she had seen how artificial that could look on a woman her age. She preferred, instead, a small amount of powder brown eye shadow just to pull the hairs together and make them look soft. Seemed that the older a woman got, the more she started looking like a man. She wasn't having that! Then some bronzer lightly across the contours of the face, a quick shave of the stubborn whiskers that insisted on showing up on her chin, and a tinted lip gloss, or if needed, a single coat of natural looking lipstick. She didn't want to go to mass looking like a TART. She let out a quick laugh, thinking that that term, and the other one her mother used to use, PAINTED

WOMAN. She thought these words sounded silly when her mother used them, but here they were inserting themselves into her own vocabulary. No surprise, Elizabeth had accepted the fact that when she looked into the mirror, her mother's face looked back at her. She had accepted it years ago, probably when she was still in her fifties. It had shocked her at first, but then she just got used to it. Genes could do a lot more to a woman's appearance than Revlon or Helena Rubenstein. Sometimes that was good, but often, nah.

At 9:15, Elizabeth left home to drive to church. She wanted to be early enough to get a good seat. These special veteran's services tended to crowd up early because many parishioners and the vets themselves showed up, even if they never set foot in Blessed Sacrament on other Sundays, or maybe just on Christmas and Easter. Didn't matter to Elizabeth. She wasn't a regular either.

***

Dora had decided to sleep late this morning. She told herself that she deserved to sleep in. Fortunately, she had read and commented on all her students' papers the day before, a few at a time, during breaks in her other responsibilities. So when the sunlight broke through her window, she just rolled over, pulled the sheets and blankets over her head and ignored the time. It was cold in the house the unseasonably warm sun had not yet reached her room. She could feel the chill that meant it would be cold when she woke up and that even though today was forecast to be warm, she knew the cold would start spreading throughout the days and into the night in the weeks to come.

After the emotional shredding of a significant part of her life the day before, she had spent three additional hours cleaning the attic and hadn't even made a dent in the mess up there. As soon as all the cleaning and rearranging began to bring back memories of the cleaning out of her father's belongings in the attic at her mother's house after he died, Dora decided she had done enough for one day. She had brewed herself a strong cup of hazelnut coffee, opened up the bag of chocolate chip cookies her mother had sent home with her on Friday night after Jeopardy and watched a few movies on TV. Old movies, ones she'd seen before but never seemed to see all the way through. By midnight, she was ready to go to bed without setting the alarm clock.

When the morning sun invaded the room through that one broken blind, she moaned, rolled over and went back to sleep. The errands could wait till afternoon and then, she would go to her mom's house for dinner after picking up a few things she needed for the week.

***

Angela Bookman spent her Sunday mornings drinking coffee , reading the *New York Times* and looking at the help wanted ads, even though she didn't need or want a job. She was retired from her position as reference librarian at the local library in her small Kansas town years ago, she didn't need to work anymore. She got into the habit of reading the help wanted ads when Rachel graduated from college, but her daughter had done quite well on her own, finding a position with a New York City publishing firm instead of the small town library opening Angela had seen advertised near Wichita. Angela drank her morning coffee and savored the crumb cake from Barrenburg's Bakery. It reminded her of Sunday mornings when she was a kid, all about church, crumb cake and jelly doughnuts. Sunday was all about relaxing, remembering and breathing deeply. She was still in her floral robe, no longer caring how long she was up before she dressed. Sometimes she thought about going to church to complete the nostalgia, but it has been so long, the thought of it didn't made her mildly uncomfortable. After all she had been to the firemen's funeral and since she believed God was right there with her all the time, why would it matter? She took a sip of her coffee, leaned back and wondered where the years had gone.

***

On the other side of the world, Bill Victor was covering up the body of a young man who should have been home waiting for the birth of his son and stitching up a kid who looked to be about fourteen, but was actually twenty one, and thinking about Dolly. She might as well have been on another planet. This war was supposed to be winding down, but the casualties kept coming, more slowly perhaps, but they came just the same. He always felt a sense of failure when he lost a patient, even now when some of them came in already beyond hope and at death's door. Neither time nor numbers changed the loss of that single life that was cut short at the worst possible time, cut short at that nexus where hope and possibilities meets the dark of finality.

***

Back in Blessed Sacrament Church, the organ struck a chord and the processional began. As the congregation rose to its feet, many veterans and active members of the military services, some in uniform, blended together in a single voice.

Holy, holy, holy, Lord God almighty

Early in the morning our song shall rise to thee…

A young man in loose jeans and a Met's tee shirt walked uneasily down the side aisle. He wore a Yankees baseball cap. An elderly man eyed him suspiciously.

"Hey kid, he said in a loud whisper, which team are you on anyway?"

"ARMY!" the young man answered proudly.

"Well you need to take that cap off, you are in church," the elderly man commented, somewhat annoyed, but the young man looked straight ahead, obviously ignoring him.

Following him, and stopping to shake hands and greet his neighbors, was Mark Michaels, a dad in his thirties with his wife and their twin boys toddling beside them. Mark's burn scars were bright and still raw on his cheek and his arm. Some well wishers got out of the pew to great him, some with tears in their eyes.

"I'm doing well. We're doing well. Happy to be here," Mark told them.

Elizabeth had found her seat in the front side pew as she usually did when she came to mass, which made her wonder if God took the trouble to save it for her, even though she didn't make mass every week. He must not be too disappointed in her, then. She was moved by the men and women in uniform, the Marines, especially because their uniforms were so colorful and striking, but mostly because Leo had been a Marine, one of the Few Good Men who served their country and never came home, leaving an indelible mark on her heart and her soul at that very young age. What was it? Sixteen? Had she not believed that he would come home and maybe ask her out when she was a year or two older? She sighed! He was so handsome, blonde hair that sparkled in the sunlight, piercing blue eyes that you could see from a distance. They were Paul Newman eyes and his voice so gentle and kind…

Lord have mercy…

So many years gone by and it still only seemed like a few. Where had they gone? Her mind wandered as the mass continued. Too bad Dora hadn't come with her. It was hard to tell if seeing the men in uniform would help her cope with Bill's absence or make it worse. This annual mass was always impressive. A veteran from each of the armed forces did a reading and some even sang.

Alleluia, alleluia, alleluia...

As Father Jim read the gospel, he looked out at the congregation, the familiar faces and the emotions hidden behind them. Over so many years of being a priest, he had developed the ability of reading the familiar words smoothly and comfortably while thinking of other things. Like Lawrence's widow sitting in the back of the church, still wearing black, unlike many young women today who have given up that custom. Seeing her with her sister, who was dressed in a brown suit and holding her arm for support from time to time, he knew she was still having a hard time getting beyond her grief as her pregnancy had progressed to the eighth month, making her look even more forlorn and heart wrenching. He had stopped by once since her husband's funeral and she had been gracious in her sorrow, but had not taken him up on his offer to call him if she needed him. Grieving is often a slow and private process.

Then in the front side row, there was Mrs. Black who didn't come to mass every Sunday, but was always there when the parish needed something. The holidays found her and her generosity to other families to be very much like that of the story of the widow's mite. When she wasn't giving from her pocket, she most certainly was giving from her heart. He usually heard her voice above the others when they sang the alleluias, but perhaps this week, she was a bit under the weather.

The McCall family was there and Sean was in uniform. How good to see him, back with his family again. His parents looked so happy and his girlfriend was clinging to him, holding onto him as if to say, "Damn the Navy. He is staying with me. You just try to get him back!"

And there was Frank, his old friend who had had open-heart surgery, a triple by-pass, and was back in church for the first time. He looked like he was doing well. And his son was still struggling with PTSD after one suicide attempt.

The gospel of the Lord

Praise to you, Lord Jesus Christ!

Now for the homily…(Father Jim took a deep breath and began.)

Dear friends in Christ, the message of today's gospel speaks to us this very moment and all the moments we spend here living our lives. It speaks of giving out of the love of God and our neighbors, not to be seen or honored, but just out of that pure love that Jesus taught us through His life, His words and His death on the cross. When Jesus watched the showy contributions and behavior of the wealthy hypocrites, and then saw the humble, but ever so loving gift from the poor widow, He recognized the intention and sacrifice of that woman as being pure and mighty at the same time. For even the small value of that sum, for her, was a large act of love. So what do we learn and take from these words, today?

These words are not meant to be a rebuke of the wealthy, who also give from their hearts, nor a call for everyone to give money as the way of showing love for God and our neighbors. The giving of money is, of course, a blessing for both the giver and the receiver. But today, we need to think about all the other ways people give and show their love of God and their fellow human beings. In this special mass today, Veteran's Day, let us not only honor our members and veterans of the military, but let us honor service itself, service given in Christian love, to God and to the community...Waterview, to our country and the world. Our service to our values, our moral strength, and the highest ideals our hearts and minds can imagine. Let us reach within to the Holy Spirit and see every day as a chance to serve.

We see here today, young men and women in uniform, and we honor them along with the veterans who wore these uniforms years ago, some in war and other times in peace, but all in service to God and country. We honor them because they are deserving of honor, for they have given of their lives and time a part that cannot be regained. We honor them for their love and sacrifice. But they do not do it for the honor. They don't wear their uniforms to be showy. They wear their uniforms to show their brotherhood and sisterhood and to honor those who made the ultimate sacrifice. We honor and pray for all whose pure love of God, country and their neighbors has led them into serving something bigger than themselves ...

Elizabeth had convinced herself as a teenager, that Leo, her senior by three years, would discover how lovely she was when he came home from the war in Vietnam. He would stop seeing her only as the little girl whose family knew his family and would one day ask her to a movie and then to Howard Johnson's for a burger and ice cream and that would be the turning point in their lives. They would get married, right here in Blessed Sacrament and have kids and ....wow, she thought, she had been a silly girl, hadn't she? But, Leo was her friend. She never got over how she found out from his sister who came running out of the house crying and blurted it out.

"He's dead! My brother is dead!" as she fell to the ground.

Leo, dead, and his sister never had the slightest idea of how Elizabeth felt about him. Tears welled up in her eyes even, today as she relived that memory while the world around her went on. Of course life went on, but she never gave up thinking of what might have been. She took a tissue out of her pocket and dabbed her eyes.

It was just three weeks ago, that we honored two men who also gave of themselves to make this community a safer place and then that night, trying to save the sacred Torah in our neighboring synagogue, lost their lives. These men also did not serve to be seen or honored but gave their service for God, community and country. Lawrence had served in the Coast Guard before becoming a firefighter and Paul served in the fire department upon his graduation from college. There are many members of both the Waterview Fire Department and the county police department that serve our community. Some have also served in the military and some have served in the Peace Corps, have volunteered in local organizations and hospitals. Some members of our volunteer fire department serve in that capacity after they complete their full work-days as members of the New York City Fire Department. Having served as chaplain to these individuals has taught me that their valor and tireless service is extraordinary.

Yes, Leo was more than just handsome. He was gorgeous. Not only did he have those eyes, but she remembered how she felt when she saw him with his shirt off, that summer day in 1968, just before he went into the Marines. He was working on his car and he looked just like *Cool Hand Luke,* all tanned and masculine and grown up. Only he always wore a cross around his neck and he didn't smoke like Luke did in that movie. And he was nice, very nice and mannerly. What a crying shame!

...and so my friends, we weep together for those who we have lost in the service to our country and our community and we honor their lives as well as the lives of those who serve us in so many ways day after day. And in the spirit of Christ, we dedicate ourselves to the promise that those who have served will never want for anything and never be lost from our thoughts and prayers.

We believe in one God...

`Elizabeth looked at the red candle holders next to the altar. Each flickered with a yellow white flame. Each represented a light for remembrance like the one she lit for Leo. She wondered who each other candle flickered for. Perhaps others lost in service for their country. Perhaps others who were lost in more natural ways, and some maybe were lit for those who were still living but near to death. It was hypnotic, staring at the candles. Meditative. Now communion as over

Among those returning from the altar rail, Elizabeth saw the man in the jeans and baseball cap. She thought it was odd that he was wearing it and that the priest said nothing as he had received. But as he returned to his seat two pews in front of her, his cap fell off as he stumbled and she was shocked to see that his head looked as if it had been bashed in on the side. It looked as if a chunk of his scalp and been bludgeoned and the skin torn away. The cap had landed in a young girl's lap and she did all she could do not to gasp. She handed the cap to him as their eyes met.

"Thank you so much for your service," she said in a trembling voice. "Thank you so very much."

"Thank you for your kindness," he answered, grateful for the words.

Elizabeth had not chosen to receive communion because she had been raised to refrain after eating. That had been changed years ago, but she just didn't feel right. Her mind kept wandering, from Leo to Lawrence and Paul and to Dora and Bill.

CHAPTER 9

By the time Sunday morning turned into afternoon, the soccer fields at the elementary school were filling up for a midday game and the handball courts were empty, but expectant. This would be the last weekend for soccer tournaments as the unseasonably warm weather was a fluke and the cold weather would be coming in a few days

Angela Bookman was just finishing up her dusting as she looked out the window at the street between her front lawn and the school soccer field where the game was about to begin. The street was lined with cars and SUVs so she could barely see. Sometimes she wandered over to watch, but today she had too much to do. It annoyed her when the parking lot overflowed and the vehicles blocked her view, making the street too narrow for the traffic that often moved way too fast for a school zone even if the speed limit didn't apply on Sunday. She thought there was something ironic about having school zone speed restrictions when the kids were safely inside school, but not on Sunday when they were all running loose and unrestricted in all directions. She glanced down the sidewalk toward the slowly setting sun and saw a boy on a bike racing toward her on the sidewalk from over a block away. It was a nice day to be out, but she had too much to do inside. She walked toward the kitchen where her three days worth of dishes were waiting to be washed and put away. As she stopped for a second to wipe a missed patch of dust from her dining room table with her sleeve, she heard a strange noise, a kind of loud thud and a crunch. She stood frozen for a moment when she heard a car door slam and a woman's voice calling out.

"Help me, someone please help me!"

Angela ran to the window where she saw the boy, who had been riding the bike, on the ground in the middle of the street crawling toward a woman who was rushing toward him.

"Oh Dear God!"

The windshield of the car was shattered with a hole pushed in where the boy had apparently made contact. Angela ran to the door and shouted.

"I'll call 911 right now." She picked up her phone as the woman looked at her. It was then she recognized Dora, the young woman from the funeral. "Oh no!"

"Please hurry, yes, the child just collapsed onto the pavement." She watched through the window as people gathered, surrounding Dora and the boy. A woman dressed in jeans and a sweatshirt pulled out her cell phone as Angela stayed on the line, shouting out the door, "They are coming. The ambulance is on its way."

The woman with the cell phone put it in her pocket and went back into the crowd as Angela strained to see what was happening. When she heard the siren, she took her phone and ran out the door.

"I can't believe it. I can't believe it…" Dora repeated over and over as Mrs. Bookman made her way through the crowd.

"Are you okay?" Angela asked her?

"No, I'm not okay."

"It wasn't your fault. It was an accident," she told Dora. Looking at the car and its position in the street, still blocking her driveway, she knew that Dora had been driving slowly. There had been no screeching brake noise. Just that awful thud. The windshield was crushed into so much broken glass and the boy's bicycle was lying against the tree just past the driveway.

"How could this have happened? I can't believe it!"

"Don't worry,. Not your fault. I am sure he will be okay. You were being careful. Things happen. You couldn't have expected it."

Dora stared at Mrs. Bookman, trying to figure out what she was saying and to recognize the face that was saying it. Careful? Yes, she was being careful, but not expected? That was the point! She had expected it, she had felt a foreboding as she turned onto the street, but it was already too late. Her head hurt worse than anything she had ever experienced before and everything was a blur. Where was the boy? She looked at him and he seemed so far away and yet there were the bright flashing lights of the ambulance and voices talking to her. A policeman?

How fast? Fast? Not fast.

"Did you move your car after the accident?" he asked.

She looked hard at him. Were the words coming from him?

"No," Why would she have moved the car? How could she? she felt like someone had poured very warm water over her head, and everything was a blur. The policemen looked at the car and at the bike and asked her again.

"Are you sure?"

"No, she didn't move the car," Mrs. Bookman came to her aid. "No, I didn't see the actual accident, but I saw her right after. She just got out of the car. I did see the boy on the sidewalk coming toward her. He must have dashed out into the street right here." She pointed to her driveway. "Should I call anyone, Dora?"

"No, there is no one to call …not right now." She looked at her finger. There was a sliver of glass lodged in it. She carefully removed it. The policeman finished the accident report and gave Dora all the info she needed and fortunately, Mrs. Bookman heard it all because all the sounds were just muddled rumblings to Dora.

The ambulance had arrived. But when? Dora saw the yellow tape and the flashing lights, but nothing fit into time, no consecutive string of events that made any sense at all. Voices, disembodied voices, in a mist talked to her, asked her the same questions over and over and she answered, *about 20 miles an hour, maybe, blur didn't see anything but a blur, no time to stop but then the car was stopped, who stopped it, did I stop it? Of course I did.*

She looked up, trying to see the boy…where was the boy? The crowd around him blocked her view, but then she saw something, something clear and familiar. "Oh blessed Lord," it was Paul, standing there in the street as clear as day looking just like every other person, not ghostly or transparent. It was Paul, first looking at the boy and then turning his head toward her. She blinked and he was gone. How foolish to blink like that, but he had been there! She saw him. Everything else was blurry and confused, but not his face. He was there and now he was gone! She couldn't have imagined it. It was too real! Maybe she was losing her mind.

But the boy…there he was….they were cutting his shirt off and there was blood running down his face from his ear and his chin. The dream was mixing with reality and the world was going mad, or maybe it was only Dora. They carefully lifted the boy onto a stretcher and into the ambulance and as it pulled away, Dora felt totally abandoned. How would she know if the boy was okay? Why did they leave her alone in the street? Wasn't there something else for her to do? She didn't feel well at all. She stared at the flashing lights until the vehicle picked up speed and the siren grew from a low moan into a full loud blast. Why did they assume she didn't need to go, too? Had anyone asked her? All she had remembered saying when asked was, "No, I am not okay." A comforting arm wrapped itself around Dora and moved her toward the house. A neighbor volunteered to move the car over to the curb, out of the way of traffic.

"Come inside and have a cup of tea," the voice said. "I am Angela Bookman. We met at the funeral for those firemen, but you probably don't remember. Would you like some tea?"

"Tea? Oh tea! I need to call my mother!"

"We'll call your mother. She can come and get you and we'll all have tea. You need to relax. Everything is going to be okay. Please believe me. Everything is going to be fine. It was an accident. You couldn't have done anything different."

"I wish I could believe that!"

"It will be okay. Let's go call your mother."

It wasn't her fault. The boy came out from behind a car and she stopped immediately," Angela told Dora's mother as she came through the door.

"Oh Mom, it was awful." Dora stood up from the couch where she had been sitting staring at the floor while Angela put up some tea and mad the phone call."

"But I am sure the boy is going to be fine. He was talking to the firemen and to his parents and he seemed fine except for some cuts and maybe something with his leg, but nothing life threatening, I'm sure."

"His parents were there?" Dora looked confused.

"Yes, they spoke to you. Briefly, but they did."

"These things happen and I know it wasn't your fault, honey." Elizabeth took her daughter into her arms and gave her a reassuring hug. "Thank you so much for helping my daughter. I was a friend of Thelma's. You still look just like her."

"This is Mrs. Bookman. We met at the funeral, Paul's funeral."

"I know."

"I can't believe it." Dora couldn't get the thought of the dream out of her head.

Angela picked up the newspaper that was lying on the table and looked at the horoscopes. She was a habitual horoscope checker and had checked her own not too long before the accident.

"If you don't think it is too silly, may I ask you what your astrological sign is?"

"Sagittarius," Dora answered blandly.

"Well, here it is, 'Luck rides with you today. You will encounter someone who will share in your good fortune.'"

"Great! That sounds like I will win the lottery, not hit a kid on a bike."

"I wonder what the boy's sign is," Angela muttered.

"I have it here on the accident report." Dora opened the paper she had unconsciously folded in quarters and put in her pocket.

"Oh my! The kid's birthday is two days before mine. So this is the kind of luck that rode with him as well!" Dora stared at the paper. Devin D'Angelo. Why did that name sound familiar? "I'm not superstitious, though. So the horoscope, just a coincidence."

"Of course." Her mother poured her some tea from the pot Angela had placed in the middle of the table. It was a pale blue teapot with an angel on it.

Angela set a plate of cookies on the table next to Dora. "Here, have something to eat."

"No thank you, I'm not hungry."

"Don't let this upset you too much. I can understand how it could, but I truly believe that everything is going to be okay and you will get past this. Can you take tomorrow off and get some rest. I'll help you get in touch with the insurance company and all that," her mother was trying to clam her but not doing a good job of it as she was worried as well.

"Oh, God, the insurance company. The car is wrecked and how will I handle all this? I wish Bill were here. Every day I worry about him and now this."

"We'll both help you," Angela said. "If there is anything I can do, I will. It's only the windshield anyway and you can get that fixed".

"How can I find out how the boy is?"

"I'll see what I can find out for you," Angela said. "Let me call the hospital now. Why don't you go lie down on the couch? If you're not hungry, maybe a little rest will help. Just close your eyes and take a few deep breaths."

Angela picked up the phone and made the call while Elizabeth poured some tea and Dora excused herself to go lie down on the couch. "Deep breaths," Her brain was racing. She only had one late class the next day and an office hour. She could deal with that, get someone to cover for her and have the office hour later in the week.

***

William Victor was just getting to sleep after a busy day of surgery on two wounded soldiers. One was a young woman who had been shot in the leg by a sniper. She would survive, but the young man from Iowa who had been hit by the same sniper had suffered damage to his brain and was not likely to be as lucky. The stress was getting to Bill and he had started calling for Dolly in his sleep. Something made him feel uneasy about her, like something was wrong. He needed to sleep, but the images of the wounded soldiers flashed on the inside of his eyelids whenever he closed his eyes. This shouldn't have been happening. All he wanted was to sleep and to dream of Dolly, but not tonight.

***

"He wasn't admitted. They must have tended to his injuries and sent him home," Angela reported to Dora and Elizabeth. "Look, since I am not family, I can make some calls for you tomorrow. Your insurance company might be a little leery of your getting in touch with the boy's family directly. They can make things harder sometimes."

"This is really nice of you." Elizabeth had an odd feeling, talking to her late friend's identical twin. "You do remind me so much of your sister."

"We were always close and now that I am living here, it is a pleasure to get to know her friends better. I knew some before of course, but I think people have forgotten me. Forgotten that there were two of us. I always liked this community and often when I came back, I thought I'd like to stay. My daughter got a job in New York City, so soon after my husband died and all the change at once was a little more than I could take. Coming here, I'm closer to my daughter and closer to the memories that make me feel better."

"I can't thank you enough," Dora added from the living room, thinking how odd that first meeting at the funeral had seemed, even a little intrusive. But now, Dora was grateful that there had been someone there for her at her moment of crisis. She closed her eyes and breathed deeply. belonged to though. I thought people might find it too strange."

"Is she asleep? Elizabeth turned to look at Dora,

"Poor girl, it wasn't her fault at all."

"She'll be okay. She was on the way to my house for dinner. She didn't even touch her scone and she loves scones. How nice that you had scones and tea."

"I am glad to have company for tea, but I wish the

circumstances were different. My sister used to love a proper British tea. She went to England once and kept that custom on weekends. I guess it is just one more way I keep her close to me in my memory."

"I am pretty sure that's where I got the whole tea in the afternoon habit from. Thelma had me over a few times and I sat right here. I have a grandson who lives in London. I rarely even hear from him but that is how things are these days, I guess. I'll drive Dora home and have someone come for the car in the morning if that's okay."

"She can leave the car in front of my house. I have a tarp I can throw over it. It should be fine."

"I'll help you cover the car. Are you awake Dolores?"

"Ummm, yes, I am awake." Dora's voice was tired and weak but she pulled herself up.

CHAPTER 10

She picked up the breakfast dishes from the table in a bit of a haze, glancing every so often at her son and thinking, "Thank, God!" The boy, sat on the couch, his back leaning against a white pillow with his leg up in a soft cast playing a video game, and shouting "Yeah, gotcha," at varying intervals of time and whispering some more choice words at others softly so his mother wouldn't hear. The sun shone on his light brown hair, making it look golden. Yes, he was the golden boy who had *cheated death,* how many times was it now? Cheated real death, and now doing the same in a video game. Life is not a video game. His mother hated the violence of the games he played and had objected a few times when she looked over his shoulder and saw blood spurting out of a neck here and a bloody head with bulging eyes flying away there. But his dad always countered with, "Oh come on Carol, he's a boy" and young Devin would chime in, "Mom, it's not real! I know it's not real okay?" But Carol D'Angelo wasn't comforted by that at all. That only made it worse. Maybe it wasn't real inside that game, but it was getting too close to reality and desensitizing the kids to violence was not a good thing. Why couldn't they make exciting games where the object was to save lives, rescue people, after all didn't they think that was important after....

"Carol, let the kid play. He's a good kid. Let him blow off some steam this way." That was always Mickey's retort. Then he would walk away, case closed. She knew she had to pick her battles and this one would never be won by harping on it.

"Next time you wear a helmet," she shouted, feeling satisfied that she had some control.

"Yes, Mom," he shouted back. He continued to play mumbling, "I am not riding my bike wearing a dorky helmet."

His mother stopped loading the dishwasher in the kitchen and went to the doorway. She paused briefly to muster up her power and her patience. "I heard that! Perhaps you forgot that you no longer have a bike. If you want a new one, you will promise me that you will wear a helmet."

"Don't see what good a helmet would do. I busted my leg, not my head. Maybe I should wear a suit of armor." He giggled, not so much because he thought it was that funny, but because he had been scared and it was easier to make a joke of it than to admit how scared he had been. "At least I don't have to go to school for the rest of the week."

"You know you like school."

"Yeah, it's okay, but I hate getting up in the morning. It's not even morning, it's like the middle of the night. Why don't they wise up and let us go to school later. "Aw sh, now you made me get shot, I'm dead!"

Carol shook her head. Raising kids was dangerous. It

was a miracle most of them actually made it to adulthood. Too many close calls, especially for her son. Like that time he disappeared in the supermarket when she turned right at the produce and he didn't follow her. When she went back to look for him, he was gone. She looked all over the store for him, getting more and more frantic every minute, and then she saw a young woman coming in the front door with his hand grasped tightly in hers.

"Devin, where have you been?" she called to him.

"He bolted out the door in front of a car," the young woman said somewhat sternly, "I grabbed him and he kept repeating, 'My mother went home, my mother went home. I told him his mother wouldn't go home without him and said we could look in here. That car would have hit him."

"Well thank you. I just turned the corner and he disappeared." She turned to her son and repeated, "I was looking everywhere for you. Didn't I tell you never to leave the store? Why would I go home without you?" That was when he was about five. The kid had already had a close brush with… NO she didn't want to think about it anymore. We were all lucky! And now this, the third and hopefully last close call.

Carol's thoughts were interrupted by the phone. She looked at the caller ID and recognized the name. It was the lawyer. Why had Mickey called that man? He knew the accident was not that woman's fault. "Doesn't matter," he had said. She had no intention of answering the phone.

Mickey could deal with that.

***

When Dora awoke she saw the sunlight peering in her window for a brief moment and everything seemed normal and then it hit her. The accident, the flashes of images, and the deep sadness. She had left a message on the voice mail at school that she would not be in today, asked her friend to cover for her, and already there were voice mails for her expressing concern and support. Messages that went unanswered as she went about, a little like a zombie, trying to figure out where to begin. Well, she'd call her mother and the insurance company and the glass repair company for the car…ugh, so much to do and so little control over her life. Even her day, no control. She would clean and tidy and clean some more. But those phone calls, she dreaded making any of them.

She looked out the window to see if her car had been towed into her driveway yet. Gee, that Mrs. Bookman, Angela, turned out to be a Godsend after all. She was taking care of so many things for her, as was her mother, of course. The two women had seemed to hit it off and it looked like Elizabeth had acquired a new friend with the visage an old one.

Dora drew the curtains back from the window and saw her car and the smashed windshield in the driveway, giving her a sudden sharp pain in her stomach and a chill all over her body. It really had happened. It was the same feeling she had a the day after her dad died when she got up and slowly wandered around the house to see if it had been a bad dream. The silence in the house, the broken tea cup left on the kitchen floor, (she never quite knew how it got there) and her mother's quiet whimpering in her bedroom, erased any possibility that her father's death had just been a bad dream…again.

She had gone out to the kitchen to pick up the pieces of the broken cup and to make her mother a new cup of tea, not knowing what else to do. Tea was always the short-term solution to everything. It was the only thing she could do. As she had picked up the pieces of porcelain, and carefully dropped them into the trash, she wondered if it had been dropped or thrown in anger, grief or a sense of total powerlessness. When she thought of it now, she knew that it had been a combination of all of the above, an almost lethal combination that made that teacup substitute for more drastic measures that may have crossed her mother's mind. And yet, in the time that followed, it seemed that her mother was able to find a new sense of independence and that as the grief faded, Elizabeth's tears were left to a few isolated moments.

But that was not anything like this. The total powerlessness of this, despite the outcome, left Dora with a whole series of what ifs flooding her mind. When she finally got to the business of calling the windshield repair company, she was glad they didn't ask a lot of questions. They seemed to assume it was vandalism. She let that go. It wasn't anyone's business. Then the phone rang and this time she had to answer. It was the insurance company.

A businesslike, but not unfriendly voice began by saying, "This must have been a horrible experience for you. You are probably still shaken up, but I do have to ask you some questions." Mr. Wood went on with all the typical questions...*which way was the boy coming and where were you headed ...* and ended with, *just make sure you avoid contact with the boy or his family. Don't say anything that could be construed as an admission of fault.*

"Fault? Why would I...but I was hoping to see the boy. See that he is alright."

"Mrs. Victor, you cannot do that. I can find out what his injuries were for you. But you should avoid contact so they can't use anything you say..."

"I wasn't at fault, not in any way but..."

"Well, we know that, but they probably will say you were, at least partially, but we never let our clients admit fault...ever. And you don't need to see the boy. He seems to be okay, just minor injuries, like any kid would get even playing, and that is all you need to know. Now you can just forget about the whole thing and go about your life. We will take care of the rest for you. Just take a day to rest and let everything go back to being normal again."

"Normal? Are you kidding..."

"Well, give it a few days then, but feel free to call me if you have any questions. We will deal with it all from here on in."

With that the man hung up the phone and Dora stood there incredulous. She had never had an accident before. What an odd conversation that had been. Why wouldn't she be able to see the boy, tell the parents what happened in detail and see for certain that he was okay. It was just stupid. Did they think she was stupid? That picture of him in the street bleeding, surrounded by glass, was burned into her mind and it was not likely to fade away. And even if it did, how long would that take? Her throat swelled with frustration and grief until it felt like it was going to burst and when she could no longer hold back the tears, she sunk down into Bill's favorite chair, clinging to it as if she were sitting on her husband's lap, and she wept.

She let her sobs come like waves, lapping onto the shore, waves from a distant place caressing her cheeks in salty and stinging tears at first but then changing into soft sweet kisses to comfort her. She allowed herself to settle more deeply into the chair letting it envelop her body in its overstuffed cushions against the soft, brown suede cloth. She closed her eyes, blinking the last tear from each of them, and imagined the softness that surrounded her was her husband's arms enclosing her in that safe world he created for her when he was home, a world he could not create for himself when he was away on the other side of the world where dusk was dawn and night was day.

***

The floor creaked as Bill walked across it. He was

having trouble sleeping. It was full of interruptions and anxiety. Something didn't feel right. He shook his head and scolded himself silently for his thoughts. How could anything feel right when there was a war in progress, death was all around and no one could see an end to it all? But, no, that wasn't it. Something else…it just felt as if something else were wrong, something on the other side of the world. It was as if Dolly were calling to him as in a dream, when you try to shout and call for someone and yet there is no sound. He felt a cold shiver and poured himself a cup of hot tea. He took a sip and then put it on the table. It tasted like nothing. Everything seemed to taste like nothing these days, just hot or cold nothing and he missed home more than ever, his home, his wife and even his favorite chair. And old chair with a cushion that once had been thick and soft but now was flattened by too much wear and too much war, would have to suffice. He sat down and put his head in his hands down by his knees and breathed deeply. Soon there would be another day to face the unknown. Another day longing to be with Dolly. Dear Dolly, the light of his life, alone and missing him, maybe… or maybe not. There was always doubt, not because of Dolly herself, but because of the world and all its unpredictability. And yet the feeling that she was calling to him persisted. It was as if he felt her hair on his face, but he knew it was only his own. He let himself drift for the short time, closing his eyes, trying to get a few more minutes of sleep. There she was, standing before him, her hand gently stroking his hair and telling him she needed him. As she moved around his chair in his mind, she slid her hands over his shoulders and down onto his chest and rested her head on his. "I love you," she whispered. "I love you," he whispered back.

CHAPTER 11

Dora had stayed home from work on Monday because she was just too distraught to think or function normally. Besides, she had that windshield to have fixed, but late Monday night, Melanie called to ask if she could pick her up and take her to school the next day.

"I figured it might be easier for you and I didn't know if your car was okay to drive. It's not really out of my way anyway."

"I would love that. I would feel much better, if you don't mind."

"Mind? Are you kidding? I know you would do the same for me. So, I'll pick you up at 7:45, okay?"

"Thanks so much, Mel. You are a huge help."

Melanie loved teaching. She had taught at the high school level before she got this position. She always seemed so upbeat and ready to get into that classroom and discuss whatever unit of American History her class was up to. She didn't teach dates and battles and all that like bullet points on a textbook page. She didn't even use a textbook, no Holy Catechism of Patriotism to be memorized, but not understood. Nope, Dr. Melanie James brought history to life by involving all the senses and making sure it was complete with no one of importance left out, black people.,women, indigenous people, everyone who was there, but may have been omitted from the all male white written history books.   She taught history the way that Dora taught English, making the poetry, the stories, the novels, and essays jump off the page and entice her students to ENGAGE! Primary sources, research, real scholarship! Sometimes the two connected their lessons by finding the commonalities between the history and literature, creating unofficial learning communities among their classes, breaking down the walls of this subject and that and just teaching LIFE AND TRUTH.! There was often food involved, and music, and even dancing. And why not? All kinds of people danced throughout history. But she didn't leave out the dark side either and she didn't sugarcoat any of it. What wasn't pretty and so much wasn't, was visible and discussed in depth in Dr. James' classroom. There had already been enough of the cherry picked history. Sometimes Mel's students rebelled and said she was distorting history and Mel even overheard one call her an angry black woman and she was, why wouldn't she be? Why wouldn't anyone who knew the truth be angry. Dora was angry, too, in her own way, even while espousing a curious kind of Anne Frank belief about the basic nature of humanity.

When Mel's blue Toyota pulled up at the house, Dora was ready, but not quite as motivated as usual. She hadn't even taken care in choosing her clothes for the day, ending up wearing gray and looking just a bit paler than usual.

Like everyone else, Dora had good and bad teaching days. She was hard on herself, wanting perfection, but sometimes she had to settle for just good enough. Lessons could go wonderfully well and then they could just flop, you never knew because there were so many variables, but she almost always started out optimistic.

"So how are you this morning? Mel said, as Dora opened the door and got in the car.

"I'm okay, I guess. A little more tired than usual. I feel like my brain has been scrambled like the inside of a kaleidoscope, only no pretty patterns are coming up."

"Well, take it easy today. Just get through the day. That's really all anyone could expect."

" I only have the two classes, the 101s, and my office hour in between. I should be able to muddle through."

"I'm across the hall from your 9 am so feel free to call me if you need me. Want to do the Brick Café for lunch?"

"I haven't been very hungry, but sure. It's Monday, oh navy bean soup, I can probably down that. I'll save you a seat as usual."

The Brick Café' was the dining room where most of the faculty ate when they weren't eating at their desks and too busy to take the time for a real lunch. Mel and Dora preferred to take the time to eat and do their paperwork later. On days when they had committees or other activities during club hour, they had no choice. They grabbed a sandwich and a bottle of water and ate at the meeting. It was awkward, balancing the lunch on those small desks while trying to review documents for whatever their agenda demanded. Such was the life of college professors. It looked easy on those schedules that hung on their office doors, but they only told half the story.

There was only one entrance to Franklin Hopper College, a large wrought iron gate with its gold letters memorializing forever, the name of Franklin Hopper, whose estate had been bequeathed to carefully chosen caretakers to create this lovely private institution of higher learning. The campus was full of winding paths and even a small stream that meandered past buildings of every type of architecture. In spring the trees were full of blossoms and in the fall blessed with bright foliage. But now, the autumn branches were half empty and their gray bones reached out like monstrous arms and finger longing to squeeze the clouds and scratch the sky. That was how Dora saw it. But today, it was just space to be traversed in a block of time that at best could only be endured. She and Mel stopped in the campus coffee shop and bought their medium hazelnut coffees in squeaky white Styrofoam cups and parted ways until lunch.

"Hope it goes well," Mel said before she crossed the small pathway heading to Cluster A as Dora went through the archway to Alumni Hall where her office on the third floor overlooked the Memorial Garden with its engraved bricks.

Dora reached into her pocket and retrieved her office key, opened the door and dropped her bag of notebooks and folders on her carefully arranged desk. Letting out a sigh, she placed her coffee cup on the desk and slid into her chair. She stared for a moment at the wall with her photos, and her eyes settled on the one of Bill in his faded jeans and green polo shirt. Nothing military looking there. Just Bill standing there smiling and leaning against a tree, his head framed by trunk and the branches extending up from it. Just a regular happy guy who happened to be a military doctor. Next to that was a picture of him in uniform. It was then she realized she would need to tell him what happened. She was hoping she would feel better by the time she emailed Bill or perhaps got to chat online.

"Oh Bill, I feel like crap!" she muttered as the door to the office opened and her office mate, Liz struggled in, balancing her coffee and her books.

"Dora, hey. How are you doing? I heard about the accident? You okay?" Liz dropped her books noisily on the cluttered desk.

"I think I need a few more days before I can say I'm okay."

"The boy okay? It was a boy, right?"

"He's okay. I haven't seen him, but yes, when they took him away, it didn't seem too bad."

"Well, as long as you are both okay…"

"I'm not really okay, but I am hoping that will pass. It all scrambled my brain a bit. I am so tired." Dora put her head down on her desk just like they did in school years ago when the teacher was tired.

"Not sleeping?"

"No, but I guess that's to be expected. I am hoping I can get some real sleep soon."

"Well, give it a few days and then when everything is back to normal, you will probably sleep better."

"I am not sure everything will be back to normal in a few days. I have been so broken apart."

"Really? It should be. If he's okay and you're okay, then it should all fall back into place, no?'

Dora looked up at Liz with disbelief written all over her face. "Maybe, it's only been two days. What am I thinking? Maybe you're right."

"It never happened to me, so I really don't have a clue. I just hope you can let go of it."

"Yeah, I'll try." Dora responded, thinking but not saying, "If only it will let go of me."

Liz was about to say what she always said, especially to her students, "You can't try, you have to do," but she thought better of it and just smiled as she sat down at her desk and opened her grade book. The time went pretty fast and Dora's first class was due to begin in ten minutes.

***

"So you have all read the Chapter on "Joy and Sorrow" in *The Prophet*, right? I would like to begin by asking you to write your overall response to the assignment, the reaction to the poem in general. Just a short free write…take a minute or two. Don't overthink it…just go

100

with it."

As Dora looked around the room, she noticed that some students were already writing, while others stared into space and pushed their pens and pencils slowly. She walked over to the window and watched as the last yellow leaf fell from the oldest oak tree on campus. Thanksgiving, a week away, she hadn't even discussed any plans with her mother. She glanced at her watch…thirty seconds…give them another 90.

"I don't get it,' one young woman with hot pink lipstick muttered while making little flowers on her paper with a just-as-hot-pink iridescent marker. *"and the selfsame well from which your laughter rises was oftentimes filled with your tears."* She let out a sigh of frustration.

"Just write what you feel about the poem. Don't need to explain it right now," Dora reassured her.

"You want me to be honest…say what I really think?"

"Sure!"

" It sucks."

Some in the class giggled, some looked disgusted and others nodded in agreement. All waited to see what Dora would say. Who tells their professor that a poem she chose to teach actually sucks?

"I'm sorry, Professor Victor but…"

"No, that's fine, but now you need to tell us why."

"Why? Why what?"

"Why, why does it… suck?"

"It just does. It makes no sense."

"Good, write that down, but now you have to tell us why you think it makes no sense."

The young woman squinted her eyes, "Are you agreeing that it ...um, makes no sense, Dr. Victor?"

"No, I didn't say that. But that's your opinion and that's okay. But, you do need to say why."

"Wait, are you going to just keep saying *why, why, why* until I fill this page?"

"No, Maggie, I want you to keep asking yourself that question until you feel you are done."

"Oh, whatever." The girl sighed and began to write, now with more fluidity, until she filled half a page with bright pink that could make a professor go blind and then emphatically slammed her marker down as if she wanted the whole class to know she was done. Dora waited a few seconds more and then asked the class to finish the thought they were on and then stop writing. Some students looked satisfied while others silently read what they had written. Others just sat staring into oblivion.

"Who would like to share all or part of what they wrote?" Dora waited until a hand shot up. Surprisingly it was the hot pink girl.

"I think this poem is difficult to understand. The guy who wrote this uses words that no one uses ...like *selfsame and oftentimes,* which nobody says. I think that people should write the way we talk. But even though I can figure these words out, they are boring. This poem is boring because he says things that I don't think he even understands. He seems fake to me."

"But this was written in 1923, nearly a century ago and people didn't speak as we do today." A male student in the back of the room said as he raised his hand. "And it's a philosophical, sort of religious poem, so that kind of language fits. It isn't that hard to understand really."

"I liked the poem," another young woman said from the front seat. "I have heard of it before, but never read the whole thing. I think there is a lot to think about. Parts of it, I had to reread and read aloud and even ask my roommate about. She is a philosophy major, so we have some good discussions."

The students were talking without hesitation now.

"Well, then" Dora continued, "Maybe we should talk about your responses to the ideas."

"I liked the line that said our joy is our sorrow unmasked. It made me think, but I am not sure I can agree. What I wrote last night was, *I can understand that joy and sorrow are related but, I think it is backwards how he explains it. I think our sorrow is our joy unmasked because when we lose someone, it was our joy that came first and that hides behind the mask we have to wear when we lose someone. And how you read this poem, what it means, is only about what has just happened in your own life.*"

"Like if your boyfriend cheats on you, you will have sorrow because when he was with you and you thought he was faithful, you had joy," a blonde girl in the back mumbled audibly as she wrote a young man's name on a paper over and over, crossing it out with a vengeance each time.

"But then that would be your sorrow that was hidden behind the mask because your boyfriend was probably always a no good rat and now you know it," another girl added with a giggle. So that makes sense…what the poet said."

"Gibran," Dora interjected. We are on a roll, she thought.

"Yes, this Gibran guy. But it works the other way around, too. Maybe you meet someone else who is better and then you have joy again and you can appreciate it more because of the grief that other guy gave you." The responses continued, one after another.

"I wrote about where he says that neither joy nor sorrow are greater, but are inseparable. Seems like a kind of double helix to me. We've all felt joy and sorrow and which one is greater to us depends on us."

The hot pink girl seemed to have suddenly gotten into the poem. "You know when I broke up with my boyfriend, my mother said, 'It is better to have loved and lost than never to have loved at all.' She actually said that. I was all crying with my mascara running down my face and feeling like I was going to throw up and she says that."

"So it didn't help?" Dora asked.

"She meant well, don't get me wrong, but no, it didn't help. It made it worse because I knew she didn't understand what I was going through. So this poet says all this stuff and it is like, don't worry, you can be happy again, but it won't last and I think, *what the fu…*I mean *heck.*"

"What her mother said is a cliché," a young male student chimed in. "My parents used to do that. Not so much anymore since my brother was killed in the Middle East. He was a Marine. No one has been the same since and no more clichés about anything. You get to feel like all that is just bullshit. My brother was a real joy to be with and now there is nothing left but sorrow."

"I am so sorry," Dora's thoughts, turned briefly to Bill. There was nothing more to say. The class went silent for a few moments before another student raised her hand and a young man shrugged.

"I found this poem to be depressing a bit because when he says, *when one sits with you at your table, the other is asleep in your bed*, it means that you can never really be happy."

The young woman who had been sitting quietly in the back doodling on her paper, added. "Maybe it means you have to take life as it comes. It is like a roller coaster and even when you can't change things, you can only change how you react."

"Well I am going to challenge you, now. This is a

more complex poem because if its language and style, but it is on the same topic, joy and sorrow." Dora handed out the poem. "It's by Keats."

"Ezra Jack?" A student in the back row shouted with a grin on his face. "I love Keats, read all his books, They were easy to understand and the pictures were great especially that one about the little kid and the chair."

"Nope, wrong Keats, although I always loved his writing and his art," Dora responded without missing a beat. "This is the poet John Keats. The title is *A Song of Opposites.* As you read this, write down some thoughts for discussion. Ask questions. You might start by asking if joy and sorrow are really opposites and thinking about how Gibran and Keats are similar and how they are different in their views in these poems. We will be working in groups and then we will discuss it as a class. I will read it once for you now and then expect you to put a serious effort into the assignment…not to get it right, but to get your thoughts out on paper so they can be shared. You can look up things you don't know just to get the references to names and words you are not familiar with, but go more for the ideas and how they relate to you and Gibran's ideas.

Dora began reading.

Welcome joy and welcome sorrow,

Lethe's weed and Herme's feather;

Come to-day and come to-morrow,

I do love you both together! ...

After she read the poem, she took a basket of miniature candies and passed it around.

"Okay, milk chocolates in the back corner, almonds in the other corner and coconuts up in front. She handed each student a copy of the group assignment and told them they could use the rest of the class time and would be expected to be ready to present what they did first thing next class.

When class ended, the students filed out the door and Dora stared out the window as if a switch had gone off, putting her back in a state of withdrawal. No more leaves were on the stone cold bareness of the tree outside. Her eyes and mind went out of focus and she grabbed onto the desk beside her to get her balance. Maggie, the hot pink girl, came back into the room to ask a question about the assignment, but Dora didn't see or hear her.

"Professor V?" the girl said softly, hoping to get Dora's attention without appearing rude. "I have a question about the homework?"

Dora continued to stare out the window while slipping down into the chair by the desk. The girl tried again. Nothing. She looked around and then tried once more.

"Professor? Are you okay?" Getting no response at all, Maggie left the room and went across the hall to Melanie's room.

"Excuse me, professor, I think there may be something wrong with Professor Victor. I was trying to talk to her, but she didn't seem to hear me and she looks weird.

"Oh, Okay," Melanie replied, hurrying across the hall where Dora was sitting very still and staring.

"Dora, you okay?"

It took a few seconds before Dora jumped a little and came back to the real world.

"Oh, I guess I was just lost in thought there for a moment."

"But you are okay?"

" I feel a little queasy, but that will pass. I have some fruit in my office. I'll be fine."

"Well call me if you aren't feeling well. Or call someone in your building. There was a student here to see you…": She looked around but the student was gone.

"No, no, don't worry, I'll be fine. I haven't been eating regularly. I'll be fine." Dora packed up her books and folders and headed back to her office. It was just too soon to be okay. No one should be surprised.

CHAPTER 12

Elizabeth set the tea sandwiches on the table. It had been a week. Mrs. Bookman had taken it upon herself to make a visit to the boy's family, explaining that she was the one who called 911. She nothing about knowing Dora or her mother. She became the unofficial and clandestine go-between for Dora and the boy. She was coming over later for a brief visit. Elizabeth knew her daughter would welcome any information about the boy. The table set and the scones and finger sandwiches covered and on the table, Elizabeth locked the front door and went out to the car, her keys in her hand. It was a short ride to Dora's house where her daughter was waiting at the front door anxiously.

"How are you doing, sweetie," her mother asked reverting back to her motherly tone as if Dora were a child who had fallen and skinned her knee.

"Hanging in there."

"Well, I guess that is the best we can do for now."

"I guess so. Thanks for coming to get me."

"My pleasure darling."

When they reached Elizabeth's house, Dora suddenly said, "I really miss Bill!"

"I know. I miss him, too. You two have been apart too long and it is time you get your husband back. This war is dragging on while people need to get back to their lives."

Elizabeth opened the front door and held it open.

"Well, I am not waiting for the war to end, Bill should be home in the spring or early summer for good, war or no war."

"That is certainly something to look forward to. The time can't go fast enough for me."

"I could have sworn that I heard him speak to me last night… I mean in a dream. He said he loved me."

"Of course he loves you. Did you ever doubt it? It won't be long before he tells you that in person."

"I know he loves me, but it seemed so real, like he was here." Dora took off her coat and hung it in the hall closet. "It is getting cold now. The holidays are going to be tough for me and even tougher for him, I suppose. Every day I worry that something bad will happen."

"I know. I worry, too and pray a lot. As for the holidays, guess you will just have to make do with me."

Elizabeth gestured toward the table and they both sat down. Te afternoon tea was comforting as usual, a ritual that would someday end, but hopefully not for a long time.

It was five o'clock when Angela Bookman rang the doorbell and Dora let her in.

"Come join us for tea." Dora tried to keep the surface level pleasantries from eroding and letting the growing depression left over from the accident show through.

Angela sat down at the table, tugged on her clothes to make herself comfortable and looked at Dora. "I saw the boy and he is fine. I went to his house and didn't say a word about you, but told them I was the one who called 911. I figured that that gave me some right to know how he was, this boy, Devin. He has a few stitches in that cut on the side of his chin and he has to wear a soft cast on his leg, but it is really only a bad sprain. He was walking around as if nothing had happened.

"Really? I am relieved to hear that." Dora was only partly reassured.

"His father said he told his son to be more careful and I am certain they know it was not your fault. The boy said it with me right there that when he got to the driveway where he came out, he looked right, but forgot to look left and darted right out in front of you. You couldn't have stopped. I think they know that."

"Well that's a big help to us, Angela. Thanks so much," Elizabeth said, pouring the tea. "So now you can relax, Honey. Get back to normal. It's done, over, and not your fault.

Dora stared at her mother for a second blankly, "But I did stop. Not sure how I did that, stopping in such a short distance…reaction time and all." Then she looked at Mrs. Bookman, "I don't know what I would have done without your help. The insurance company said I can't talk to the boy or his family, until this whole thing is settled which could be, like forever."

"They don't think the parents will sue or as anything do they?"

"You never know, I hope not."

"Well they know it is not your fault, they did everything but say those exact words, but if they did, I would be there in a second to tell anyone what they told me."

"That certainly is reassuring. I'd still like to see the boy, just to get a new image of him in my head where the one that was burned into it on the day of the accident is now."

"Maybe you will see him around town. Maybe that would be good."

"Yes, honey, you may just see him, you never know. Try not to think about it too much."

Mrs. Bookman's information should have helped Dora feel better, but what it did was only to make her feel less worse. She took a deep breath while her mother and Angela made small talk or drifted off into talking about the good old days, old residents of Waterview who had moved away or died and Dora began to feel isolated even as she sipped the herbal tea in her heirloom teacup and watched the crumbs from her scone crumble and fall onto her plate.

Dora thought she should have felt a hundred percent better, but she didn't. There was still a numbness about her that made her uneasy and made it hard to pinpoint what was wrong and what she could do about it. As she got ready for bed and the next day, collecting her school papers and putting everything in her brief case, she felt more and more like she knew this boy, somehow before the accident. She couldn't place anything or remember anything specific, but it was an eerie feeling that overtook her. It was almost as if some voice inside her was urging her, no compelling her, to remember something she had forgotten. Something important. Maybe that was just a normal part of the aftermath of a traumatic event. Still, she wanted to know more about Devin D'Angelo.

That night she didn't sleep well. She tossed and turned and when she started to doze off, her heart woke her up with its pounding, and when she was asleep, she had disturbing and fragmented dreams that made no sense, making her feel only that she was losing her mind. There was a doll in the road that she picked up and as she touched it, it disintegrated in her hands. There were images of her father clutching his chest and of Paul, his hands on fire and a child in flames running away and disappearing into the air. She got up frequently, to get some water, to wander around the house, check the locks on the doors, all while trying to avoid the shadows. She tripped over her own shoes in the living room and fumbled her way to the desk drawer to get a flashlight to chase away whatever might be lurking in the shadows. She opened the drawer and took the flashlight out and played with it turning it on and off, not really knowing why. Then, she noticed that something had fallen to the floor as she played with the flashlight. She bent down to pick it up. It was the newspaper clipping she had saved, the one with the picture of Paul saving the child from the burning house. She took it into the kitchen, her hands trembling, and turned on the light for a closer look. As she focused her eyes on the clipping, she felt an odd coldness and a strong force as if something were demanding that she read the story. She had read the same clipping many times before, but she felt she needed to do it again, carefully.

Firefighter Paul Hicks was praised for his bravery when he saved five-year-old Devin D'Angelo from his smoke filled home as the flames approached the child's bedroom. The boy was frightened and called for his mother repeatedly, but was otherwise unharmed. ...

Dora drew the clipping closer to her eyes and stared at the photo. She stood silent for a moment, taking it all in. Then it all fell into place.

"Oh my God," she shouted, "Oh Paul, it's him! Oh my God!"

CHAPTER 13

The night was unusually silent. Bill sat looking at the computer screen. The connection was intermittent and he wanted to check his email to see if Dolly had sent him any messages. While this kind of thing happened at home, too, since he'd been here, it made him feel more isolated, as if time were slowing down to a groan and his upcoming return home to Dolly was moving farther and farther away. It didn't help that Thanksgiving was only a week and a half away. The only family he had left were Dolly and her mother, so holiday dinners tended to be much the same as every other dinner when he was home. Dolly's brother was so far away that he and his family were never a part of these celebrations anymore. Bill felt sad, not only because he would be missing Dolly's pies and Elizabeth's old-style home cooking, but more because he knew the holiday would be empty for his wife as well. He kept hoping that one day they would grow into a real family again, if Dolly weren't so hesitant about having children. This year he would spend his holiday with more people and more food, but he knew he would still feel horribly empty.

He hungered for a normal day with the familiar and nostalgic menu, but he hungered even more for his wife's touch, her warmth, and her passion. So many times he ran those memories of their lovemaking through his mind. The longing could be unbearable and it made him wonder if things would be the same as they had been when he

finally made it home. Her emails always said, I love you,"
but he was especially happy to see her include something
more intimate and intense. Now and then, she would write,
"I ache to hold you, to become one with you," or
something similar. When she left that off, he would worry.
But part of him knew that even in a private email, she
would sometimes feel like the world were reading her
messages and be embarrassed by them,

"Damned computer," he said audibly. "We might as
well be on separate planets."

Dolly checked her email, but found nothing new from
Bill. Nevertheless, she composed a message for him.

*Darling, I hope you are keeping safe and well. I miss
you so terribly. Keep your spirits up by knowing how
much I love you and miss you.*

*Mom and I are keeping each other company. Mom
found a new friend, or an old friend, a woman who was
raised here and moved away, but is now back here. I think
it is great that she has someone besides me and some
church friends she sees on Sundays to have tea with
occasionally. She loves her tea. She is keeping you in her
prayers and asks about you all the time.*

*Things here are going okay. I did have a scare and I
am still shaken up, but nothing really bad...just an
accident with a kid on a bicycle. The boy darted out from
behind parked cars over by the school and I stopped as
soon as I could, but not until he smashed into my
windshield. But don't worry, it sounds far worse than it*

was. I was shaken up, still am a bit, but his injuries were minor and I got the windshield fixed already so as of now, all is well. Nothing for you to worry about.

So, I hope you are not too stressed out. I know my little troubles are minuscule compared to what you are faced with. I am not sure what Mom and I are doing for Thanksgiving, but I think maybe she would enjoy volunteering at the church. They have a turkey dinner with all the fixings for the homeless and folks who are alone. She talks about you all the time. She misses you, too. With just the two of us here, it may be the only meaningful way to celebrate Thanksgiving. I hope you get to spend the day with less stress and at least some pleasant company. This is not a year I ever hope to repeat. So stay safe and know that I love you. Managing without you is empty and cold. I can do all the things I have to do but none of the things I want to do, if you know what I mean, (wink.)

Email me when you can.

Send...click.

Dora thought about telling him that the boy she hit was the same kid that Paul had saved from that fire, but she realized Bill might not even know what she was talking about and she felt uncomfortable talking about Paul with anyone, thinking that something might give away the secrets she hid inside her. It wasn't relevant anyway. Bill had enough to deal with.

She turned on the television and surfed until she found

the movie, *Somewhere in Time,* and watched it from the middle for what must have been the fiftieth time. It was a wonderful movie to escape to. Fantasy about any kind of time travel was where she found comfort, but time travel to reconnect with a long lost lover? She put her feet up, put a pillow under her head and before her eyes closed she watched a forlorn Richard sitting on a white bench outside the Grand Hotel as his love, Elise emerged from the trees far below. When the actress sees him, she calls out his name and the two run to meet each other on the long winding staircase. The music swells and Dora is once again transported to a place where the impossible is not only possible, but enchantingly real. Perhaps this night would bring no nightmares. Perhaps she, too could escape to a better time and have her husband back again.

CHAPTER 14

An extraordinary sunrise is wasted when seen from behind barbed wire. That's the way it seems at first, but then, as the remnants of plastic bags and other debris tangled in the wire are silhouetted against the orange and blush sky, they transform themselves into vines and blossoms welcoming a new morning, a new day. It can be breathtaking in a melancholy way. Early morning, this brief calm, could bring anything from relative quiet to a barrage of explosions of human suffering beyond what any civilian mind could fathom. In the distance, prayers had already been offered up to Allah.

Bill looked at the torn leg of a young man, almost young enough to be his own son if he hadn't been so involved in medical school and the military when other young men were having kids. The explosion had done so much damage and tattered it from the knee down, Bill didn't know how much of the leg could be saved and there were broken bones in the thigh and the pelvis as well. The soldier was unconscious, resting now and unaware of what was to come. Bill had cleaned and treated the remaining flesh and bone, but now all that could be done was to wait until the soldier could be airlifted out and transferred to Landstuhl in Germany, if that were even possible. He would consult with other doctors in the next few hours..

In the dining facility, early preparations were

underway for Thanksgiving dinner. The naked white turkeys were being handled by diligent hands. Butter was slathered on the skin, butter and oil and salt and pepper.

"Is there any rosemary?" the woman in the white apron asked. "I like to use some when I do Thanksgiving turkey."

" I don't know. What does it look like?" the young man replied as he searched about the pantry shelves.

"Oh, just see if there are any herbs, fresh or dried…green things. What do you have for Thanksgiving dinner when you are home?" She made idle conversation as she massaged the pudgy flesh of the poultry.

"Ham hocks and collard greens."

"Okay then, pull out whatever you see that looks like home. We have ham. I don't know about the hocks, but once we get it all together, I will do my best to make it just like mama does."

"Like mama did. Mom's been gone for three years now," he said with a quiver in his voice.

"Oh honey, I am sorry to hear that." She paused a moment and looked at the young man. He was far too young to have lost his mom. "Did she teach you how to peel potatoes?"

"Indeed she did." He was composed now, his voice took on a more cheerful tone. "Fast and accurate, no waste. We weren't wealthy."

"Well, great. Can't have Thanksgiving without

mashed potatoes and gravy. Just be careful you don't cut yourself. We have enough blood around here."

"Haven't done that since I was ten. I hope we are not the only ones making dinner."

"No, Sweetie," the middle aged woman with the hair net smiled. "We have a whole army of cooks, no pun intended. They will be joining us at 7 am. Got volunteers like you and the rest of the food service personnel. We even have two who actually graduated from culinary school and are trained chefs. We are in good shape."

***

Dora had mixed feelings about Thanksgiving. Being without Bill made it bland and empty, but each time she heard from him and found out that he was okay, her gratitude was renewed. These weeks had been a mix of all kinds of feelings, but amid all the emotional turmoil, she knew she had much to be thankful for. Bill would finally be ending his time in the military in five months or so and her mother was still in good health, and those many shared cups of tea, although sometimes taken for granted, were most certainly a blessing. It was often the little things that turned out to be the ones we miss the most. Someone had told her that. She couldn't remember who. Having her mother to confide in with Bill on the other side of the world did help, even though Dora would sometimes cringe at the way her mother worded things, a minor idiosyncrasy in the grand scheme of things.

Even Mrs. Bookman had turned out to be a good

family friend and not nearly as much of a busybody as Dora had first suspected. It was good that she had finally heard from her daughter and would be spending Thanksgiving with her and her fiancé. Elizabeth and Dora had decided to spend their holiday volunteering at the Church, helping prepare and serve Thanksgiving dinner. It was the best choice. Dora was sure of that. And one more thing to be thankful for, perhaps the most important, the D'Angelo boy had not been seriously hurt in what could have been a tragic event. He was back in school and moving on and Dora's nightmares had subsided some, although not completely. Dora slept better now, sometimes with the aid of medication, but often not. The meds were only temporary until her body got back into the habit of following a natural rhythm. She would go back to sleep and sleep well until morning while the house still smelled of freshly baked pies for the church dinner. Her last thought before she fell asleep was of Bill and the Thanksgiving Dinner he would have on the other side of the world in just a few hours. "Happy Thanksgiving my love," she whispered as she nodded off.

***

Brenda Gabriel had just finished taking care of a young woman that reminded her of herself a few years back. Like Brenda, she had left home to join the military right out of high school hoping to find some meaning in life after a series of losses and disappointments. For Brenda, it had been the loss of her parents in a tragic car accident, leaving only herself and her older brother who saw her into adulthood and then sadly kissed her good-bye as she went after her freedom and he went after a life of marriage and children. They kept in touch of course, and looked forward to the day when she would come home and they could catch up on the years that separated them. There were no more Thanksgivings and Christmases with family for her, for even as she tried to get back home, other things seemed to get in the way. Most of the time, it was weather, illnesses or just bad luck. But she had resigned herself to observing holidays wherever she was with people who had chosen a life in the military, at least for the time being. As the early morning turned to noon, the smell of turkey and pies wafted through the building. Brenda walked into the hall and she called over to the kitchen staff, "Can I do anything to help?"

"Nope. We have it under control, but you can find a seat as we will be starting the early seating. "We should have the turkey and fixins," ready soon." The woman wore a white uniform and a welcoming smile. Brenda had never. seen her before, but she brought back an air of Mama and home that Brenda found comforting.

***

Back in Waterview, Father Kelly greeted everyone individually at the door to the large multi-purpose room which was now set up for Thanksgiving Dinner. One shift of volunteers, including some homeless people and a few veterans, had decorated the room with turkeys, pilgrims and cornucopias with fruit pouring out. A real one was in the middle of the buffet table with fresh fruit the poor in the community rarely got to enjoy. Even though it was one very large community geographically speaking, the poorer areas were isolated and there were few places to buy fresh fruits and vegetables. Father Kelly and Father Joe found it hard to explain to some people who didn't have to worry about where their next meal came from that there were those hard working poor who, at the end of the day, couldn't scrape together enough money for bus fare. That's why, along with nonperishable foods in their pantry, they also requested that people donate Metro cards that could be used on the buses. But usually, people preferred to donate canned and boxed goods. Metro cards were too much like money. Maybe that was it.

Sister Marianna entered the room carrying a large sweet- smelling ham on a platter with roasted sweet potatoes. Her face beamed as she inhaled deeply in anticipation of carving it up enjoying it with so many hungry and good people.

Elizabeth and Dora brought their contributions to the kitchen and set them on the counter where there was just enough space for the pecan pie and the cheesy mashed potatoes they had made. Dora found them two seats together and put her jacket and her mom's Public TV tote on them. They mingled for a while making small talk with those they knew and some they didn't, and then sat down when Father Kelly got ready to say Grace.

CHAPTER 15

After Thanksgiving, the days flew by, rushing toward Christmas., For Dora, the holiday season only meant more emptiness. She would go through minimal rituals, mostly for her mother, but her heart was not in it. Not even close to it. The sadness clumped up in her throat. She had a little tree that came out of the box all decorated from her office and she stuck it on the coffee table on top of a red and green plaid placemat. *Deck the Halls,* she mumbled to herself, in a bah-humbug tone. In all due respect to the Prince of Peace, it was not about bells and tinsel and lights, but she couldn't even summon up the real meaning of Christmas, not at all. Sadness, bordering on depression, was not uncommon during the "festive" season. But it was also wrong to let that take away the joys of others. Mom would get whatever merriness Dora could muster up, even if it took an academy award level performance.

On the first Friday in December, Waterview pulled out its Christmas spirit and traditions with a grand celebration on Main Street. They closed the block to traffic, kept the stores open and made sure all the lights and decorations were placed just as they always were. Santa Claus appeared in a horse drawn white carriage, and carolers from the Methodist Church sang Christmas carols in Victorian costumes. Their rendition of *Hark the Herald Angels Sing* was impressive. Down the block where there was the smell of roasting chestnuts, the high school students were singing *Silver Bells* as puffs of white vapor came out of their mouths to meet the cold air.

Dora and Elizabeth were bundled in winter coats and knitted hats and scarves handmade by Taylor's wife, Miriam and sent down just in time for the cold weather. They walked along the street searching for the spirit they remembered from Christmases past, not the ghosts, just the spirit. Sometimes the ghosts crept in anyway. Why wouldn't they? They were always there. Christmas drew them all the closer.

"I remember when your dad used to wait until 7 pm on Christmas Eve and go down the block to Mr. Schmidt's house where he had all the freshly cut trees from upstate," Elizabeth reminisced.

"Yeah, I remember that," Dora said. Even the mention of her dad made her sad again. It had been 15 years now. 'He and Taylor used to argue about which tree looked the best and whichever one Dad chose, it would be the wrong one according to her brother. I never cared, but they would bicker until bedtime over it."

"Yes indeed they did. But I loved the smell of the tree and didn't care as much what it looked like. By the time you got the ornaments and the tinsel on it, it didn't look the same anymore anyway.

There was a pause in the conversation as Dora wondered if she would ever feel the Christmas spirit again. Thoughts about Paul filled her mind as if a dam had broken and the waters of memory surged like a flood. They used to go over each other's houses and see the tree. Going to visit to see people's trees was a big deal back in the day. They used to keep them up at least to New Years Day or even until the Epiphany, the 12th day of Christmas, when the wise men finally showed up in Bethlehem. Those were real trees then and needed to stay watered so they wouldn't catch fire or lose needles all over the floor.

"We never put our trees up before Christmas Eve back then," Elizabeth said. And we left them up until the Christmas season was over."

"I was just remembering that." Dora said, feeling a bit like her mother had read her mind. He mother probably could read her mind. That thought made Dora shudder, but she pretended it was from the cold.

"Pull your scarf tighter, dear," Elizabeth said, helping her daughter wrap the woolen scarf around her neck and looking deep in to her eyes. "I know you are sad. When spring comes, you will be better."

"Long time till then."

"I know, but it will come and Bill will come with it."

"A lot can happen between now and then."

"Gotta stay positive." Her mother gave her a quick hug and they moved along. "Let's have a hot chocolate."

"Sure."

A woman dressed as Santa's helper poured the free hot chocolate into two paper cups and stuck a marshmallow in each one. "'ave a lovely evening, "she said in a fake cockney accent.

"I didn't know Santa's Helpers were British," Elizabeth giggled.

"Neither did I, but why not?"

Up ahead three Marines, two men and one woman, stood outside the old bank-turned-restaurant beside a large box labeled Toys for Tots.

"Wouldn't they do better to be outside the toy store?" Dora commented, wondering why they hadn't thought of that.

"The toy store closed. It has been gone for a few years now."

"Well, I guess I haven't been paying attention. I wish I had brought a toy. I like to donate to them."

"Don't worry, they have a box in the library, too."

"Good to know." Dora couldn't help being reminded by the uniforms that there were more in uniform on active duty around the world. Sometimes she could not even wrap her mind around the reasoning that sent so many to fight a war that was not going to stop anything, change anything for the better, or ever be a war to end all wars, unless the whole population was annihilated and the only thing left was a huge sign saying, *Here lies mankind. Killed by its own stupidity.* Elizabeth remained silent and then suddenly dropped the hot chocolate on the ground splattering it on Dora's pant leg and shoes. Dora looked at her mother who was doubled over, her face grimacing with pain.

"Mom, are you okay?" Dora grabbed her mother. The drink was not that hot, barely hot at all. What was happening?

Her mother didn't answer, but tried to straighten up, only to collapse to the ground as Dora followed her to the sidewalk. "Oh my God, Mom!"

Several passers-by rushed over. It was evident that the lady was in distress and was not going to get up.

"I'll call 911." It was a man's voice. "Please send an ambulance…" The voice trailed off as the man paced on the sidewalk.

"Mom, speak to me."

"Pain," her mother mumbled, conscious, but obviously in extreme discomfort.

"Okay, Mom, we are getting an ambulance. It's not far. You'll be okay."

It was only about five minutes, when the familiar sound of the siren instantly connected Dora to the accident, but then her mind flooded with thoughts of her mother, as Santa's Helper and the Marines called for people to clear the way. The red flashing lights mixed with the festive decorations turning the scene into a strange irony of ritual celebration and urgency. It all happened fast and before Dora could even think straight and the paramedics were loading the stretcher into the ambulance while Dora rushed to her car so she could meet the ambulance at the hospital only two miles away.

Dora was running now, heading to the parking lot as if racing to th finish line of a major event. Once again everything seemed to be happening in slow motion, and she opened the car door and got in, fastening her seat belt without even knowing what she was doing. She could hear the siren rising to a full blaring sound. Dora headed to the exit and moved quickly toward the sound of the ambulance and emergency room. *Be careful*, she reminded herself, as other vehicles blocked her movement and lights seemed to remain red far too long. She took a deep breath and made her way into the ER parking lot after pulling over to let yet another ambulance go ahead of her.

Elizabeth was just being transferred to a hospital bed in the ER when Dora got there.

"I'm her daughter," Dora told a dark-haired woman in a blue tunic who was hooking up the monitors. The woman nodded as she continued, while another woman, a redhead, in a similar tunic asked Elizabeth her name and date of birth.

"What happened?" a doctor asked as he came in from behind a curtain where a man was moaning.

"She was drinking some hot chocolate and then had these pains and collapsed.

"Hmmm," the doctor said, turning his attention to Elizabeth. "What's your name?" he said in a loud voice as another woman came in with an ID bracelet and placed it on Elizabeth's wrist. "Having some pain? Um, Mrs. Black?"

Elizabeth responded with a nod and a moan.

"I'm here, Mom," Dora said taking her mother's hand lightly in her fingers, trying to offer comfort without disturbing the wires from the monitors.

"Hurts," her mother said.

"Mrs. Black? I am Dr. Reyes. I am going to press on your abdomen and you tell me if it hurts." He began pressing firmly and got no response until he hit the spot, between the ribs and a few inches down. "

"Ow," she gasped.

"I am not feeling anything where she has the pain. Nothing abnormal, but we need to do some tests."

"Let me get you a chair." It was the woman in the blue tunic who had hooked up all the monitors. "Sammy, can you bring over that chair for this young woman?"

A young man in green scrubs dragged a chair over and motioned to Dora to sit down as the doctor and the women in blue moved away to the man in the next cubical who was moaning louder now.

"Mom, how are you doing?" Dora squeezed her mother's hand gently.

"It comes and goes. Feels not as bad right now."

"Well, that's good. Just relax. They are going to do some tests."

" I know. I heard."

"Well, just relax, Mom. We will be here a while."

"Sorry to ruin your evening."

"We have seen it all and done it all before. Not a problem for me. Just take it easy.

"I feel like taking a nap."

"Go ahead then. I am sure they will wake you up if the need anything. I feel a bit like dozing, myself. Not the most comfortable chair, but I can make myself more comfortable. "Dora shifted her body around so she could pull up her knees and rest her head on her hand. Elizabeth closed her eyes and fell asleep.

Dora watched the clock as the hands clicked the minutes away. She looked at the monitors. Blood pressure was pretty stable. Little green mountains all looked normal to a non-medical eye. Now it was just about waiting.

After waiting about an hour, Dr. Reyes decided to admit Elizabeth for observation, Dora went home to get some real sleep. That was all she wanted, maybe six or seven good uninterrupted hours of sleep, but that was rare these days. Now added to the flashbacks of the accident, her worries about Bill and regrets regarding Paul, she had to face the reality that her mother wouldn't always be well. Hopefully, this was not serious. These things happened, even to the healthiest of us. Even though her mother had been very stubborn about getting that flu shot, she usually took good care of herself. She got her tests and checkups every year and saw a whole team of doctors just for the sake of precaution. She seemed to be energetic most of the time. Maybe it was food poisoning or something, although she and Dora had pretty much eaten the same things and Dora felt fine except for some depression and anxiety.

Her sleep had been interrupted only a few times and fortunately, even with all that was going on, Dora got enough hours to get up in the morning and get herself back to the hospital in time for visiting hours. She decided to go there as soon as she was dressed and have a bite in the coffee shop before going up to see her mother. They sold a nice breakfast sandwich with eggs and ham, but she couldn't finish it. She had two cups of coffee and then headed up to the second floor, following the blue line on the floor as the lady at the reception desk has instructed.

"Really, this is all I get for breakfast?" The voice was clear and familiar as Dora approached the room, relieved that her mom was awake and sounded fine.

"Is that my mom complaining about the food here?"

"We have her on a liquid diet just until the doctor says it is okay to eat solid food," a woman in white said.

"Apple juice and orange jello. Not even colorful. What's this supposed to do for me?"

"Hi Mom. I am glad to see you are feeling better."

"Yes, my darling. I think I am fine and don't have to be here."

"Well, let them check you out to be sure. You don't have any pressing appointments today, do you?"

"What day is it?"

"Saturday, remember last night was Friday."

"Oh, okay well, plans…let me see…just that tryst I had planned with Paul Newman. Four o'clock, I think.

"Mom, he is dead."

"Oops, better cancel that, then. Don't wanna go there. Who is still alive that I can have an affair with? Anyone? No? Then I guess I can stay here till tomorrow. I need to be out by tomorrow."

"What's tomorrow?"

"Sunday!"

"Yeah, I know that, Mom but why do you have to be out by tomorrow?"

"Gotta go to church." She turned to the nurse's aide who was bringing in a pitcher of water. "I never miss mass on Sundays."

"Right, Mom. Never."

"We have mass here. And if you aren't up to going, the priest will bring communion right to your room."

"You mean like take out?"

The lady gave a short laugh. "You seem to be doing very well, Mrs. Black. I bet you will be just fine."

"Ha, ha Mom, she got you. No reason to leave the hospital too soon."

"They have all bases covered, don't they?"

"Sure do, so drink your juice and eat your jello."

Elizabeth picked up the juice from the tray and downed it like a thirsty man who has been in the desert for a week without water.

"That was apple juice right? They were in here with a cup asking for a specimen earlier. I don't know what they did with it."

"Mom, you are in rare form."

"I only like hospitals for giving birth."

"You wouldn't want to go through that again."

"No, been there, done that. But it was worth it. You are a great daughter, you know that?'

"Thanks Mom. I couldn't ask for a better mother." Dora gave her mother's hand a squeeze as Dr. Reyes walked in.

"Good morning, Mrs. Black."

"Good morning, doctor," she said flirtatiously.

"So how are you doing?"

"Anyone I can," she said, quickly putting her hand over her mouth in mock embarrassment.

"Mom!" Dora wasn't used to this side of her mother.

The doctor stopped, grinned and replied, "I said HOW are you doing?"

"Oh I am feeling much better thank you. My daughter, maybe not so much. She looks a little pale."

"I'm fine, but not sure what has gotten into you."

"Let's not go there."

"Is your mother always this funny?" the doctor asked.

"She is funny but, she is not usually so…"

"Risque'," her mother knew the right word.

"Well, here's the thing. You seem to be doing well enough, but you do have a slight fever and we need to keep an eye on that so we'd like to keep you here a few days."

"Who's gonna do my Christmas shopping? And where will I get my afternoon tea? My scones? "

"Mom, you don't have any Christmas shopping to do. You only have me right now and you have time. You need to get well."

"I am sure we can get you some tea whenever you want it. I don't think there are scones here, but I have been to England and had tea. I am sure we can find you a biscuit or two. Fill out the form on the tray," the doctor said.

"Can I have some real food?"

"Let's stick to the liquid for now until we see how you do with that. A piece of toast or a cracker wouldn't hurt. Maybe some pudding, but no steak and fries tonight, okay?"

"Okay, doctor." Elizabeth was resigned but not enthused. She would be confined and limited, She hated being confined and limited.

"It's a good thing we didn't make plans to go to Mohonk."

"Maybe next year with Bill. That would be nice wouldn't it?"

"Yes, wouldn't be so lonely."

When visiting hours were over, Elizabeth told Dora not to bother to come back at night because there was no problem and nothing Dora could do anyway. She would see her the next morning. Dora wasn't sure what she should do. At least being at the hospital with her mom was a change from moping around the house and trying to feel normal. But she did have some student papers to read and some last minute plans to finalize as the semester came to a close. From that point on, it would be turning in grades and going to luncheons and "parties" and then facing Christmas. She could get that done. You never knew what the next day might bring.

Dora returned to the hospital the next day to find her mother's fever was still high and although she could have some solid food, it was what her mother referred to as "mushy stuff." The flirtations with the doctors ceased and Elizabeth was resting comfortably as possible after a night of diarrhea and even vomiting. The doctor she usually went to came and did her rounds, having been surprised to see her there.

"Elizabeth, what happened?" she asked.

"Hi doc. I don't know. Got sick and here I am."

"Well, we'll have to make sure you get better. Your fever is 101 so we need to get that down. You need a lot of fluids as you are nearly dehydrated. I see you have the

IV so that should help. There is a virus going around. It could be that, but we need to be sure, you know, at," she paused.

"Yeah, I know at my age, everything is a big deal."

"No, you are generally in good health, but let's not be careless. A couple more days and we should get it all cleared up."

So that was it. Dora would be there whenever she could in her workday and all would work out. Sunday rolled into Monday and after she taught her class and held her office hour, she went right to the hospital to see how her mom was doing. Each day she looked better and she was eating regular food by Tuesday and on Wednesday her fever had broken and was back to normal. Her doctor decided she could go home on Friday morning.

Dora brought some fresh clothes early Friday morning and had a quick breakfast in the coffee shop, something she couldn't do on weekdays. Friday was her day off so her mother's release was convenient. She finished her coffee and donut. There was no egg sandwich this time, she was just not that hungry. She looked at the clock and took the elevator up to her mother's room. Elizabeth was awake and eagerly awaiting her discharge.

"The doctor hasn't come in yet, but when she does, she will discharge me and we can get on to Christmas shopping."

"Oh please, Mom, don't worry about me. And you can send up a fruit basket or something to Taylor and Miriam."

"Okay, if you say so."

"Hello Elizabeth, Ready to go home?" The doctor looked cheerful as she patted Elizabeth on the head. "I signed your discharge papers, but I would like you to take it easy for a while and call me if you have any problems at all."

"I have trouble finding a boyfriend." She seemed to be back to her old self.

"Yeah, don't we all, "the doctor laughed. "Mrs. Black, when you are feeling better, you should get a flu shot."

"Yes, doctor."

"I'll make sure she behaves herself, Doc. I'll try to get her to get the shot."

Dora was happy to see her mom happy, even if this was not a side of her she had seen before.

"Okay, I will have a wheelchair sent in and you are free to go. The nurse will give you instructions, but all they are is what I said."

The nurse came in and handed Dora the papers. "We will call you tomorrow to make sure you are doing well.

"I was going to go out dancing."

"Well, maybe wait a week or so for that." The nurse smiled and the aide came in to wheel Elizabeth down to the elevator and out to the car."

"I'll spin around to my house and pick up the mail," Dora told her mother. I will run in and get a coffee cake I baked last night. I'll only be a few minutes."

"Sounds good."

Dora pulled the mail, a few catalogs and some bills, out of the mailbox at the bottom of the steps. As she climbed the steps to her front door, she saw what looked like a newsletter stuck in her door, but as she got closer, she realized it was not a newsletter. It looked more official than that and when she took it from the door, she realized what it was. It had her name, Another name….DeAngelo and the words, SUMMONS AND COMPLAINT. *Oh shit.* They were suing her for the accident. Really? Like things weren't bad enough. How was she going to deal with this crap? Why should she even have to? She saved that kid's life. *Bastards.*

CHAPTER 16

Christmas at the field hospital was solemn. In less than two weeks, eight soldiers had been killed when two helicopters were shot down, one exploding immediately, and the other so damaged that it crashed. Add to that, three Navy Seals who were ambushed in the mountains, and you had nothing to celebrate. The wounded continued to come in, be treated and if possible and necessary, sent to Landstuhl. All of it was wearing heavy on Bill and the others. Bill had always stood up tall and proud of his ability to keep his strength even in times like these, but then he thought, there had never been times quite like these. He had seen blood and bone and minds trapped in a loop of the most horrendous images and sounds. But this was worse. He wasn't sure why, but it was far worse. He started having nightmares and flashbacks that he had never had before. On the one hand, it helped him understand what the wounded were going through, but on the other, it made him feel even more powerless and to question why it even mattered to go on with it all.

Dora hadn't shown her mother the summons and complaint. There was no reason to bring that up the first day she was home from the hospital. She felt it in the pit of her stomach, but she tried to act normal. Christmas came and went with church, of course, and whatever spirit they could muster up. The whole idea of going to a resort in the mountains had fizzled away when Angela was invited to her daughter's apartment for Christmas. Instead they had taken the train and eaten out at a nice restaurant in the city and watched the skaters in Rockefeller Center. It was very crowded, but it was better than sitting alone at home staring at each other. Dora had helped her mother get the gifts sent off to Taylor, Miriam and their daughter who was beginning to think about college. Now it was that interim time between Christmas and New Year's Day when the only purpose seemed to be clean up get some things in order even as parts of her life were in disarray.

Dora held the legal papers in her hand. She read them over and over. She new that the ten million dollars wasn't serious and that according to the insurance company was more like $15,000, but they would fight for her, whatever that meant. She suspected that what they would fight for had nothing to do with her but was only about not paying too much money. The plaintiffs were crazy, the claims adjuster had said, to expect even that. First, it was the kid's fault and his medical bills were being paid by his own insurance, and second, Dora was not at fault and it was bad precedent to settle a claim for anything more than $2,000 for his minor injuries.

"If it were up to me, Mr. Wood said, "They wouldn't get a penny. But don't expect this to be over any time soon. They will hang on and hang on and so will we. That's how it works."

Dora had found the conversation depressing. Just one more thing to pile on her already burdened mind. The nightmares had continued. On and on and on, the thoughts were like a hundred people trying to get through a doorway all at once. Sometimes she was so low down she just curled up into a fetal position in her bed in the dark and other times she let out a silent scream. *Paul, Bill, Mom, Somebody, Help Me!* She believed that if she could see the boy walking around and being normal, that at least some of the images of him bleeding in the street might go away. Knowing without seeing was not enough. Then there was the memory of seeing Paul standing on the side of the street, just for a second and then … gone. Could she have made that up? Was she going mad?

Dora showed her mother the complaint and read it to her the day before New Year's Eve.

"But the boy is okay?"

Dora nodded.

"Then why worry? I am sure the insurance company will take care of it."

"Mom, I am not okay. Just because there are no marks on my body doesn't mean I am not wounded, emotionally, mentally. I cannot function. I can't sleep and I get angry and then sad just at the thought that I cannot get closure, a way to see the boy and get the negative images out of my mind."

"You can't just think of other things? Nicer things? Take a sleeping pill?"

"No, Mom, I can't. This is something my mind has no control over. And no, I know what you are thinking, *Mind over matter,* but my mind isn't working and I can't get it to work and it is driving me crazy."

"Oh, okay. I think I have been there at least once in my life. Are you depressed?"

"Depressed is part of it, a big part of it. I cry a lot. Everything comes together and I cry and cry. Paul's death, Bill, and I worry about you." Dora realized she had mentioned Paul, suddenly afraid that her mother would figure something out. She let it go. It was too late to take it back.

"Oh I know, but maybe with time, it will go away. We get over things in time. It is just so wrong that these people are letting you go though so much when all you need is to see the boy."

"And talk to them, explain how I couldn't have done anything different. I would even prefer to go to trial so I had my day in court, but I don't have control over that either. The insurance company controls everything and I have control over nothing. It's my life, but I can't do anything. I am totally not in control and it makes me feel powerless and useless."

"Well, Honey, I hope things get better for you. Talk to the insurance guy and maybe he can do something to hurry it all along. Bill will be home in less than three months now and that will make you feel a whole lot better."

"If I can last that long."

"Oh dear. You must."

CHAPTER 17

Dora didn't want to complain about what was happening to her in her emails. It wasn't going to help Bill and because he would probably be preoccupied with real problems, real pain and suffering, hers would only make her look petty perhaps in his eyes. It got harder and harder to read her husband's feelings in those emails. Sometimes she wouldn't know if he was trying to protect her from the grisly details of what he saw everyday. She couldn't help but wonder how different he might be when he came home in a few months. He had to be different, but what if he could no longer relate to her? What if he no longer really loved her?

She knew she had to tell him about the lawsuit. They were on the same insurance policy, for one thing. His name appeared with hers on the summons and complaint. Mr. Wood had explained that even if he had been home, Bill would not have had to go to the deposition, which would be held in a month or so, maybe. He really would not be involved and no, since she was not at fault, the insurance premium would not go up.

"Forget what you have heard, that's not how we do it," he had reassured her. But she still felt that Bill should know. If she just skipped it, he would ask why she didn't tell him when he got home and the stupid lawsuit was still not settled.

Dora opened her inbox. It was January 3rd. Back to

work tomorrow. New Year's Eve and Day had gone by without much ceremony. Both Dora and her mother stayed home and watched the ball drop in NYC and then went to bed. The hope that this would be a better year crossed Dora's mind, but she really didn't expect any miracles. Her prayers and hopes for world peace had turned to "Just get my husband out of there!" She was happy to see an email from Bill in her inbox.

Hi Babe, miss you. Things here are no better. Christmas, I think I told you, was dismal. The New Year came with little excitement. Someone had some confetti and threw it up at midnight. But here, we don't even think about the hopes and expectations most people have when the year changes. Here, nothing changes. I am looking forward to coming home and finally being with you. I worry about you sometimes, okay, all the time. I was sorry to hear your mom was sick but glad she is doing better. Thanks you for keeping me updated on family things like that. I love you and want to hold you again. I may be a little different from all this blood and death, but if you understand that, then we should be fine.

Reply: January 3

Oh Bill, I miss you so much and don't want to burden you with my little problems, but I think you should know that I am being sued for that accident with the kid I told you about back in November. It will be fine. I still have flashbacks and nightmares, but from a practical standpoint, it won't do anything to us financially. The man from the insurance company assured me that our premiums will NOT go up. So I am just angry that people sue when they know it was not the driver's fault. What does that teach their kids? Now when I say that, it is usually the beginning of a rant so I will stop. I pray for you everyday...all day actually. Stay safe my Love. I began counting and marking off the days on the new calendar. Stay safe.

Reply: January 4

Don't worry about sharing your problems. It's good just to connect with you and know I am still important enough in your life to share them and hear of things going on, even the difficult things that have nothing to do with war. But you know what they say? Lawsuits are like war, but without the blood. Don't underestimate your feelings and what you are going through. I wish I were there to help you. Broken bones, broken minds and broken hearts, damage is damage and you need to address it before it gets worse. Think about the possibility of finding a therapist who deals with PTSD because I think that is what you have. Take a week or so. Maybe just knowing you are doing something about it will make it a little easier, but find someone who specializes in that. Maybe someone who uses EMDR. You can look that up. They are using it even here with soldiers who have the symptoms, so they will already be started before they go home. Let

Dora felt a little better after the email exchange with Bill. And he was right, as soon as she decided to look for a therapist, the burden lightened a little. It would take time to find the right person and she didn't know how to do that, but she began looking on the Internet. She was a little unsure of how to find someone who would understand and not think she was overreacting. A therapist who was more into the human side than the textbook side of his or her profession was what she wanted. She looked at the newspaper on the coffee table. Maybe there would be something in there. A therapist that advertised in the classified section? Maybe not the best idea.

Dora searched the newspapers and then the Internet using the terms PTSD, therapist, and EMDR. She found a few in the area, but none really clicked as far as that something she was looking for, that something that made things hit a nerve, light up and connect. There were seemingly good therapists with impressive credentials, but it just wasn't feeling right. Deep inside, she feared that even a professional would think she was making far too much if all this. After all, the boy was all healed and back to his activities as if nothing had happened and she was okay, physically, but physically isn't all there is, not by a long shot. No, she was not okay. She just wasn't, and she wouldn't be until she could meet the boy and his family, face to face and get this behind her for good.

Every night, she wondered if she would sleep peacefully or be haunted by images of what could have been had even a single factor been different. Obsessive? Of course! Horrible images, unbearable grief that she imagined led her to question her sanity and see the world as both hostile and dangerous. Once, she had felt in control of her life and then she met Bill whose connection to the military removed that control. Then there was the accident. Not much was left for her to feel in control of anymore. And her mother's increasing frailty, although not apparent to Elizabeth herself, was something that Dora thought about often.

But then there were nights when she went to bed so tired that she did sleep and there were the rare, but welcome dreams that comforted her, dreams where Bill held her and told her everything would be okay. She longed to hear his voice and feel his arms around her. He had already been gone far to long. Two months were all that were left now. Bill would be coming home in a few months if all went as planned.

His arms wrapped around her, enclosing her and enveloping her in his scent. He smelled like fresh-cut wood and his skin was smooth but just a little weather-worn. She could feel his heartbeat and his soft breathing as she wrapped her legs around his. She wanted to feel as much of him against her bare skin as she could. Both were silent, the I love yous having already been said many times over. His fingers tangled themselves in her hair as she ran her own fingers through his. There was a little less of it than before. Her heart quickened as she let out an audible sigh, causing him to tighten around her. Their bodies rocked together slowly. "Oh Bill, I have missed you so much."

She didn't dare to think of more. This was enough for now. She could keep this dream going all night. She drifted through the levels of sleep like the bubbles in a lava lamp. Now he was holding her less tightly and his scent became more musky. "Oh Babe," he sighed. You will never know how much I have loved you." "I love you, too, Paul." Her voice faded into the distance as she fell deeper into a dreamless sleep until morning.

***

She finally found him in the newspaper as she drank her morning coffee, before she went to work. It was yesterday's paper and she found his letter among the complaints about local political issues and other mostly trivial subjects. But this man, this therapist's letter resonated with her. He identified himself as the therapist that worked with the railroad union and was called upon when a train engineer was thrown into depression because someone chose to end their life by standing on the track in front of his train, knowing there was no way the engineer could stop in time. He described their agony as they felt the crunch of bones beneath them, ending a life and deeply wounding the lives of the engineers that experienced this more often than most people realized. Then there were those important letters, PTSD and EMDR. And there was one more thing. "These situations are made worse when the engineers have to face lawsuits...." Yes, this was the one! Suddenly Dora felt as if a great heavy curtain had lifted. She would tell Bill, but she knew this was the therapist she needed. It was as if he had written the letter just for her. She knew Bill would approve. She finished her coffee and headed to work.

CHAPTER 18

Elizabeth felt the need to attend mass on Sunday. She felt useless when it came to helping her daughter these days and hoped to find some divine inspiration in the church. When she saw Angela Bookman in the pew across from her, she was surprised. She was sure that Angie had been raised Catholic, but when she married Solomon Bookman, someone in town said she had converted to Judaism. But there she was, so she must have kept her spiritual ties to her roots. Not that Elizabeth really cared because she always thought people should worship God wherever they wanted despite the label that had been placed on them, usually not by choice. When Angela looked her way, she gave a friendly little wave to make sure Angela saw her. She needed some companionship and thought maybe they could have coffee together after mass. When mass ended and the two women met in the center aisle, Angela wasted no time asking Elizabeth to go across the street to the neighborhood coffee shop for coffee and a chance to catch up.

"Coffee?" is all she needed to say as she pointed across the street.

"Love to."

"Missed you."

"I spent the holidays with my daughter."

Elizabeth nodded with a smile. She could tell Angie was happier than she had been in a long time.

It was an unusually warm day for January, making it all the more pleasant, although the air had that feeling of impending snow flurries. The sun's brightness was muted behind a light gray veil of clouds. Wintertime in Waterview was often mild, but then just before spring, it could all let loose with an all out blizzard. You never knew.

"I am so glad to see you, Liz," Angie said, as she took her coat off and folded it over the chair. " I heard you were in the hospital."

"It was nothing serious." Elizabeth liked to keep her coat on until she warmed up a bit. "Got a little out of whack just before Christmas and was dehydrated, but that's all they said was wrong. Gave me an IV and pumped me full of fluids. I could have just done that myself, the water part anyway. But now I make sure that doesn't happen. Not beer, not coffee, not tea, but lots of water."

"You can't have tea? Oh no!"

"Oh, I can, as long as I don't stop drinking water. They told me to make sure I got enough good plain water. So how was your visit with your daughter?"

"Oh, it was lovely. She invited me to come over before Christmas and stay until after. We had a nice time. I had expected to see her and her boyfriend, but she was alone until after Christmas when I met her friend, Rita. She came to stay and she was very nice." Angela paused and looked deep into Elizabeth's eyes. "She and Rachael are very close."

"What happened to the boyfriend?"

"There will be no more boyfriends. Not sure if I will ever have grandchildren, at least not in the usual way."

Elizabeth looked puzzled.

Like I said, Rachael and Rita are very close." She paused and took a deep breath. "Sleep in the same bed kind of close."

"Oh, oh well how do you feel about that?" Elizabeth asked as the waitress approached.

Angela sat back, ordered her coffee and danish and Elizabeth did the same. When the waitress left, Angela leaned forward.

"You know, Liz, I always considered the possibility that Rachael might be a lesbian and always knew that when she told me, it wouldn't be a problem. I was worried that the boyfriend wasn't really what she wanted, but I didn't want to butt in either. It's so hard for a mother to know when to offer advice and when not to. I mean when our kids are grown. She looked so happy and I told her that that was the most important thing to me. I think she read my mind because she told me that she and Rita were talking about getting married and finding a way to have a child, maybe two someday. She emphasized the word SOMEDAY." Angela gave a little giggle.

"Well, look at Dora. She is married and her husband will be home in a couple of months, but I can't find out, even now, if she wants to have children. She is in her thirties. I really hope she will decide she does. I think Bill would like to be a dad."

"You can't be pushy."

"I know. I try not to be."

"I told Rachael that her dad would have been fine with it, although the idea of marriage might have taken an adjustment. Things have changed a lot in a few years and in many ways. I think that's great. I'm not sure the Church will ever catch up, but that's okay. I am not leaving my church and I most certainly am not going to distance myself from my daughter. She's a Unitarian now. They are very accepting."

Elizabeth nodded. She had visited a Unitarian church once and found it very open and welcoming to all kinds of good people.

"I feel so much closer to my daughter now. I had a problem adjusting to the whole empty nest thing, especially because Sol was already gone and I was so alone. But those ten days with her made things so much better and now I feel like I have two daughters. Rita doesn't make me feel like an outsider like her boyfriend did. He seemed very controlling, too."

When Dora married Bill, I gained a son and he is a good man. I just wish he'd come home safe. Two or three more months and I won't have to worry any more.

"So how is Dora doing?"

"Oh I am so worried about her. She's not herself.

She's still having nightmares about the accident and she tells me she is not okay. I think she found a psychologist or therapist. She told me she talked to Bill about it online and he advised her to get some help. I hope it all works out. I hate to see her like this."

"I hope so. She doesn't need this. It wasn't her fault and why should she suffer?"

"Sue-happy world we live in."

"Sad."

The danish and coffee arrived and there was a short pause in the conversation while the two women enjoyed both. In the corner, a middle-aged man with a guitar had just finished setting up.

"Looks like we are going to get some music, "Angela commented.

"Lovely, I am glad we decided to stop over here."

The man began singing a Harry Chapin song. *A ll my life's a circle, sunrise and sundown...* His voice was more like velvet than Harry's raspy tone, but he sang well as the women enjoyed the coffee and thought about their personal moments of joy and grief, his words meeting their thoughts until he got to then end. *... and so far no dead ends.*

"Let's hope not," Elizabeth mumbled to herself, but just loud enough for Angela to hear.

"Amen to that."

CHAPTER 19

On Monday school was closed for Martin Luther King's birthday and Dora had been lucky enough to get an appointment with Dr. Davidson, the therapist from the newspaper. She was a little nervous, never having been to a therapist before and even though she was an educated woman, there was still a stigma she was very aware of among people who thought you should be able to get over anything "mental" by yourself. Just do it. Mind over matter. Yes, even though she was about to see a man who specialized in exactly what was troubling her, the voices of those who would never understand rang in her head. Fortunately, she had Bill and now Dr. Davidson.

The day had begun with a chance to sleep in a little and then have a slow breakfast and get ready to leave for the therapist's office. Her nervousness had shrunken down to a little marble sized ball in the center of her abdomen. For only the second time since she could remember, she awoke without that intense anxiety as if the world were on fire, or that someone close had died. She was able to awaken slowly and feel refreshed when she finally did get out of bed. What she had once taken for granted had now become a luxury she valued more than anything else, sleeping and awakening like a normal person. That, and knowing Bill was safe and her mother was still okay, kept her going. But it was a fragile peace that could be disturbed at any time by the mere whistle of the wind.

She slipped on a denim dress and her favorite turquoise necklace. What, she had thought, does one wear to a therapist? Something familiar and comfortable, she decided.

The waiting room was the warm color of sunrise with Native American paintings that reflected community and calm. There was no receptionist, just a quiet waiting room with comfortable chairs and closed door behind which there were distant muffled voices. Dora took a deep breath and sank into the chair looking for a clock. There was none. Her watch told her that she was fifteen minutes early. Her nervousness was minimal and overpowered by her feeling of anticipation, knowing she had taken an important step. If she could be helped, cured even, it would happen here. She was sure of that. But that was a big if.

There was no clutter of magazines typical of waiting rooms, but there were a few small collections of poetry, anthologies and a scrapbook of letters thanking the doctor for his help. Dora looked through them briefly. The testimonials encouraged her to feel even more confident. After about ten minutes, the muffled voices behind the door became louder, indicating the end of the session and a switch to more casual conversation as the door opened slowly.

"Thanks, Doc. I'll see you again next week."

"Remember to write any thoughts down so we can begin with that next time."

The man walked past Dora and nodded with a smile as Dr. Davidson stepped out of the door.

"Dora?" he said with a gentle smile. "Please come in."

Dora rose from her chair and walked toward her only hope as he extended his hand. "It is good to meet you."

"And you doctor."

"Please have a seat." The therapist pointed to a comfortable-looking chair that faced his desk. He took a seat at his desk as she settled in.

"I'd like to begin by explaining what it is I do. We are talking about PTSD, a very natural response to an unnatural event or chain of events. This is what I specialize in, dealing with that. You told me you had an accident with a boy on a bicycle and he was not seriously injured, is that right?"

"That's right. He has recovered from minor injuries so that's why I think I should be okay, too, but I am not,"

"Why do you think you should be okay? What happened was something you could not have prevented. You believe that?"

"Yes. But you always wonder if you could have, even when reason tells you that was not the case."

"Well let's begin with the acceptance that things sometimes happen because of someone else's actions and we are not at fault. When the unexpected happens and a life is in danger, our thought processes are disrupted, sometimes severely and they need to be fixed. It is not just an emotional response that we can just get past, but a cognitive dysfunction of some kind that we need to fix. You have heard of EMDR?"

"I have heard of it. My husband is a doctor in the military serving in the Middle East. He told me to look for a therapist familiar with EMDR."

"Your husband is there now?"

"Yes and I am lucky to be able to communicate via email sometimes. He was the one who said I might have PTSD. He encounters that a lot there. "

"Wow, you are fortunate to have his support from such a long distance. Do you know when he will be coming home?"

"Hopefully in a few months. He is supposed to be home in

the spring, but you never know."

"So you have that weighing heavily on you as well. Much uncertainty and this accident only reinforced that for you. Well let's hope he comes home when you expect him and your life becomes more predictable. In the meantime, I am sure I can help you."

"Thank you."

" Please put on the headphones that are hanging next to you. Close your eyes. You will hear a clicking sound and when we are done, we will talk about some of the things you experienced."

She put on the headphones and closed her eyes gently

as the alternating clicks brought images to the space behind her forehead, as if it were a movie screen. The images were blurry at first, but then cleared, becoming sharper. The sound of her heartbeat relaxed itself into her body, providing a sense of calm as it seemed to let go and break down rigid walls that blocked her from an openness that she had been longing to see for a very long time. She was running now, able to see herself running through a field of obstacles on an endless field of green grass. She watched them approach like dark boulders as she moved toward them. She jumped effortlessly, barely clearing them as more and more appeared on the horizon. She was both athlete and spectator, able to see herself running, while not being distracted by her different perspectives. She was inside herself and yet somehow beyond herself. Then the boulders turned into large panes of glass, slowly changing from a foreboding opaque to hauntingly odd translucent. She ran,, she jumped, and each time her soul rose higher, clearing the edges with more and more ease. The clicking in her ear took on the sound of her feet hitting the ground. Then suddenly one large pane of glass shattered in front of her, a boulder falling from the sky and pounding the ground in front of her. This time she couldn't jump over it. This time it was not a boulder or any kind of rock. It was a body. A wounded human lying in front of her.

Then, suddenly, the screen went black and a rush of dread fell on her, crushing her.

"Okay, you can begin to open your eyes, now and take off the headphones. Take your time. Whatever feels comfortable."

Dora slowly opened her eyes and removed the headphones. The therapist was sitting back looking at her. Waiting.

"How did that go for you?" he asked gently.

"I was running. Not away from anything, but just running. I felt free. I was able to jump over the things in my way and I felt like I could do anything."

"You felt..."

"Unbound," she replied. "But then the obstacles became sharp and dangerous and I barely was able to clear them until one large piece of glass came crashing down on me and when I walked around it, I saw it, a body."

"What do you think this means?"

"You know it is a lot like my nightmares. I see a body and I think it is the boy, but I have no way of knowing if he is dead or not. Then I wake up."| I was carefree and then the accident happened and that ended that."

"What did you feel when you had the headphones on?"

"A feeling of carefree and then sudden dread followed by anxiety and deep sadness."

"Are these feelings creeping into your life?"

"Not creeping, flooding, like a tsunami." Sometimes I am so full of anxiety, I don't want to go anywhere or do anything. Other times I feel like I can't move and feel so depressed."

"What do you do when you feel anxiety? How do you cope?"

"Sometimes I start cleaning the house, tidying up mostly. I know that while I am doing that, I am also trying to get my thoughts in order. I know that it is about control and getting it back."

"Yes, and does it help?"

"Only temporarily."

"What else do you do? Anything else?"

"When I have time, I paint, sleep."

"Well, what I would like you to do is to write, keep a record of any thought you have related to anything we talk about in our sessions, thoughts, nightmares, whatever you think you would like to talk about."

"Okay. I like to write things down. Writing comes easy to me."

Dora eased into the therapy, starting to feel more relaxed and calm, even though she knew that most of what she was feeling was only temporary. It would take time. Dr. Davidson explained that it was a process that would take time and many visits. When she left the office, she felt that even though she was unsure of what was ahead, having someone who knew what she was going through and how to address it would make all the difference in the world. As she walked down the hallway, out the door and into the light, she felt a relaxed and hopeful feeling that she had not felt in a long time.

CHAPTER 20

Valentines Day came and went with nothing from Bill. They had spoken via Skype shortly after Dora had her first therapy session. It was a little silly to expect a Valentine's Day message from Bill with everything else that was happening, but under the circumstances, she worried when she didn't hear from him and she thought he might be in touch around February 14th, because he had always been aware of the date. But he was a bit inconsistent when it came to being a romantic and he certainly had enough occupying him now. Still, she worried about him all the time when she didn't hear from him. She had had only one strong anxiety attack two weeks ago, but she still felt that there was a storm rumbling in the distance. The sensation was always with her. Sometimes she felt she had risen above depression only to be walking a tightrope just above a deep pool of it, fearing it would only take one slip on that rope to fall in. But even small steps were progress. Every time she checked her email, and that would be a few times some days, and found nothing, she got a cold hard lump in her stomach. It felt a little better if she sent him an email, something short, something that let him know she was thinking of him and missing him, but not something that required an answer. Even with her own husband, she feared she might sound too desperate or too aloof. Getting the right balance had been hard early on in their relationship and it seemed that the awkwardness of those early days were coming back with his absence. Now she was drifting, feeling sleepy. She got up and slid out of her clothes, burrowed under the covers and fell asleep.

***

Bill looked at the calendar on the wall by his bed. It was down to the wire now. He'd be headed home soon. Somehow knowing that intensified his fears, his doubts and his inability to believe it was true. He would see Dolly and time was moving more quickly. Maybe he needed more time to prepare himself. But how? Why? There was a numbness where excitement, even joy, should have been. He didn't understand it. He loved Dolly and couldn't wait to see her again and the sooner the better, but there was also a sense of foreboding. Hell, he had avoided injury and death all this time, why did he feel more vulnerable now. SHIT, he realized that Valentine's Day had passed and he didn't even send Dolly an email message. What must she be thinking? He went to his computer, opened his email account and saw a few short messages from his wife, messages that had gone unseen and unanswered. What was wrong with him? He clicked on reply and sat until the tears came running down his face and then closed it. Maybe later he would know what to say. She would be asleep by now anyway.

***

Dora's nightmares continued, but now they were different. Now, sometimes, she saw Dr. Davidson in them,

168

but somewhere in the background, a Where's Waldo kind of thing and often she would hear a ticking sound that was like the clicking in the headphones used in the EMDR sessions. This time he was off in the distance behind a smoking campfire. She seemed to be camping in a big woods like she did once as a child, with the 4-H, a bunch of preteen girls trying to sleep in tents. But there were no girls in her dream. She struggled out of the tent so as not to disturb the invisible sleepers and looked at the clear star-filled sky. It was so quiet and beautiful. The moon was full and lit up the area. But there was that smoke and the image of the doctor behind it as if he were walking away. She tried to call to him, but all she could utter were dry-mouthed grunts. He didn't respond. She decided to follow him. She knew that she wouldn't make it out of that woods if he were to leave her. She needed him to be in her dreams, even if he were hiding as part of a tree or back in the distance, a face on a mountain top. She could not let him disappear from her dreams because then he would disappear from her life. She quickened her steps and started running, but then he stopped and turned around. Her heart beat faster as she realized it was not Dr. Davidson, but a weary and worn Bill, an aging Bill. He said nothing, but motioned to her to go back. Then, his breathing grew loud and coarse until she woke up to the sound of her own snoring. She sat on the edge of the bed trying to leave that space between dreams and reality, neither being in focus. She pulled herself up as the room cleared before her. She headed for the computer which was sleeping, probably better than she slept, and pressed the keys to wake it up and open her email inbox. Maybe Bill had… nope, there was nothing new. The house was eerily silent. She knew she couldn't go back to sleep. It was too quiet and she needed a distraction. There were always old movies on the TV, the kind you could watch with little effort because you'd seen them dozens of times. May be not all the way through, but you could watch and it would be like staring into a campfire, letting your mind go to a special place where different images and sounds cut through your anxiety. Dora's thumb clicked the TV on and pressed the channel key as it took on a rhythm of unconscious monotony. But then, there it was, like an old friend and she has caught it near the beginning.

High Noon. *…twixt love and duty, sposin' I lose my fair –haired beauty…Do not forsake me oh my darlin' although you're grievin', don't think of leavin', now that I need you by my side.*

It was such an old movie, but she loved it. It was way before her time when Gary Cooper played the sheriff who walked the streets looking for someone to help him carry out the last responsibility before he went off with his new bride who was still wearing her lace wedding dress. Yes, torn between love and duty, sometimes she saw Bill in the Cooper character. She inherited her love for the movie from her mother who watched it every time it was on. But they liked it for different reasons. Elizabeth was in love with Cooper when he played the strong silent type who never wasted words but always stood up for what was right. She used to point out to a young Dora that any actor who could play that role and also be believable as Lou Gehrig, the Pride of the Yankees, was truly an artist. Dora got it. But what she saw in this movie was different from others of that time, the fifties when women were supposed to be weak and fragile beings. How many movies had she seen where men fought each other, punching and rolling on the floor, as the women who loved them cowered in the corner waiting for the outcome, but not playing any part in it? Dora often found herself shouting to take the vase and smash over the bad guy's head. No spoiler alert here, the blonde actress soon to be a princess, would pick up a gun, aim it carefully and save her new husband's life after a dramatic gun battles in the empty streets where the townspeople would not come to his aid, despite his dedicated service protecting them. What was a choice between love and duty for some was no choice at all. Fear and cowardice was the only option they knew. Dora was glad she had married a man for whom the choice between love and duty never came from the end of a gun, but from the scalpel, the bedside manner, and the ability to stitch someone up and make them whole again. When he could. Dora watched, occasionally whispering the dialogue until she began to fall asleep. When she woke up, the end credits were rolling and the theme was playing. She instinctively switched to CNN where a breaking news alert was on the screen. *Hospital Explosion in the Middle East,* Oh God!

CHAPTER 21

Dora was determined not to let the lawsuit go on and on indefinitely, postponing her full recovery until so much damage was done that such a recovery would be impossible. She called lawyer after lawyer and counted every dollar she had in the bank. None of them really heard her. She wanted to have her day in court. Didn't the Seventh Amendment guarantee that? She could read. She knew. Everyone sued for $20 or more had a right to their day in court to tell their story and present their evidence. It wasn't about money, but about sanity. As long as the images continued in her mind and the accusations against her, no matter how routine, were not answered, they and the words that went with them would continue to destroy her. The therapy was helping, but it was only half of what she needed to be free.

She couldn't believe the responses she got from the lawyers she called and from Mr. Wood. When she told them she had money to pay what the insurance company covered, they suggested she use it for therapy or a vacation to the tropics. One lawyer she asked to take her case refused and when she asked why, he said, "Because it is not the way I do things." One, who sounded more concerned and seemed to listen, asked why she would be willing to spend her own money when the insurance company would handle it all, listened as she explained that if she had a terminal illness, no one would question how much she was willing to spend for a cure. He listened without interrupting, without offering an instant judgment. She explained what she was experiencing along with some information about PTSD and he listened. When she was done, he paused before speaking.

"I never heard that about an accident causing PTSD."

"I am getting therapy and my doctor specializes in PTSD, He treats train engineers who have hit people committing suicide on the tracks."

"They must be horrible, but the boy is okay, right?"

"Yes, he is, although they try to make it seem like he isn't, at least on paper, but the brain doesn't always stick to what is, but also embellishes on what might have been."

The lawyer waited a second and then responded. Dora thought he was thinking "psychobabble" and not taking her seriously. that's what they all did. She had to admit that when she heard herself, it did sound unreal sometimes, even though she knew better.

"You know I am usually on the other side, representing the plaintiffs. I have never heard of a defendant in an accident case who actually wanted to go to court. Most want to avoid that. It can be very stressful even when the insurance company pays everything. But most insurance companies will hold out if their clients are not at fault, even till hell freezes over and the lawyers for the plaintiffs will do the same. It is a game and it is about money. I'd like you to take some time to make sure you know what you want to do. Let's say a week or two and then call me back. Who is representing the plaintiffs?"

"The firm they call, Sheister and Shiester," she said, expecting the response she got.

`"You know they have a reputation for winning every case if it goes to court."

"So I have heard. Only makes it more of a challenge for me. Maybe it is time for them to lose, get a little push back for their arrogance."

"Oh, okay. I know them well and may not share your opinion, and I certainly don't agree with calling them that, but I get what you are saying. Are you one of those who would defend herself in court if she had the chance?" he said with a laugh.

"Yes, probably would if I had to. I was there. I know what happened and I know you can't stop a car within 20 feet if you are careless, reckless and negligent."

"Well, let me check it out and talk to you in a week or two. Maybe we will have a better idea with a little time."

"Thanks for listening. You have no idea how rude and insulting some lawyers can be,"

"I think I do."

When they hung up, Dora felt better and hoped this would not be just one more disappointment. A few minutes later, the phone rang and she saw that it was a call from the insurance company. She shuddered, not wanting to pick it up, but she knew she had to. Could be good news, but she doubted it. She reached out and took it from its cradle and pushed the button.

"Hello, Mrs. Victor?"

"Yes?

"Joseph Wood calling about the accident and lawsuit?"

"Oh yes."

"The lawyers set the date for the deposition."

"Okay," Dora said, waiting for more, as her heart began to pound rapidly.

"They want to meet at the plaintiff's lawyers' office on March 3rd at 10 am. They are at 458 Main Street."

"Yes, I know where they are. I pass there on my way to work. I will be there."

"Mr. Graham is the lawyer assigned to your case. He will brief you before the deposition. That will only take about 15 minutes and the lawyers for the plaintiff will do the same and them you will all be present for the deposition."

So I will get to see the boy?"

"When the deposition begins, yes but you cannot talk to him or his parents at all."

"I see. As long as I can see him, but I don't know why they have to make this into a stinking war"

"I know, but we have to protect everyone. Some people would harass the kid and make a scene. That has happened, so these rules make it easier for everyone."

. "Okay, I will be there." Dora thought it was lucky that that day she only had one class late in the afternoon.

"We were lucky to get a date so soon. It usually takes longer. But this is better for you and better for the plaintiffs."

"Yes, thank you."

"Have a good day, Mrs. Victor."

"You, too, Mr. Wood, and it's Doctor Victor," she added with an indignant whisper.

When Dora hung up the phone, her heart was still beating fast. She went to the couch to help it calm down. This was a good thing. Maybe like a light at the end of the tunnel, but she wasn't sure. She was not afraid of the questioning the lawyers would do. She had gone over everything they would ask in her mind since the accident. Over and over, she had mulled it all. It would be a welcomed opportunity to be heard and maybe that would be enough. She let herself relax, sitting back and clicking the TV on button.

There it was, the news about the hospital, a civilian hospital was attacked, but by whom? While she knew, of course, that it wasn't Bill's hospital, she also knew that it was in the area and that was never a good thing. She wanted Bill to come home, but she was afraid that when he did, she might not always say the right thing, that he would be changed, or that she would do something silly like call him Paul. She had never told him much about Paul except that they grew up together and that he became a fireman. She hadn't mentioned his death in her emails and that seemed both a good idea and a bad idea.

Now as the time grew closer, her longing for her husband was mixed with trepidation. Perhaps he hadn't told her everything either. You never know. You don't always have to know.

***

On the day of the deposition, Dora was filled with anxiety, but also with anticipation of some kind of closure. She sat in the waiting room of the plantiff's lawyers' offices as the boy and his father came off the elevator and headed toward the other end of the room. Her heart beat fast at seeing the boy, the first time she had seen him since the accident. He seemed bigger, older, despite the relatively short passage of time, real time, not the eons if felt like. The image of him lying in the street bleeding was replaced by a strong-looking young man with no limp, no visible scars. Yet, he seemed nervous. Both the boy and his father avoided looking at anyone other than each other when they took their seats. The mother had not come. Dora had expected to see three of them. It wasn't long before she was called in to get a briefing from the insurance company lawyer, Harold Graham.

Dora got up without looking in their direction. It wouldn't be long now before she would be able to say what she had to say in front of the plaintiffs She was confident that the lawyers would ask the right questions, even though she has been told just to answer the questions and not to elaborate, instructions that the insurance company lawyer would repeat. The briefing at the big table in a room with just the two of them was simple and short.

`"If they ask you if you can tell them your name, just say yes. Answer the exact question they ask, no more and no less. A few practice questions about the date of the prepared enough.

"You have nothing to worry about. The boy and his father are in the other room being briefed by their lawyers and we will join them when they are done. Do you have any questions? "

"No." Dora inhaled deeply. She was ready.

When Dora was ushered into the small room where the deposition was about to take place, there were only the insurance company lawyer, Mr. Graham, a stenographer and five empty seats at a long table.

"You can sit right here, "Mr.Graham said pointing to the closest chair. She sat down and he sat beside her.

"The plaintiffs should be in soon. Try to avoid looking at them. I know that is hard, but just don't want to intimidate the kid. "

"I know, I know." Dora replied impatiently.

The lawyer for the plaintiffs led them in and they took the two seats opposite Dora and her lawyer..

"I am Len Parker, "the other lawyer said. "I am representing the D'Angelos today. We will begin with Devin D'Angelo. Are you ready?" he asked looking at the boy who was chewing on his fingernail. The boy quickly took his hand away from his mouth and answered, "Yes sir,"

He asked a series of short questions, all with short clear answers. What was the boys name, address, basic things. Dora watched the boy, as if by looking at him, she could absorb enough of his face and his voice to make up for the time she wasn't allowed to see him.

"What kind of a bicycle were you riding?"

Many questions about his bike, the brakes, the size, all of which seemed irrelevant to Dora. A woman at the end of the table typed away vigorously. Then came questions about whether anyone else in the family, or friends ever used the bike. No. Where was he going? What direction was he going while riding on his bike? Was there any time when he left the sidewalk and enter Schoolhouse Road?

Just before you entered the road, did you notice any parked cars ?"

"Yes."

"Were there any cars coming down the street in either direction?|

"Not that I could see."

"You couldn't see any cars?"

"Did you have a clear view of the street before you entered it?"

"No, I didn't."

"What blocked your view?"

"All the parked cars."

"So there were enough parked cars to block your view of the street you were about to enter?

"Yes."

"But you entered the street anyway?"

"Yes."

"Did you hear any cars on the street?

"No."

"So you thought the way was clear so you could safely cross the street on your bicycle? Then what happened, Devin, when you entered the street?

"I got hit by a car. Mrs. Victor's car."

"You mean the car she was driving?"

"Yes."

So far everything the boy said was just as Dora remembered it. The questions went on, slowly, methodically.

"About how far away was the car when you first saw it?'

"Three feet."

Now Mr.Graham was asking about the impact, the injuries, where he was on the road in relation to the car. Where the car had stopped. All his answers were were accurate and coincided with what Dora remembered.

"Now, Devin, do you recall talking to anyone after you were hit?

"Yes, Mrs. Victor."

"What did you say to Mrs. Victor?

"I said I was sorry... because I hit her."

There were more questions about what he felt, how he was injured, the ambulance and how much school he missed and then Mr. Graham appeared to be done. He tooka moment to look ar some papers in front of him and then said, "Okay, thank you, Devin.

Next to be deposed was the boy's dad. He was asked how he heard about the accident and he described how someone in the neighborhood came to his house. Questions centered on what insurance paid the bills for medical treatment and that all the medical expenses had been covered. The plaintiff';s lawyer clarified that Dora's insurance company had paid the boy's medical expenses under no-fault. Then it ended abruptly and a voice said, "Thank you very much. You are free to go now."

Wait. Free to go? Dora's heart fell as she looked around frantically. As they stood up and moved toward the door, Dora looked at Mr. Graham.

"They aren't staying to hear what I have to say?" She couldn't believe it. Every step of the way in this process, she had felt like a nail being hammered into a piece of wood. She knew she wasn't familiar with how things worked in lawsuits, but wasn't there supposed to be some element of fairness. Wasn't the defendant supposed to get to be heard? She repeated her question again, this time loud enough for the plaintiff's attorney to hear.

"Why do they get to leave before I get to be heard?"

Len Parker looked confused and mumbled.

"Mr. D'Angelo has to get to work.

"I had to take a day off to be here. I expected they would get to hear what I had to say. Don';t they want to know what I have to say?"

"Probably not," Mr. Graham mumbled barely audibly. "Oh, they will get a copy of your deposition as you will get one of theirs as well. The entire deposition of all three of you will be provided to each of you. Nothing to be concerned about. If you want to take a break, say 5 minutes, before you are deposed..."

"No thank you., Dora said, as her lawyer handed her a cup of water. Mr. Parker left the room briefly and then returned.

"The plaintiffs wanted me to tell you that they bear you no ill will. They know it was an accident," he said.

"Then why can't I talk to them, to the boy?"

"Why would you want to talk to the boy?" Mr Parker looked at her with a strange empty look. Dora just threw up her hands in frustration as Mr. Parker took a deep breath and began.

The questions she was asked made Dora feel like she was just repeating the same things the plaintiffs had said and that there was no real in depth of questioning about what really mattered. How she was able to stop the car within 15 feet? He didn't ask why her foot was already on the brake before she even saw the boy. He didn't ask... she sighed. The father and the boy had no ill will toward her, she thought, wasn't that just dandy! They accused her of everything unholy and they had no ill will. There was anger mixed with what felt like a big lead ball in her stomach. When it was allover, she headed for her car knowing it was not over, not out of her hands, and not going to be business as usual.

CHAPTER 22

While the attack, the bombing, had not been on Bill's hospital, it affected him more than just emotionally. Others in the area, even those who were not doctors, went to the site and started working to set uop some makeshift hospitals in heavy duty tents for the survivors. Two medics and one of Bill's colleagues went over to help out as well. Only one doctor had been killed in the attack, so the need at the bomb site was temporary until another doctor could be transferred from a hospital in a less active place, perhaps even outside of the war zone. Bill offered to go, but they needed a surgeon where he was. So he stayed. They still had a surgeon at the other hospital, but he was scheduled to go home in a few months, too. Bill knew that this might delay his return home, as the doctor scheduled to replace him permanently might be the one who was going to be assigned at the other hospital. He wasn't sure who was replacing whom, but this couldn't be good. He also knew that Dora was going to ask him about all of it so he had to find a way to be truthful, yet cautious.

Even before the destruction of the hospital, and the feeling that he was needed here now and had to postpone his departure, he had acknowledged some ambivalence to going home after his service ended. One evening, he looked out over the barracks and across the dusty field where the helicopters landed and realized that a person could be drawn to a place they very much wanted to get away from. Held by some familiarity and attachment, even to the most horrific memories, brought an odd nostalgia while at the same time depressing him. He would never be the same as he had been when he first arrived and he knew that the changes were major and yet he also knew that Dolly was the love of his life and he longed for her. But no one stayed the same. To stay and never change would be a kind of death of the soul. When lovers were together, the real ones, the meant for each other kind, they changed and adjusted to the modifications on a daily basis, but this, this being so far apart and sharing only the most obvious of changes through email or even face to face on Skype, was not the same. It was sometimes too much like play acting as each censored out that which they feared would harm the tenuous balance of their relationship. Oh, the conflict of longing and loving, leaving and lingering...Bill shook his head vigorously. What was he supposed to be doing? He had come into the room for some purpose.

"Do you need anything?" the voice came from the doorway, a familiar and comforting sound.

"No, I'm good" he replied holding up his half full cup of coffee. "How are you doing?"

"Hanging in there, same as always," her a soft smile hid so much pain. He knew she had been struggling, knew she was fighting the stress, the sleeplessness, drawing on her determination to do her job while missing home and family and longing to just be as far from this place as possible.

"Well, find some time for yourself." He knew she wouldn't because she couldn't. Even this stolen moment he was having, trying to sort everything out, his thoughts, his fears and his feelings, this time for half a cup of coffee would be short lived.

Did he need anything? Oh he couldn't even begin to answer that, but every time he heard the young nurse's voice, something stirred within him, and the need was strong. He didn't know if her question held in it something more than a can-I-get-you-some-coffee innocence. Sometimes he thought it was more than that. There were those times she would come back and sit with him and talk. She would share her innermost feelings, her hopes to take a few courses and maybe become a school nurse and maybe teach some health classes in a nice quiet school where she could live a normal life, meet a nice man and settle down and raise a family. But she also talked about her fears of PTSD and never being normal enough to have a relationship with a man who could love her with all her war-induced flaws. Sometimes, he would put his hand on hers and offer words of comfort, but what he felt was more than that and he had begun to believe that she was feeling the same way. Once, when he hugged her and told her it would work out, something he didn't really believe, he wanted to draw her even closer and hold her so close that she could feel his heart beating and maybe she would put her arms around him and pull him tightly to her. She was a gentle kind of beauty with soft auburn curly hair and a natural rosy complexion, young, but not too young. Did he need anything? Oh for God's sake, he needed her, he needed comfort and he needed Dora to be waiting for him when he got home. But right now, he needed so many things and he felt like he was holding back a raging river and that the dam was about to break.

***

Dora was in a kind of sad and restless mood. She felt a longing for normalcy and an even stronger longing for Bill's physical presence. She wanted to feel him, run her fingers over his skin, get back some of what his departure had taken from her. She wanted to feel his breath on her neck and hear his voice whisper in her ear. He could say anything as long as he whispered it in her ear. This desire mixed with trepidation made her uncomfortable, emotionally and physically. She shifted her body so it made greater contact with the overstuffed chair, a chair made more for comfort than beauty. She wrapped her arms around herself, giving herself a hug and closed her eyes. She wanted to pretend Bill was holding her. Her eyes closed, she let herself fantasize, hoping to bring him so close in her mind that she could feel him, really feel him in a way that would satisfy some small part of her longing, her desperate needing. There was only so much she could put on hold. When he left, he just hadn't left enough of him to bring her this far. Her imagination didn't satisfy her anymore. She wished that she had a recording, a video, something from before he left her this last time. Yet she tried. Tried to bring him up in her mind so that she could feel his touch, his kiss and his body loving hers. It was getting more difficult now, but there were times when she got lucky.

***

He came up behind her as she sat resting in the chair. He kissed her on the head, something she didn't like that much, but she knew it was always followed by the things she did like, the things she loved, the things she craved. As he let his lips linger on her head, his arms slid down to her shoulders. As he massaged her, he kissed her ear and whispered, "I love you. God, how I love you." Her arms would reach up and as she placed them on his hands, he moved them down to her breasts. She could feel them tingling, her nipples rising to meet his caresses, and she moved her body again to make more complete contact with the chair. Yes, now she could feel him. He was there, really there. He kissed her neck and she could feel his tongue on her skin. She turned her body, reached up for his head and kissed him passionately. As they kissed, she felt the hunger inside her grow and she let out a sigh, shouting out his name, PAUL! It took her a few seconds for her to realize what she had said. She opened her eyes and felt the shock of her mistake run through her. Oh no. She couldn't let this happen again, when Bill was home. Her heart beating fast, she remained unsatisfied and confused. She pulled herself up from the chair and walked slowly to the bedroom, trying to imagine that Bill was with her, but as she reached the bedroom door, she thought that she saw Paul standing by the bed waiting for her. She took a deep breath and walked toward him closing the door behind her.

***

Bill's coffee had gone cold, but not his longing. It was hot and strong as ever. When Brenda came back to say good-night, he got up to talk to her. She didn't say a word. He made some mindless small talk, when she asked him to walk down the hall with her. She seemed a little upset, mumbled about her brother's being ill back in Pennsylvania, but seemed preoccupied by something else. She stopped at her door and reached up to touch his face. She said nothing as he put his arms around her and kissed her gently on the lips. Hearing someone approaching, they released their grips on each other and Brenda started a conversation in the middle. "...seems to be doing better. I think a few more days and..." The man passed without looking at them or saying a word. She looked at Bill with a look that was deep, desperate, and pleading. His tender gaze and touch of the hand on hers made her tremble. She opened the door to the room. "Are you alone tonight?" he whispered. "Yes, all night. Please come in." He followed her into the dark room and closed the door behind them.

CHAPTER 23

Elizabeth put the plates out, paper for pizza, and tall glasses for the peach iced tea that Dora liked to drink with it. She heard her daughter's car door, a sound she could tell from all other car doors, and opened the front door to let her in, even though it was unlocked and Dora never had to knock.

"Hi Mom, I can smell the pizza and I am so hungry.," she said in a lilting voice that sounded almost like a song." She walked over to the table where she set down the ice cream she had picked up on the way. "Pizza looks delicious. Where did you get it?"

"Belaggio's. I had a coupon, so I called them and they delivered it in just twenty minutes. I'll put the ice cream in the freezer."

"Actually, it is gelato. I saw it and I couldn't resist last time I shopped. Pistachio, and chocolate. I keep looking for melon like I had in Italy, but no one makes it here."

"Well, you made good choices. Do you want wine instead of the tea? I have some in the cabinet."

"No no, thanks. The iced tea will be fine. You make the best iced tea." Dora thought that even a drop of wine would not be good if she was going to drive home. Never could be sure some kid on a bike might not dart out in front of her again. If they asked her if she had been drinking, the amount wouldn't matter. If she couldn't prevent an accident when she had no alcohol, then what would it sound like if she had even a drop?

Elizabeth was excited about the news she had for Dora. She wasn't sure how Dora would take it and she hoped she would just accept the gift. She put the red folder on the table next to her, and continued with the small talk about weather, neighbors and church. Dora was curious about what was in the folder, but she held off asking. Her mother unconsciously moved the folder a little closer to her while talking and sipping the tea. Dora watched as Elizabeth caressed the folder, a habit her mother had when she was nervous. It annoyed Dora when she did it, caressing a cup that had coffee in it or a glass of ice tea, the way you would caress...well, it was annoying to watch. But there was obviously something that she was nervous about in that folder and Dora began to think it must be something related to her health, medical reports, test results, or maybe a living will to instruct her as to when to pull the plug or something else unpleasant. Finally she asked.

"So Mom, what's in the folder?"

"I was about to get to that. I was looking at my bank accounts and I am doing pretty well and I have that pension along with the social security, so I put some away in a certificate of deposit for you, in trust so you could get it when I die."

Dora didn't respond. She was still thinking there was bad news attached to this so she took a deep breath and waited. Her mother continued as she opened the folder and slid the papers out.

"But," she paused to look at Dora with a smile, "I don't see why I shouldn't give it to you now so I can watch you enjoy it."

"Mom, you don't have to do that. I am doing well financially, well enough and maybe you should spend it on yourself." Dora didn't like the idea of taking money from her mother and she imagined it was probably not much anyway.

"Now wait, think about what I am saying. I have plenty of savings for whatever I need, or to splurge now and then. Your dad and I saved up over the years and I am fine. I want to give it to you, not because you need it, but as a gift from my heart. An inheritance only make sense if the person leaving it doesn't have enough to enjoy their lives, but giving you this gift would make me very happy."

She turned the papers around and showed Dora the amount and the due date. There was $15,000 and it matured the next week.

Wow, that's a nice hefty sum," Dora said. "Are you sure you don't want to use it for..."

"No Babe. I want you to use it for whatever you want. You don;'t even have to tell me. It is yours. It was always meant to be yours, but I want you to have it before I die. There is no use in waiting. This way, I can live a long time and know you have the money I want you to have."

"Well, if you put it that way..."

"I most certainly do."

"Thanks so much Mom. Yes, I hope you will be with me a long time and this is so kind of you." Dora put the papers back in the folder and put it on the chair with her pocketbook. She was relieved that it hadn't been something else, bad news or something to worry about. She was happy to know that her mother's finances were doing well and that she had such a positive outlook. Dora wished that she didn't have this very heavy weight around her neck and could get some help dealing with it so she could just live her life the way she wanted to. The accident, the lawsuit and of course missing Bill and fearing that something could still happen before he headed home wore her down. But now she was just going through the motions of being okay for her mother, and because others were probably sick of hearing her talk about her problems. The pizza was even better than expected and the gelato was superb. Jeopardy was a repeat, but neither Dora nor her mom seemed to care that much. They only remembered half the answers anyway, so by the time Dora was ready to go home, they had had a predictable, but pleasant time together.

Later that evening when Dora was back home, she looked at the CD and her name on it. Next week she would go down to the bank with her mom and they would do the transfer into Dora's account. They would make it an occasion with lunch and maybe a short walk on the boardwalk by the lake. That always helped her clear her mind and it was always where she and he mom bonded and rebonded over and over.

Scattered around her on her table were her bank books and other financial statements. She added them all up and thought about what she could do to end the stupid lawsuit so she could heal. With money came options and even if they were unusual options, she had to consider what was best for her sanity. If money could bring her husband home sooner, wouldn't she use it for that? But that was not a possibility, so maybe it was time to re-evaluate her priorities, think outside the box., She had an income and in a week she would have a bit more to use to take the power back. Even before her mother gave her the gift, Dora had had just enough money to insist on implementing her plan to end the lawsuit her way. Now she had a cushion and nothing would stop her. She wouldn't tell Bill because she was afraid he would not support her crazy scheme, but she knew what she had to do. She just needed someone to help her do it. A lawyer who was willing to follow her directions instead of insisting she take his or her advice, claiming that was the only way. She added up the numbers in her accounts one more time. Nearly 100 thousand dollars, the same amount her insurance company covered her for. To create a win/win and just let the conventional wisdom about money and made-up fault go. Her life had been joined with Devin DeAngelo's in a split second when her windshield made contact with his body and despite the lawsuit and the very harmful words in the summons and complaint, there was a higher law, a better way and she was going to follow that. In a few days she would set it all in motion. She wondered what Paul would have thought.

CHAPTER 24

If dreams could be made into reality, and we could choose which ones to keep, would it make our lives better? How useful the brain can be while we sleep and dream of the things that will not happen, but perhaps should!

The disembodied voices kept asking her questions as she sat on the hard wooden seat beside the judge in the courtroom.

"How fast were you going just before the impact?"

"Twenty three miles per hour. "

"Do you have a digital speedometer? How did you know it was 23?"

"No, a regular one. The needle was right between 20 and 25."

"Did you take your eyes off the road to check your speed?"

"Briefly, after I turned the corner , I checked it and then let up on the gas."

It says here that there were no skid marks suggesting that you didn't try to stop."

"There were no skid marks because I already had my foot on the brake before Devin D'Angelo darted out in front of me."

"You had your foot on the brake, why?"

"Because it was a dangerous situation. There were

children playing on the left side of the street, on the curb and that's when he came out from the right."

"You were braking because you saw children on the left ,but you didn't see Devin D'Angelo on the right. Is that what you said?"

"Yes, I saw a blur and stopped the car as he hit my windshield, throwing him into the street."

The questioning went on and on.

"So where did the boy enter the street from the sidewalk?"

"From the driveway of 163 Farmer's Path."

"And where was your car when it stopped,?"

"The back bumper was still at the western edge of 163."

"And you say you were driving in a westerly direction."

"yes, and my car stopped in front of the same driveway the boy came out of."

"How far past the driveway did you stop?"

"I was not past the driveway. I was blocking the westernmost 1 foot of it with the back bumper."

"So you were not looking to the right and thus didn't see the boy coming down the sidewalk on the right?"

"No, the sidewalk on the rights wasn't visible as there were cars and SUVs parked all along. The boy darted out from behind a line of parked cars. He had been riding on the sidewalk. Had he been in the street, he would have been going in the wrong direction."

."Please just answer the questions and not speculate as to what would have happened if. Do you know how far a car travels after deciding to stop, with reaction time and all?"

"I have it written down..."

"Objection, she already said she stopped in front of the same driveway the boy came from.

"How is that possible?"

"She said she already had her foot on the brake because she thought it was a dangerous situation. The police report said her car stopped in front of the driveway of 163 Farmer's Road. At the property line with 161."

Dora looked for the people who belonged to the voices but all she saw a was thick fog, She looked at the rows where people usually sat but they were filled with mannequins, unresponsive grinning and naked. She turned her head left looking for the judge, but could only see an endless sea of black fabric. Then the jury box. She saw no one. There was supposed to be a jury. Where was the jury?

"Excuse me your honor, where is the jury?"

There was no response. Dora would have preferred to have been yelled at, threatened with contempt or admonished by her attorney, but nothing.

Useless dream. Even in her own dream, emanating from her own mind, she could not get anyone to listen to her. Fuck futility. She was done with it!

CHAPTER 25

Early sunrise made the sky over the mountains look deceivingly peaceful and beautiful. The sun's rays created a halo over the rim of the far off range and lit up the sky enough to illuminate the scattered clouds of dark gray. It looked as if God had taken them and pulled them apart like cotton candy. All was quiet except for the beating blades of a far off chopper. The shift change at the field hospital was orderly and routine. With all the talk of a major reduction of troops and eventual pull out of the country, people were unsettled. Bill was getting ready to leave, this time with no extensions and no more commitment to the military. Finally he would be able to join a medical practice at home or even open up his own, treat his neighbors, and live a normal life. He had repaid his debt and paid his dues to his fellow Americans many times over, and whatever was left would be paid on the civilian side. By noon, he received the official papers confirming that he would be leaving in three and a half weeks. He wanted to email Dora with the good news, but he kept reading the letter in case somehow there was a catch and it was not really going to happen. Having the date and the details of how he would return home in his hands only increased his anxiety that something could go wrong in the next twelve days. But he had no time to be negative. He had a wife waiting at home and a lot to do ahead of him if he wanted to return to civilian life, a transition that should have been joyous, but was also plagued with self doubt and worry. Bill started going through his belongings and sorting them. After all this waiting and some setbacks, this was what he had been waiting for. He wandered out into the hallway and down to the door that led to the mess hall where breakfast was sending out smells of sweetness and bacon. When he went in, Brenda was already sitting at a table alone. Bill grabbed a tray and picked up some scrambled eggs, a banana muffin and bacon and went to sit with her. As she looked up from her coffee, he noticed that her eyes were red and as she wiped them with a tissue mumbling a weak, "Good morning".

"Are you okay? "Bill asked and then added, "Something wrong?"

"No, I am not okay. You know I have been waiting to hear how my brother's operation went."

"To remove his kidney? Yes, your twin.

"Well he finally got in touch and told me that when he went to get clearance for the operation from his cardiologist, the doctor refused. He said he didn't believe my brother would survive the operation because of his heart. I knew his heart was bad, but I didn't know it was that bad that they wouldn't allow him to have a life saving operation for kidney cancer."

"Oh Brenda, I am sorry to hear this." Bill took her hand in his and gave it a squeeze.

"He said he found a doctor who said he would do the surgery, but that that doctor also believed he would die on the operating table. So now my brother has to decide if he wants to die during the operation or die of kidney cancer. What a choice."

"Is there any other option? Chemo, radiation?"

"Not for my brother. He doesn't want to be kept alive just to suffer. I think his kids want him to try it, but he is adamant."

"I am so sorry, Brenda." Bill wanted to kiss her, to comfort her, to hold her close the way he had the other night, but all he could do was offer empty words and squeeze her hand again.

"Last time we talked, before he knew he had cancer, we talked about going down to the beach as soon as we were together again and walking on the boardwalk. He wanted to have a lobster roll by the ocean. He lives too far inland now. Looks like he will never see the ocean again, or me." She started to weep again. Bill handed her a napkin and moved his chair closer so he could put his arm around her. She rested her head on his shoulder.

"We were always so close. Even though we are the same age, well he was born first about 10 minutes before me, he always played the part of big brother. We have been apart for almost two years, since our last visit, but knowing he was there, I really can't believe this." She paused and wiped her face again. "Well I need to pull myself together. It was a shock. I don't know how much time he has left, but it can't be more than a month or two at best. He TOLD me that. I asked him to hold on until I could get home, but he calmly told me that wasn't going to happen. Now all I can do is wait for the end to come. I don't know how I am going to be able to function."

"I don't know how to help you, Brenda, but I am here for you. To talk, whatever you need,"

Brenda smiled at him and squeezed his hand. "Thanks. Do you know when you are going home?"

"Yes, I will be leaving here in twenty-four days. Finally it is over. Sounds like many of us will be leaving in the next few months. That's good news."

"I am skeptical, but even in the best case scenario, I am afraid many of us will be taking this war, these wars actually, with us. One end only leads to a new beginning. Sorry, I am getting cynical in my old age."

"Old age" Bill laughed. What are you twenty five? "

"Forty two, but thanks. My brother is going to die at forty two? That just doesn't seem fair does it?"

"No, it doesn't."

"He has abused his body. Too much smoking from the teen years and he has been very overweight since he was fourteen. Depression too. I never understood why. Fraternal twins, we hardly look at all alike, not even like brother and sister, but we are twins and I feel close to him in a very special way. I never smoked, never suffered depression, well maybe now, and never had to watch what I ate. I feel so bad for him. Probably be even worse when I go home. Seeing places where we used to go with the family, I can't even bear the thought. Mom must be in terrible state right now. My brother was always there for her after our dad died, wow, twenty years ago. I will have to help her out. I feel so empty now over here where I can't do a goddamn thing."

Bill and Brenda remained silent for a few minutes and then Bill asked her if he could get her more coffee.

"No thanks. I have had so much coffee I am wired now. I need to get going." She looked at her watch, stood up and gently pulled her hand away from Bill's. "Talk to you later. Have a good day. Hope it is uneventful."

"Thanks, hang in there, Bren, love you."

"Love you, too."

They both knew what they meant.

CHAPTER 26

Dora took a deep breath and dialed the number of her insurance representative. She would ask a simple question, whether it would be possible for her to add money to the settlement to end the lawsuit so she could go back to normal life after meeting with the boy and his family to get closure. Seemed simple enough. It would create a win/win/win. The boy would get money to put toward college or whatever, the insurance company would settle for amount they had offered, and Dora would get what she so desperately needed to go on with her life and be ready for Bill's return. As she waited to be connected with Mr. Wood, she thought about how wonderful it was that Bill was going to finally be home. When she had read his email, she was totally elated.

"Robert Wood," his voice triggered anxiety in Dora and she never knew what to expect. She took a deep breath and told him what her plan was.

"..so you could just settle for the $2,000 and I would give the boy enough to make up the difference and this would be over and we all could move forward." She held her breath. There was a long pause before Mr. Wood spoke.

"That's is not how it works," he replied coldly. Another pause. "Look Mrs. Victor, you just have to let us do what we are contracted to do. Why would you give these people anything. You know it was not your fault, we know it was not your fault and the family of the boy, damn well know it was not your fault. Don't be a f... I mean don't let people take advantage of you."

"Well I would make sure they knew I am not giving them money out of any kind of guilt. It is just..."

"Look, you are a nice woman, I get that, but you just can't do that. It is not how it is done."

Dora felt a deep feeling of disgust. Being called a nice woman in this context was really an insult, especially when it was followed with BUT. What it meant was that she was naive, foolish and not worthy of being heard.

"Look, Mrs. Victor, we will keep on doing what we are doing. We will do our best to get this settled, but these things can take years. I told you that. It is about not giving in when we are defending our clients."

"It's about money..." Dora slipped it in.

"Yes, of course it is about money, but you were not at fault so it is also about integrity. If you want, call back in six months and maybe things will be a little better. In the meantime, please do not contact the family or try to do this yourself. That would be a bad precedent and you don't want us to drop you."

Dora hung up the phone. The light she thought she saw at the end of the tunnel was quickly extinguished. The lump I her throat made her feel as if she were about to choke. She should have known it would not be that easy even when it made sense to her. The rest of the world wasn't thinking as she thought, about making everyone win, but so many were so brainwashed by the us vs them mentality, that they couldn't even think of any other way. Dora decided to open her email again and reread what Bill had sent her, to make sure she read it right.

Hello Sweetheart, well I got the official letter. I will be leaving here in three weeks and then I will be in transit, probably two or three days, but then I will be coming right home to you. It seems like this day would never come, but it is here, just tying up my last loose ends, saying good bye to everyone and then, it is over for good. Back to you and a normal life. I will give you the specifics when I know them, but I can't wait to be with you again. I hope you are doing well and are ready to start a new normal. I love you so much.- Bill.

Dora read it exactly three times and then just sat holding the letter and letting it all sink in. She wished that the whole lawsuit thing were over already and that she wouldn't have to deal with it when Bill was home. But she had just over three weeks and she would make sure she was able to do something. There had to be something she could do.

Bill sat at the table eating a light lunch, a salad with walnuts, pears and blue cheese, a glass of water and coffee. It was a stunningly beautiful day outside, and very quiet. The hospital was almost empty with an unusual pause in activity. Bill knew it was unlikely to last, but he held onto the calm that enveloped him. Brenda had met him in the hallway, only to tell him she had received an email from her brother's wife telling her that the doctor had only given him one week to live. The family back home was gathering to sit by his side to share childhood memories when he was awake and just be with him when he was not. Brenda was already grieving and could only be with him via the Internet. She told Bill that she just wanted to be alone as she headed back to her room.

"So I hear you are finally going home." a voice interrupted Bill's thoughts. It was his friend and colleague Johnny Bellamy. Doctor Bellamy was an anesthesiologist with a quick mind and a sarcastic wit. But today he seemed serious.

"Yeah, I can hardly believe it. I've been in the military for what seems like most of my life."

"Well, I guess it's time for you to enter the next chapter of your life. Have any ideas what that will be like?"

"Well I am not sure. I can't wait to see my wife. I miss her so much. But career wise? Not entirely sure yet. Maybe I can join a practice and start treating patients who have not be blown up or are at death's door every single day."

"Have you considered working in a hospital?"

"I haven't ruled anything out. Whatever I do, it will be a bit of a challenge just to adapt to civilian life."

"But you are up to it. I know you and any job that you get will be lucky to have you."

"I don't really know where to start, but I guess I should get started now, not waste any time waiting to get home. While the idea of taking a break, a real vacation sounds good, I will need to go back to work and who knows what will be available."

"How about opening your own practice? "

"I am not sure. I think I would rather do something where there are other doctors to cover for me in the same practice. Something already established. To be honest, it is all overwhelming. I have no idea where to begin."

"Well, whatever you do I am sure it will work out for you."

`"Thanks. "

"You will be fine. Congratulations and best wishes. Talk to you later."

"Have a good day."

In the morning, after having a quick and very unhealthy jelly donut for breakfast, Dora nursed a tall cup of black coffee and prepared herself for the next step in trying to get beyond this very rigid system of making people miserable for no reason and pretending there was some sense to how lawsuits are settled.

When Mitch answered the phone she began again. She explained what she wanted to do and insisted that she understood it was not the normal way to do things.

"You can't just let this play out then?" Mitch sounded as if he were trying to understand. To think outside the box. But in the end she said he couldn't do much and that he didn't want to charge her what the law firm charged. There was a pause and then he finally spoke.

"Let me give you the number of a lawyer who might help you. He is not a personal injury lawyer, but he is qualified to do what you are asking. If you fire your insurance company, and settle this yourself, it just becomes a matter of signing the right papers and filing the rights fees, clerical legal things. His name is Joseph Brown and you can say I recommended him. See what he says. Explain it all to him. And I wish you good luck."

Mitch gave her Mr. Brown's phone number and Dora felt like she was making some progress. She refilled her coffee cup and sat for a bit, trying to get her courage up. She wasn't even a phone person. She didn't like talking to people she didn't know on the phone, but she had no choice. Maybe this would turn on the light at the end of the tunnel.

"Mr. Brown, Mitch Anderson gave me your phone number. He said you might be able to help me." The voice on the other end sounded friendly and helpful, so she slowly explained what she wanted to do. He seemed to be listening, although he did try to interrupt her once to tell her that the insurance company would take care of all of that and that she didn't have to worry, because she wouldn't have to pay anything. She tried to continue and explain why she needed help and when she was done, Mr. Brown said, "I am sorry, but I won't do that."

When she asked why, he responded, "Because it is an unusual thing to do."

That's when she lost it, replied, "Thank's for your help," sarcastically slammed the phone down and broke down in tears.

"You are what's wrong with the world," she yelled at the phone, already disconnected from the brainwashed lawyer who obviously did everything by some antiquated book and couldn't think outside that book to save his or anyone else's life. Dora called Mitch, but his office was closed. Still very upset, she let loose and told him no one would help her and that Mr. Brown was useless, too. She had hoped that would make her feel a little better, venting about the legal profession, but she only felt worse. She was alone in every way. In her thinking, in her need to make things right, in her righteous indignation and her anger that people just went on with their lives hoping to get as much money as they could while allowing their lawyers to make false accusations against someone who had done the right thing. She not only had not been at fault, but she knew they knew it and yet that was not enough. Had anyone else been driving that car, there would be no okay ending. She deserved better and this time, she would not let go just because people thought what she wanted was, "an unusual thing to do." And it had never been just about her. Some things are just wrong and this was one of them.

CHAPTER 27

Thank God, Brenda sighed when the Skype link to her brother's room opened up and she saw him on his hospital bed with his wife and her sister nearby. Upon seeing and hearing Brenda, Brenda's sister in law Linda moved the laptop closer to her husband. Although he looked weak, he was awake and was happy to see her.

"Hi there, twin sister," he said as if nothing were wrong and they were just about to have a friendly chat. "You are looking good."

"How are you feeling?' she asked. She had been told that his kidney was gone from the cancer and he was in a lot of pain, but he didn't show it and was in much better spirits than she expected.

"I am just so tired. They keep me medicated, but I feel so tired."

"I wish I could be there with you," Brenda said, trying to keep from breaking down. "But this is the best I could do."

"Well, I am glad to see you, Sis. I wasn't ready for this, but what can you do? Seeing you makes all the memories come back. Like all those trips to the park and the water fountain by the playground..."

"And how you used to trick me into putting my face way down and then turning the water up high so it went up my nose."

"Yeah, you hated that," he said with a chuckle.

"And when we were on the seesaw and you sat down and made me go all the way up and wouldn't let me down again?"

"Yeah, I was such a tease."

"But I always loved having a twin brother I could play with and tell my troubles to."

"I know Brenda, me too. "His voice became somber. "Hey Sis, I hope you are staying safe. I worry about you every single day."

"Well, I am doing my best. I get tired, but I do my best."

"I am proud of you, You were always the one to take care of people to give your efforts to something bigger than yourself."

"I really wish I could be there to take care of you."

"Well, I have two daughters, both nurses, and both are here. I couldn't be in better hands."

"How are they doing?"

"Celia is expecting her second baby, a boy this time." He paused, starting to tear up, then inhaled deeply, "That's the hardest part, leaving my granddaughter and not being able to see her grow up. And the boy," his voice trailed off .

Brenda waited and then asked, "And Emily?"

"Oh she is great. Still single, but very happy. Travels a lot. But now she is here with me. Making the best of it.

But" he adjusted his frail body, "I am so damned tired and weak. Maybe need to sleep some more now.

"Okay, you get some rest and I will try to get back again tomorrow."

"Love you, sis."

"I love you, too."

"See you tomorrow then. I promise to hold on so we can talk more tomorrow."

Celia, came into the frame. "Hi, Aunt Brenda. Hope you are doing okay, Stay safe. I am going to give him some morphine so he can rest comfortably. "

"Okay, I will be back tomorrow. And Celia, take care of yourself and the baby. You and Emily, take care of your Mom. I love you all."

Brenda had not expected to have even that short a chat with her brother. At this point it was comforting just to see him and to talk to him. If she hadn't known better, it would have seemed like a normal face time visit, although short. She worried that there might not be another, but she reassured herself that he would hold on until she could talk to him at least one more time. She washed her face, brushed her teeth and headed back to work, down the hall, out the door and into the patient area. There was a lull in the madness and there were no preparations for surgery, and it seemed more like an outpatient clinic than a hospital. A helicopter pilot who she had seen but didn't really know, was sitting up in a bed waiting for an IV.

Brenda gave a quick look around the room checking to see if Bill was there, but he was not. She hadn't expected him to be, but it had become a habit.

"Hi, there. Are you being helped?" Brenda asked, sounding more like a department store salesperson than an ER nurse.

"I am waiting for an IV. A young man named Charlie, I think, went to get something."

"And why do you need an IV?"

"Well, I was sick with a really bad bacterial infection and they tell me I am dehydrated and need an IV. Don't know why I can't just drink some water."

"Well, its quicker this way. And if you are not fully recovered, maybe your body is not absorbing the water you drink. I am guessing you had pretty bad diarrhea right?"

"Very bad. Worst ever."

"Well there has been a bug going around."

Charlie appeared at the door. "Okay, ready? We are going to hydrate you so you are as good as new. "

"Yep, ready as I will ever be," the pilot answered.

"This won't hurt." Charlie started flicking his finger on the veins. "See that was easy, found a perfect vein. Here we go, you will feel… nothing." As Charlie taped the IV in place, the pilot said, "Wow. Didn't even feel that."

"Ask anyone. That is my specialty, painless IVs."

"Someone should clone you, Charley," the pilot said making Charley smile.

"Well, now you will get some fluids and you will feel a whole lot better."

Brenda sat down at the desk and started looking at some charts and records when Bill came in.

"How is it going Bren?"

"Not bad." She looked up at him, her eyes dry and she sounded fairly cheery. "I got to see my brother."

"That's good news. How was it?"

"I was able to talk to him. It was a short visit, maybe five minutes from start to finish, but he was was just very tired. My nieces are both nurses and they are there with him. We reminisced a little, but then he needed to sleep. I let him get some sleep. I want to try again tomorrow."

Bill walked behind her and put his hand on her shoulder. "Glad you got to talk to him."

"It helped me a lot. I know it will be tough when he's gone, but talking to him meant so much. Took the lump out of my chest even if it is only temporary."

Bill gave her shoulder a squeeze and let go. "Well let me know if there is anything I can do."

"Thanks."

✳✳✳

On the other side of the world, the phone rang and went to voicemail as Dora sat in the in the alcove at her desk sorting through the mail and taking out the bills. Usually, she ignored incoming calls when she didn't expect to get anything important on her landline. There were all sorts of calls trying to sell her things she didn't need or want or to scare her by telling her the IRS was coming up her driveway to arrest her for tax evasion, even though she always paid her taxes on time. Scam after scam came into her voicemail from truly stupid people who didn't even know her name or who offered to help her pay her mortgage even though she hadn't had one of those in over a decade. But this time, the voice was familiar. She stopped what she was doing and listened to what she suddenly recognized was Mitch Anderson's voice.

"I am sorry you didn't get any help from Joe. You have a right to representation so I will do what I can. I will have to charge you, of course, but give me a call back and we can talk. I will be here till seven tonight and pretty much all day tomorrow."

Dora ran to the phone, but he hung up before she could answer. She sat down in the chair and took a deep breath. Maybe this would finally be the beginning of the end. She didn't need to carry this burden into the first few months of Bill's homecoming. If she had a plan and was on track to get beyond this, she would be fine. There would be things she needed to help her husband with and she could only guess at what that would entail. She collected her thoughts, took another deep breath and called Mitch.

CHAPTER 28

Bill was taking a break and drinking his third cup of coffee. He had printed out a list of job openings from the Internet, not so much because he was intending to apply for any of them, but just to get a feel for the next step in his life, the one that didn't involve the government or the military. A colleague had suggested he look at openings in a veteran's hospital, but no, he wanted a practice, something not remotely connected with the military. He wanted a brand new start in a place where there was some kind of normalcy, a practice with other surgeons commutable from home. Hopefully, near home so he and Dora would not have to relocate. Dora's mother might need family nearby and Dora had always been close to her so moving away wouldn't be ideal. There was a lot to think about.

"How is it going, Bill?" Dr. Bellamy asked as Bill looked up from his screen.

"Good."

"Oh, I was just looking at some ads for surgical jobs back home. Not that I am interested in any of these specifically, but I wanted to get back in the groove of job hunting. I haven't had any experience with that actually, having been in the military most of my professional life."

Johnny sat down and pulled a piece of paper out of his pocket. He opened it up slowly as if it were some precious document.

"So my brother-in-law is a surgeon in Logandale, I believe that is near where you live?"

"Yes, Bill replied. "about 45 minutes away."

"Well, he is in a practice he describes as bread and butter surgery. I think that means basic surgery, not heart transplants or anything like that."

"Bread and butter, that's general non traumatic surgery. Not like we have been doing here. Less stressful."

"Well his partner is retiring and he will be starting to look for another surgeon to join the practice in a few months. He is going to start searching in a couple of weeks. I was thinking how opportune this would be for you."

"Seriously? Couldn't be more opportune."

"I think you would like him, too. Easy going

sense of humor. I told him about you and I wrote down some information. But when you get stateside, you might want to give him a call."

"Thanks." Bill took the paper, looked at it briefly and thought it was too good to be true. Logandale, he had been through there many times. He always thought it was a nice community. Logandale, bread and butter, Dr. Michael Swan. Yes, he most certainly would give him a call. This sounded ideal, almost too ideal. Things just couldn't be so easy. But a step forward was a step forward. He wouldn't share this with Dora, not yet. Might jinx it.

Brenda came in, got herself some coffee and headed

for the empty seat at the table where Bill was sitting with Johnny Bellamy. As if on cue, Dr. B. started to get up, but Brenda motioned that he should sit and spoke to him before she said anything to Bill.

"How's it going, John?"

"Oh, same old same old. You doing okay?" He had heard about her brother.

Brenda sat down, nodded at Bill and gave them both a smile that could have meant anything.

I got a message from my sister in law that my brother passed away last night. He just closed his eyes one last time and that was that." She took a deep breath and continued. "You know when he decided he didn't want any treatment to delay his death, I wasn't sure, but after seeing him, I know he did what was right for him and I feel better about it."

"I'm sorry, Brenda,"

"I am glad you got to see him and talk to him," Bill added.

"I was so depressed, but when I saw him joking with his kids and he even was eating a Strawberry Shortcake ice cream bar as if everything was fine. It felt natural and I will miss him, but it made it better for me. It gave me closure and a transition for him that we all shared. I know it seems odd."

"No, not at all."

"After all we have seen here with pain and suffering

and death, it was such a difference to see a loved one just accepting and going peacefully. Now I can focus on the memories we shared."

All three were silent for a minute and then turned to small talk.

***

Dora drove to the huge three building complex made of glass and steel. This was where Mitch Anderson's office was. It was impressive. She looked at the paper where she had written the address. Room 1400 Monument Drive was about three miles from Waterview. She felt like Dorothy Gayle when she first saw the Emerald City, only this was white and silver, but it sparkled just the same. There were three buildings, the 1000, the 2000 and the 3000. She pulled her car into a space by the entrance of the 1000 and took a deep breath. Would the Wizard grant her wish? Well at least he had agreed to take her case and see what could be done. It was a huge move forward. She parked her car and headed for the 1000 building. It was massive. She couldn't even imagine what kind of work people did in that building, besides legal cases. She entered the outer door and headed for the elevator, pressing the button for the fourth floor. The ride was smooth and the elevator opened on a richly carpeted floor where a woman in a designer suit waited, a bunch of folders in her arms.

"Good afternoon, she said as Dora got out. Dora was glad she had dressed up a bit, not in designer clothes, but in a nice-enough dress that fell just below her knee. Gray with a burgundy light jacket. Her hair was tied back, making her look like she could have worked in that building. "Afternoon" Dora replied, holding the door open button for the woman and then watching the doors close. The directory was on the wall in front of her, and she saw room 1400 was just to her right. She opened the door and entered the plush waiting room where the deep blue carpet continued, leading to a very large counter where a young woman with thick black hair and a pleasant businesslike smile made Dora feel confident and at ease.

"How may I help you?"

"I am here to see Mr. Anderson."

"And what is your name?"

"Dolores Victor."

"Oh, yes, Dr. Victor. Have a seat and Mr. Anderson will be with you in a few minutes."

Dora sat in a deep blue velvet chair. She looked about the room and marveled at its luxury. The woman had called her Dr. Victor, but she didn't recall telling Mitch Anderson about her degree. Maybe she had. Everything had been a bit of a blur, especially the past few weeks and she didn't always remember what she had told whom but still she was confident that her memory of the accident was clear and spot on.

In a few more minutes, Mitch came to lobby himself

and ushered her into his office and to a chair that overlooked a park with a bridge and a small stream.

"Would you like some coffee?" he said as he poured a cup.

"Yes, please. Just a little milk, no sugar."

After delivering her coffee and placing his on the other side of his huge mahogany desk, he said, "Okay, so I need to know exactly what you want to do. If it is legal, I will do it and will only charge you what I have to."

"I am not worried about the money but..."

"I just want you to know," he interrupted politely. "that I may not agree with what you want to do but, at this point, and after what you have told me,. I am pretty sure you have thought it through and if it doesn't work out the way you expect, you will just have to accept it."

"I only want to be heard."

"And you will do whatever is necessary to be heard, right?"

"Yes."

"And you are willing to spend money, even give the kid money just to be heard?"

"Seems odd?"

"Yes, it does."

"I can't process the events around the accident. I need to be heard to remove whatever is blocking my ability to process it all."

"You mentioned PTSD."

"Yes, I was diagnosed with PTSD and have been going to therapy But until I have closure, this just isn't enough."

"Well, I hope I can help. Mitch pulled a pad and pencil over. "Tell me exactly what you want me to do."

I want to give them a choice. I will give the 15k now if they meet with me and just listen to what I have to say. Or I will bypass my insurance company and insist we go to court.. They already treatened to drop me if I did that but..."

"They can';t do that. They are trying to intimidate you." Mitch looked at Dora before continuing. He wanted to jump in and tell her how crazy this was, but he knew that wasn't the way to go, so he paused. "While it sounds simple, it could backfire. You never know with people. And I am fairly sure I can get the plaintiff's lawyers to support the first option to avoid going to court, but as long as you know and are sure about what you want to do."

Well they will end up with more money if they take my offer as well as what the insurance company will settle for. I believe it is 2,500 now. "

"Remember, their lawyers will get a third of the whole amount."

"Okay, lets make a change in that then. Offer them 20K added to the insurance company offer." Dora took a sip of coffee and waited.

"I can't, I mean, that is a lot of money. Are you sure..."

"If you won't help me out, I have nowhere else to go!"

"I know. I said I would help you. I wouldn't do this myself but I am not in your shoes."

"I have been told I needed therapy, that the plaintiffs would end up taking all my money, that I should just get over it and even one lawyer told me I had no right to a trial."

"Well of course you have a right to a trial. Okay, so hopefully this will only require a few phone calls, but if you insist on going to court, I will defend you. I am usually on the other side but I can do this if that ends up being what you need."

"Thank you."

"Just give me two days before I make any calls and that'll give you a chance to change your mind if you want to."

"I am on a tight schedule. My husband ins coming home from the military in three weeks. I'd like this over by then."

"That is very tall order and if they refuse your offer, a trial may take a very long time. But okay. Give me 24 hours then. It still is going to take time but you can always change your mind even after I make the offer."

"Thank you. I won't change my mind."

"Okay, consider it done. I will get back to you as soon as I get a response from the plaintiff's lawyers. I'll talk to you soon."

"Thank you," Dora finished her coffee and stood up."

Mitch stood up and led her to the door.

CHAPTER 29

Dora sorted her mail as she sat down at her desk. The next few days would keep her anxious for some news in the hope that the plaintiffs would agree to end this insanity and make a profit by doing so. But she needed to focus on her work as the semester's end involved all sorts of forms to fill out and records to keep. The office had only one small window at the top of the wall and it was hard to open and the one time she was able to get it open, a bird nearly flew in. She had closed it so fast that the mockingbird on the other side collided with the glass and fell onto a branch where it took a few seconds to regain its bearings. Then it hopped up to the higher branch by the top of the window and squawked at Dora who stood there staring at it. Mockingbirds, she knew, were fierce at defending their nests and she decided that the window would remain closed from then on.

As she shuffled through her interoffice mail, opening each yellow envelope to see if the contents were memos about required meetings or some new guidelines for turning in grades, not accepting free lunch from publishers or perhaps a new scholarship she needed to tell her students about, But as she opened the next envelope, the contents made her pause. It was a memo about how to apply for a sabbatical. She skimmed through it and then read it again more slowly and thoroughly. When she read the requirements, she counted the number of years she had been working at the college on her fingers as she lay the paper down, pushing away less important papers and making sure there were no crumbs or coffee spills. Under the memo was the application. Her heart started to beat faster as she wondered if she could possibly be awarded a sabbatical and what on earth she could study.

The sound of footsteps approaching her door distracted her. It was Anna Duffy, a friend from the Foreign Language Department. Anna stopped at Dora's door and waved a piece of paper in her hand.

"You get the memo about sabbaticals?"

"Yes, I just opened it"

"Are you interested, Dora? We could both apply for sabbaticals. Wouldn't that be awesome? If we both were approved?

Dora and Anna had started working at the college the same year. They both got tenure the same year and here it was the time they were finally eligible for sabbaticals. Dora continued reading and motioned to Anna to come in and sit down. Anna quickly pulled the chair out and sat. Dora read aloud. *Six sabbaticals will be awarded for the upcoming academic year. Applicants can choose one semester (either fall or spring at full pay or the full academic year at half pay.* Dora set the paper on her desk.

"I don't know. It seems unlikely that I would get it even if I had the slightest idea what I would do with it.

"I know, it may be a long shot, but we wouldn't lose anything if we applied., Even if we didn't get it next year, it might be good practice for another year and maybe one of us would get it. I heard that if you choose the full year at half pay option, you have a better chance, but I would only want to do the single semester myself. I want to go to Brazil and study Brazilian culture and Portuguese. I have heard that the department is thinking of adding Portuguese to the courses and that they might be focusing on Brazil."

"You know we would be competing against each other."

"Yeah well, we are always competing against someone, but hey you never know. I could travel to Brazil and develop some course materials and lessons. And if I applied for a semester and you for a full year, we wouldn't really be competing at all.

"That sounds great for you and the department. I can see why they might want you to do that, but what would I study? Hemingway, Chaucer? Um no. And now is not the time I would want to be traveling."

"Well you know, Dora, I was thinking. Why don't you study something relevant to your life like maybe PTSD. I know you have been having some trouble with it and your husband will be home soon. I am sure he has had his own experiences with it."

"Anna, as much as I would love to have time to research that topic, I cannot justify it as a sabbatical project in the English Department. I have read some poems by veterans and a few essays, but not really enough to be the basis if a full year sabbatical."

"But think how it would help you. It might help you as well as giving you insight into the problems of our veteran students. We have a lot of veterans. I have an older student who was in Vietnam and he says he still suffers and you know we have young ones who just came back from the Middle East."

"But that would be good for anyone in counseling or even in psych, but English? I am not sure how I would make it seem like something I should do."

"I saw your dissertation. You did a great job of laying out a structure to use literacy to address problems of the farm workers. Just do the same to address the problems of veterans dealing with PTSD."

I see you have thought this out," Dora said smiling. Anna was selling an idea, a product and it was beginning to sound feasible.

"Besides, I heard yesterday that last year the year-long sabbaticals were not awarded to anyone because no one applied."

"I guess most people wouldn't want to give up half a year's salary."

"Is that an issue for you?" Anna asked knowing Dora and her husband weren't ever going to live paycheck to paycheck."

Dora looked down again and was silent for a few seconds. "No, money is not the problem."

"Then what is?"

"Nothing I guess."

"Didn't you tell me you did some volunteer work at a psychiatric hospital once?"

"I did. It was volunteer meaning I didn't get paid, but it was not really by choice. It was fieldwork related to a social work course I took in grad school when I was getting my masters."

Dora began to think seriously about this opportunity. She looked at the deadline for the application, only 10 days away and decided she should go for it. She separated the application from the notice. It required the title of her topic and how it was relevant to the college. Next she had to give a detailed history of her experience, coursework and credentials related to the research she would be doing. Then an outline with a timeline, and a summary statement. This was no easy task, not to do it correctly and it had to be reviewed by her department sabbatical committee before it was delivered by hand to the Faculty Senate and the Senate committee. While it seemed a little overwhelming in light of everything else she had on her mind, she decided it might also be a positive distraction from her problems and worries.

CHAPTER 30

Three days passed with no word from Mitch. Dora realized how silly it was of her to expect to hear from him in so short a time. She tried not to get too excited about the idea of having a full year sabbatical, but it simmered somewhere inside her mixing with the fear and hope of hearing news from her lawyer.

The emails from Bill were coming every single day now. He talked about things he looked forward to seeing, his favorite dishes that she had cooked for him over the years, asked about her mother and all sorts of things. And while he sounded anxious to get home, he also sounded a little like a stranger in some ways. He asked about people he had known and some of them had died. Dora realized that she didn't tell him about many things that had happened in Waterview, and she should have. But she did her best to update him and apologize for her omissions. She had spent the day finishing up her sabbatical application and was ready to hand it in the next morning. She was just getting ready to turn in a little early, hoping for a good night's sleep. As she was brushing her teeth, the phone rang. She ran to pick it up as while it seemed a little late, it was not too late to be hearing from Mitch. She was right, his name came up on the caller ID.

"Dora, how are you?"

"Good, do you have any news?"

"I do but it is not good."

"What, tell me."

"Well the plaintiff's lawyers presented your offer and they rejected it. The boy's father said he doesn't want your money and he is willing to wait until he gets what he is entitled to from the insurance company.

"Entitled?"

"Well, yes, but they tried to explain that that meant he would have to go to court for a trial and he said he was fine with that. But here is the thing, his lawyers don't want to go to court. Jason Hall is handling the case and he said if the case when to court, you would win. He explained that to his client, but the kid's father said he would take his chances. Their law firm always says that they have never lost a case that went to court. They say that in all their ads. It would be a horrible precedent for them. They usually settle out of court when they think they could lose. But now you have presented them with a problem. Jason said they asked Mr. D'Angelo to come into their office, thinking that maybe a face to face meeting would be more conducive to making him understand what is at stake. So he is meeting with Jason tomorrow afternoon. They can't make him do anything, but hopefully the second attempt at persuasion will succeed."

"Well, I hope so. Please keep in touch and call me as soon as you hear anything."

"I will do that. I just wanted to update you. I thought you might get some satisfaction from knowing they think you would win. "

"Well yes, some, but I still need to speak to them."

"Even if they agree, they might just sit there and say nothing."

"I know, but at least I would get my hearing."

"I understand. I will probably call you around seven pm if that is okay. They are meeting in the afternoon, but by the time they call me, it could be after dinner."

"That is okay. I will be in." Dora's heart was beating faster. She took a deep breath and let it out slowly.

In the morning, Dora headed to the college. Things were winding down now with finals graded and only a little paperwork left. She walked her application over to the department office and found the three committee members in the office of the chair.

"Since we are here, why don't we go over this now?" They agreed and told Dora they would let her know when they would be done. Dora knew that that meant they would put little stickers all over the application and ask her to correct, add and clarify before they turned it in to the senate committee. She hoped that this wouldn't happen more than once. These committees were there to help make sure the best application possible was turned in, but sometimes the do-overs got to be cumbersome. especially at the end of the semester when she just wanted to go home. But back at her office she had one more set of forms to fill out and they were the official grades of her students. So, she grabbed a cup of coffee and headed back to her office where she spent the next hour carefully transferring her grades to a sheet with little circles under each grade next to each student name. Tedious but necessary. When she was ready to put the forms into her folder, the phone rang. It was the department chair.

"Hi, Dora. The committee finished reading your application and they decided that any changes they would recommend would be minor and not worth doing. We think you have a solid plan and it will be hand delivered to the senate immediately. Congratulations and good luck."

"Thank you." Dora didn't want to get her hopes up but a positive comment from the department committee made her relieved that she wouldn't have to keep revising over and over so that she could feel she was moving forward. Her grades in hand, she returned to the department office where the secretary looked over them once and signed her off.

"You're done. Enjoy your summer. I will forward any important mail to your home."

Summer began early in the college calendar. Graduation was a week away and this year it was not Dora's turn to attend. She enjoyed attending graduations with all the pomp and circumstance and enjoyed wearing her robe and academic hood and her beret which she had chosen over a mortarboard. But she was only required to be in the academic procession, every other year. This was a good year to be home, instead of sitting out on the lawn on what could be a hot day or a rainy day. Even for a small college, the ceremony was impressive, but this year her thoughts were elsewhere.

All Dora had left to do was to write a few letters of recommendation for a half dozen for grad school and employment. She could get that done later, maybe in a day or two. She picked up a food magazine and put her feet up as she tried out the new recliner she had bought for Bill. Halfway through the magazine and the recipe for chicken paprikash, she dozed off and was awakened by the ringing of the phone. She just made it to the phone before it went to voice mail. It was Mitch.

"Okay, Dora, it took some persuading but Mr. D'Angelo finally decided to accept your offer and they set a date for next week, on Tuesday at 4 pm. I hope that will work for you."

"It will. After all this, I would make it work, but I happen to be free that day."

"Good. I will be there and will handle the transfer of the money. You will need to write a check to their law firm, but I assure you the plaintiffs will get their money. As you know, the firm will take its cut, but the good news is that they are only taking their percentage of the 15 K and not the entire 20. It will be over and even if it doesn't end perfectly, maybe the way you wished, it will be done and you will be able to go about your life without worrying about ho you are allowed to talk to."

"I will be free." She took a deep breath and the air entered her lungs like new air giving her new life.

"Is there anything else you need?" Mitch asked.

"No, I'm good. Oh, how much do I owe you for this?"

"The firm will send you a bill. I think for everything, it will be less than five hundred. I personally..."

"I can afford it. Don't worry, I am grateful for your help. Especially since it is..."

"...an unusual thing to do."

"Right."

When Tuesday came, butterflies took up residence in Dora's stomach. She felt a little numb as she climbed the stairs to the office where she would get her chance to be heard. She knew she had to make sure this would be the closure she needed to put the accident and the legal absurdities behind her. With Bill coming home, the timing had been close but sufficient to clear the slate and set her mind on happier things.

Perhaps the meeting could have been more satisfying had the boy and his father connected with her on a friendlier level but it was polite and at times as she talked about the day of the accident and the months that followed, she felt there was an occasional glimmer of human empathy. At one point when she explained about her PTSD and how it kept her awake at night, someone on the other side of the table mumble, "I'm sorry" but she wasn't sure if it was the boy or the father. She thought it was the boy. When she spoke of the wording on the summons and complaint, their lawyer used the words, boiler plate and said everyone knows those words are standard. Dora responded, that they were still a lie when they knew no one had lost "community with his son" and that his life was never in danger. The lawyers grinned but then kept their silence. When Dora said that the words "careless, reckless and negligent were particularly offensive when she had done everything she could to prevent the accident, they just listened. At one point, Dora heard the plaintiff's lawyer whisper "OCD" almost inaudibly and saw Mitch stare him down, clearing his throat so his stare would not be missed. Then she continued to speak to make sure they fully understood that the money she was giving the boy had nothing to do with fault and everything to do with gratitude that things came together in the street that day to make sure the best possible outcome was achieved.

"Something or someone warned me, before Devin ever turned to enter the street so that my foot was on my brake before so I could stop in 15 feet of when he entered the street. Something or someone spoke to me silently and for that I am grateful."

Devin looked up and made eye contact with her, and she thought she saw a tear in his eye, but when she blinked it was gone. Maybe her imagination, or maybe not. When she felt she had almost said enough, she finished off by saying if she met them on the street, in a store or at the local pizza place, she would say hello but, that was enough and otherwise she would leave them alone.

There was a pause and Mr. D'Angelo said he hoped

she would do better now."

"Thank you," Dora said. "My husband is coming home from years of service in the military, coming home for good. He is a doctor and I am hoping we can finally begin a normal life. Life is so fragile and I am blessed that now he has left the Middle East and although I will always worry, about those who serve our country, those who protect our lives and property here in our communities, and kids who have lapses in focus and dash out into dangerous streets, I am going to be more positive and hopeful and, well enough of that. "

Devin spoke up, "Please thank your husband for his service and if you ever want to stop by the baseball field when I have a game, you will be welcome."

"Yes, I will send you his schedule. You come with your husband," is

dad added,.

"I will do that, thank you."

"Okay, and thank you," Mitch said. I have turned over the check from Dr. Victor and your lawyers will send you your portion. "I think this pretty much concludes ..." He wasn't sure what to call it as it was not anything anyone had done before, at least not to his knowledge. He looked at Dora and softly said, "Are we good now?"

"Yes, and Thank you. Dora felt a rush of clean air flow into her lungs as everyone stood up and Devin was the fist to extend his hand. After the handshaking, they left the building, the D'Angelos heading for the parking lot in one direction and Dora turning in the opposite. It was done.

CHAPTER 31

As long as Dora had been waiting for her husband's return, when the day came, she didn't feel ready, as if there were things she should have done but neglected. Why hadn't she lost some weight, redecorated the house, gotten her hair trimmed, added more highlights, and more. She had read every article about how to respond to a loved one coming home from war and yet, she felt totally unprepared. Her heart was beating fast as she looked at the clock and tried to decide when to leave for the train station. Of course, she would arrive at the station early. She was always early, more a sign of anxiety than punctuality. What was that saying? *To be early is to be on time and to be late is to be left behind,* something like that. She took a deep breath, took out her keys and headed out the door.

The drive to the station was not like any other time she drove there. Her palms were sweaty and every now and then her breathing stopped and then a rush of air filled her lungs while she made a loud gasping noise. Yup. nerves. The dashboard clock confirmed that she was going to be early. Good. The sky was clear, the temperature outside, a perfect seventy three, and she was going to see her husband, the love of her life, and he would not be leaving again. What more was there to ask for?

Dora parked her car and got out, giving her dress a tug to make sure it wasn't wrinkled and that she was presentable. It was an old dress but still looked like new and was one of Bill's favorites. He always said she looked great when she wore it. Even though she doubted he would remember it, she hoped it would spark a feeling in him that said HOME. She was wearing the same perfume she had used for years, hoping that would add to the familiarity and feeling that he was finally a civilian again. Her hair was full and loose.

She gave a quick glance at her watch, the one Bill gave her for their third anniversary, the one with the brown leather band. It was 9:17. The train would be in at 9:31. She approached the station, climbed the stairs and found an empty bench where there was some shade. Then she waited, checking the large station clock on the platform. Still ten minutes to go. The rumbling of the 9:22 to the city shook the platform as the train pulled in behind her. The lit up sign nearby said Bill's train was on time. No delays. Finally, no delays, and no going back. Bill would never be going back to the military. He belonged to himself now, and to her. It was almost too much to believe. A new start, a new chapter was awaiting them. She stood up to get a better look down the track. Dora felt like she was floating on air and not sure where her feet would come into contact with the platform again as the 9:31 from Penn Station came around the bend in the distance. Feeling weak in the knees, she moved to the nearby light pole and slid her hand around it. No, that looked silly, holding onto a pole for dear life. So she just leaned against it. Oh my God, no, now she probably looked like a hooker.

"Hello Soldier..." She stood up straight and sucked her stomach in and pulled her stray hairs out from under her collar. Unsteady, she decided to go back to the bench until she saw him. The train was pulling into the station as her heartbeat quickened and she took a deep breath. The brakes screeched and the train came to a stop. There was a pause before the doors opened and her heart was racing. She leaned forward, but stayed seated. She didn't see him. He had left a text message on her phone, one she found after she came out of the shower. The 9:31. But where was he? She saw two men and a women in camouflage uniforms carrying dufflebags, but no Bill. She released a sigh and then heard his voice.

"Dolly!"

She looked up and she saw him. He was dressed in fresh new denim jeans and a blue and white striped polo shirt, a black suitcase wheeling alongside him.

"Bill!" Her voice betrayed any calm she was hoping to project and broke, as if she were about to cry. She swallowed hard as she jumped up and ran toward him and almost knocking him down when they collided. Laughing, and then bursting into tears, she threw her arms around him as he pulled her close to him. He hugged her so tight, neither of them wanted to let go.

"Welcome home baby."

"I missed you Dolly. I missed you so much."

They held each other close for a full minute, as passersby took no notice. Had Bill been in uniform, they would have turned their heads and shared briefly in the moment, but not this time. Dora and Bill dropped their arms and clasped hands so they could stay connected while looking at each other. Tears streamed from Dora's eyes.

"I hope those are happy tears." Bill said softly. "I have so much to tell you.

"I couldn't be happier."

"Let's go home." Bill loved the way that word sounded. "Home." he repeated "I am finally home."

They walked to the car holding hands like young lovers.

"Do you want to drive?" She offered him the keys.

"Not today. I'll let you take the wheel today. I want to look at the scenery and get adjusted to what has changed. I know some things have changed since I was home last."

They got into the car and she started the engine, put on the AC and had one deep kiss before heading home. Bill named the things that were the same, as they moved along the small familiar street, the elementary school, the supermarket, new name but the same otherwise, the library, and strip mall with a Tae Kwon Do school where the barbershop used to be. They stopped at a red light and he reached over and touched her arm kissing her once again.

"Oh, Dolly, Dolly, Dolly. Is this real? I can't believe it is real."

"Oh it is real. I can't even begin to tell you how happy..." she said interrupted by the car behind them, honking its horn.

As they turned the corner, Bill saw a big change.

"What is this?"

"It's a Toyota dealership. They sell new Toyotas and used, excuse me, preowned cars of all kinds."

"Can you pull over here?"

Dora pulled the car over to the curb.

"What happened to the amusement park that used to be here?"

"It was torn down. They extended the parking lot and put the Toyota showroom where the roller coaster used to be."

"They took paradise and put up a parking lot," he said with a sigh.

"I thought you knew they shut it down last time you were here."

" I remember that it was closed down, but I thought someone would reopen it. And what happened to the carousel?"

"Oh they saved that, thank God. It's in a park a few miles away.

"Sad. I always thought we would be able to take our kids there."

"Well, there is another one not too far away. We can

take our kids there," Dora didn't look at him when she said it. That was something else they had to talk about, but it could wait a few days. No pressure, not on either of them. But yes, kids were going to be part of the equation if all went well. Bill smiled. There was hope.

"How's your mom doing,? Bill asked.

"She's doing fine. She can't wait to see you. I thought we could stop by if you have nothing planned for tomorrow."

"Planned? Not yet. I am just going with the flow right now. But sure, that would be great. I miss her, too. I miss family. You two are all I've got. "

"She wants to make us lunch."

"Nice."

"Are you hungry? Have you eaten?"

"Not really, just coffee and a donut. I can wait until lunch. I look forward to seeing your mom.. She is a good cook. "

"Taught me everything I know.

"I missed your cooking. "I can't wait to set foot inside our house. Maybe just catch up on some things. There is so much I want to say and do. But we have plenty of time, now. Plenty of time."

When they got home, Dora prepared a full welcome home breakfast, of biscuits, eggs, bacon, orange juice and coffee while Bill wandered around the house, looking at all the rooms and letting it sink in that this was his home.

She enjoyed the moment, even though it felt strange and she had to keep reminding herself that Bill was home to stay and not just there on a visit. There was so much to talk about, but she had decided she would focus on listening.

"I don't want you to fuss. I could have waited until lunch,' he said coming up behind her and putting his hands on her shoulders.

"Well, I didn't have breakfast either so, we can call it brunch if you want."

"Brunch it is then. I'll make the coffee." He went over to the counter where everything was ready and all he had to do was to push the ON button.

"Thanks," Dora said as Bill ceremoniously pushed the button and the coffee maker began to gurgle.

"Why don't you go sit down, maybe turn on the TV or read something. There are some magazines on the coffee table."

"Okay. But let me know if I can do anything to help."

"I will."

She had felt happy for sure, but also a little odd when she fully realized that nothing would ever be the same again. Yes, it was a lot like the day after they got married over a decade ago. All the preparations and the wedding and the romantic honeymoon in Bermuda and then, the realization that life would be very different from then on. But this time, there was a whole lot more that she didn't know and she was going to let it unfold slowly. So far, it was a new, but very welcomed new normal. Only time would tell. There was this whole reintegration process she had read about. Whatever problems and trials she had had here at home, were nothing like what he had experienced. So it would begin with breakfast, a good place to start to face reality after the romance and comfort of Bill's return.

"Somethings smells wonderful." Bill's voice came from the living room. Wow, I still have to pinch myself. It seems too good..."

"...to be true? But it is true, Dear Husband," she said with a laugh. It is ready."

Bill got out of the chair and met his wife at the doorway to the kitchen and put his arms around her. She drew closer to him as he kissed her hand, noticing that she looked a little more tired than he remembered, but still so beautiful.

"Thanks," he said.

"I hope you like it. I'll get your coffee and some marmalade for the biscuits."

"Oh my dear Dolly, you know what I like. I have something I want to tell you so when you are ready," he said as he sat down at the table.

"Good news or bad news?" she asked as she grabbed his coffee and marmalade.

"Not bad at all, but too soon to tell if it is good news."

Dora went back and picked up her own coffee and

breakfast and Bill jumped up to pull her chair out as she sat down."

"You are still the gentleman. One of the reasons I love you." She reached over and caressed his face, looking into his deep blue eyes. "No more military, right?"

"Absolutely not. "

"No more answering the call of duty?"

"I promise."

"You did your time and now we can be a family?"

"Yes, whatever you want." Bill wondered if "family" meant children, finally, but he would leave that for another time. Normal takes time. It would not happen in the blink of an eye, but for sure, they were headed in the right direction.

Dora set the coffee mug Bill had always used before he went away on the table in front of him. He looked at her, winked, but said nothing. It was a white cup with the inscription, "A wise doctor once wrote..." the rest was written in illegible doctor's handwriting.

"I love you," she suddenly said, not even expecting what came out of her mouth.

"I love you, too Babe. Especially for keeping my favorite mug."

"I have a favorite mug, too?" she said, cradling his face in her hands."

They gazed at each other for a moment and then Dora

asked, "So you said you had something to tell me?"

"Okay, I don't want to get my hopes up but I actually have a job interview this upcoming week. On Thursday."

"A job interview, really? Tell me more." Her heart began to beat faster in anticipation.

"Well, a friend at my base, connected me with a surgeon here who is looking for a partner. I was able to get in touch with him and he said I should come in for an interview. It seemed absurdly fortunate and easy."

"Wow!"

"I am not kidding. His partner is retiring and he needs a replacement. He seemed impressed by my time in the military and sounded interested."

"And the interview is this coming Thursday? Can you be ready in time? Do you need travel arrangements? Where is it?" The thought were flowing.

"I think you are going to love this."

"What, tell me, tell me now." She was almost out of her seat and the pitch of her voice was rising with every word.

"The office is in Logandale." He waited.

"Our Logandale? Logandale? Really?"

"Yes, my love, our Logandale. What is it about 45 minutes from here?|

"I think so. I would say that. More or less depending on traffic, oh my God, Logandale? Could it get any better?"

Well, only if I get the job. That isn't guaranteed and I am looking at other options, but yes, It would be great if I did get it. Okay. Maybe I don't want to talk about it anymore for now. But yes, so we will see."

"Okay. It is a lot to take in but that's great. Let's just hope...Okay let's talk about something else."

"Thanks for the great brunch," Bill said as he finished eating and nursed his coffee before getting up and adding a little more to the mug."Can I give you more?" he said holding up the coffee pot.

"No thanks, I'm good. Why don't you finish your coffee in the living room. Put your feet up. Relax a bit."

"That would be great.

"I have some work for school so maybe while you relax, I can finish that up so we have more time together later. Try the new recliner."

"Good idea." Bill walked into the living room, sat in the gray recliner with a tray attached and pushed himself back. When he finished his coffee, he began to doze off.

Dora got her folder with the names of the former students who needed letters of recommendation and where they were to be sent. Then she sat at her desk, quietly arranging her work. She could see Bill in the chair and smiled to herself as he dozed. His presence was comforting and watching him sleep made her feel a new sense of peace. She felt excited inside about the prospect of a job just a few villages away. But, like Bill, she didn't want to get her hopes up. Still, her mind kept taking her back to imaginings of how it might be watching him leave for the office, and how she would expand her own geographic horizons and perhaps even make some new friends. Please God.

The sunlight came through the window, shining on Bill as he turned his head away and continued sleeping. Dora went to the window and closed the blinds enough to keep the sun out of his eyes without making the room dark. Streaks of diffused sunlight came through the cracks and cast gold highlights on his light brown hair. Only a few silver hairs here and there indicated that he was in his late forties, forty eight, to be exact. The last time he had been home seemed too long ago, and then there was the time he was supposed to come home but caught a bug and ended up in a hospital on the other side of the world. How she had worried about him then. But now, to say it was all too good to be true was just a cliche' and didn't scratch the surface of the reality. She had the urge to touch him, to run her fingers through his hair or kiss his forehead, but she didn't want to disturb him. These things would come later and they would spend the night holding each other. Any uneasiness she had had about his return was gone now. She left him and went back to her work.

CHAPTER 32

Angela sat on the balcony outside her stateroom. Such luxury, she thought. She had never imagined that one day she would be on a cruise with her daughter and her new daughter-in-law. Who ever heard of a mother going on her child's honeymoon? But the two women had insisted. All three of them knew Angela's health was failing and that instead of sitting in some hospital, being treated for what would eventually take her, they had decided to spend this precious time together. The ocean moved past with the invigorating sound of waves splashing against the ship as she watched the horizon sliding by. The sun was about to slip into the water. It looked like a big red ball bouncing on top of the ocean and it made her feel peaceful. Her life was like the sun going down, and the end would come naturally. But the week long cruise would not take any time away from her. In fact, it was giving her time she never imagined she would have and she was filled with satisfaction that her daughter was happy and with the one she loved. The wind blew across her face, sometimes even a bit harshly, but she didn't care. It made her feel alive and for now, she was and that was all that mattered. A knock on the door and the two young women entered, joining Angela on the balcony.

"This is really nice.

"We brought you some fruit."

They both pulled up chairs and sat, one on each side

of her.”

“I love you both.” Angela said as she took a plate of grapes.”

“Are you warm enough, Mom?”

“Yes, I am fine, thank you.”

“We could get you a sweater? Let us know if you want a blanket or a jacket.”

:”Dinner is in a half hour.”

“Good. I can’t wait to see what is on the menu.”

“I saw the menu and there are many things you would like, Mom”

“It might get a little colder as we get farther out away from the coast.. It is two and a half days at sea before we get to Bermuda.”

“You wearing the bracelet?”

“Yes, the one so I don’t get seasick? Yes.”

***

Elizabeth set the table and took the brisket out of the oven. It looked great and smelled even greater. The sauce was rich and smoky, with deep flavors of onion and tomato and just a touch of spices and herbs. Roasted potatoes and fresh green beans, recipes she hadn’t made in a long time but remembered that they were Bill’s favorites. There was a nice fresh side salad, watermelon cocktails and gelato from the Italian grocery, brought the meal full circle. When she heard the car drive up, she was full of joy and could hardly contain herself. She flung the front door open and almost fell down the front steps, but caught herself in time so as not to make a scene. She wore a flowery dress, a sundress with a light sweater for the joyous occasion. Pinks and blues and yellow. She had even colored her hair three days before so that the gray was now a golden blonde making her look 10 years younger when she looked into the mirror.

"Bill, "she shouted happily. "I am so happy to see you!" she held her arms out to hug him and he hugged her so hard he lifted he off the ground and took her breath away.

"Oh, Mom, I missed you. I am so happy to b e home," he said. "You look great. You've been taking care of yourself?"

"Well, I've been trying. Get my daily walks in."

"Good for you. I smell something delicious.|

"I hope you like what I cooked for you."

"I will."

The table set in the screened in patio and the meat resting, Elizabeth offered them watermelon cocktail that she had recently learned to make by watching the food channel. She motioned for them to sit outside on the patio.

"I love the summer, but it always goes by so fast," Elizabeth said.

Bill agreed. I love the autumn in Waterview and I look forward to doing some hiking and outdoor things, maybe go fishing."

"That would be great. Get back to a less stressful life," Elizabeth said smiling. This was the kind of conversation she was longing to have with her son-in-law. How things should be.

"This is delicious, Mom" Dora said as she lifted her glass, prompting the others to raise theirs as well.

"To home and family, Dora toasted.

"Amen," Elizabeth replied.

"To the best family on the planet," Bill added.

"You will have to give me the recipe for this drink," Dora said.

"I will be happy to." Elizabeth set down her drink on the nearby table and got up to bring the food out to the table.

"Mom, let me help you. Oh and I didn't tell you, both of you, that the accident and all that has been settled amicably. It is over for me."

"Great to hear." Bill said

"Best news, and thank God, "her mother added..

Bill finished his cocktail and breathed a deep breath. This was Heaven.

Elizabeth took her sharpest knife out of the drawer and began to cut the meat."

"Oh let me do that." Dora paused as her mom handed her the knife. "I know, against the grain." She remembered the time she was scolded for cutting it wrong .

"Oh, I know you know how to cut it." Elizabeth drained the green beans, the steam rising from the colander. "I could get a facial while doing this, "she quipped. It was something she said when she drained hot vegetables. "I kept it simple. Meat, beans and roasted potatoes."

"That's fine. I brought the dessert as you asked. Black Forest cake."

"Bill's favorite?"

"Used to be. Hope it still is."

"So, Mom, have you heard from Angela Bookman? You haven't said anything about her for a while."

"Her daughter called me a while back. I meant to tell you. |Her health has been failing. She has some kind of blood disorder, a kind of leukemia, or something like leukemia, they really didn't seem to know much, other than she was getting weaker and sadly, was not going to get better."

"How awful!"

Her daughter and her female um, partner, decided to get married while Angela was here and to take her on their honeymoon with them on cruise to Bermuda."

"Okay, wait, Angela's daughter got married and Angela went on a cruise?"

"You knew she was gay, right? I am sure I mentioned it."

"Yes, now that you mention it. The daughter had broken up with the man she was with...yes. So did they get married or...."

They decided to have a small ceremony at the Unitarian Church in Yonkers. Just close family and friends. They invited me, but I said no. I think they were just being kind. I would make it sad. But I sent them a nice tea set. Angela told me they like tea."

"Well, I am sad to hear she isn't doing well, but how nice of them to take her on a cruise."

They continued placing everything on the table.

"I hope she is up to the cruise," Dora said.

"They chose a stateroom with a balcony where she can sit and be served and where she can rest when she needs to. Oh, and they hired a nurse to go with them just to help and be with her if they go ashore on excursions. They thought of everything. I hope the end comes peacefully for her."

"Okay, come and get it," Elizabeth called to Bill, cutting off the conversation about Mrs. Bookman.

"Let's enjoy this sumptuous feast,' Dora said with a smile.

***

Hundreds of miles away, sixteen-year-old Ellie Black sat in a waiting room at Harvard. She was dressed in a beige summer dress, her dark hair tied back. The sunlight through the window made her hair glimmer with copper highlights. She was excited about meeting with the woman she had spoken with on the phone, the woman from the admissions office.

"Ellie Black?" The young woman who had opened the door smiled and motioned for her to come in. "Have a seat. I am Millie Moore. I am a grad student and an alum of the gap year program." and this is Sarah Elliot. She is familiar with several gap-year programs here and at other colleges. We are excited to help you with your plans for this upcoming year so it will be a worthwhile experience you will never forget."

"So many students that have been accepted to Harvard are taking this option and since you are only sixteen, this will be a great opportunity for you to explore the things you are interested in and still start your freshman year when most freshman do."

"Thank you. I am excited about it."

"Have you read the brochures we sent you?" Sarah leaned forward resting her hands on the knees of her chino pants.

"Oh yes, "Ellie answered. "It was exciting to see so many options and a little overwhelming as well. I was happy to see that there were half year programs as I would like a few months off before I join a formal program.

"Oh like a gap semester before your gap semester. Sounds like a good idea," Millie said with a smile.

"Yes, maybe do some community service, take art

courses at the local art's council, and visit my grandmother who I have not seen in years."

"Those sound like worthwhile things to do. So when do you think you would want to join one of the programs? Do you know yet?" Sarah asked.

"Well I was looking at the January to April programs. Not sure if I would like to go to Seville or Dublin. I do speak Spanish and would love to use it and improve on it, but Dublin has always enchanted me."

"Do you have an eventual career goal in mind?" Millie was leafing through all the destinations and the new ones they had added recently.

"No, I know I don't want to do anything in technology. I lean more toward the arts, language and people. But that's as narrowed down as I got because I need more experience and exposure to he world. Even though I finished my high school career at the top of my class, a lot of what I excelled in was narrow and I need a broader education."

"Wise woman," Dr. Elliot smiled.

"We will be lucky to have you here."

"We have some new programs that we didn't send you. Maybe Costa Rica?"

"'I have heard that is beautiful," Ellie was feeling like a hungry kid in a candy store. "I do care about the environment and I think anything about climate change, rain forests and saving the earth..."

"Sydney, Australia?"

"Too far away. At least for now."

"You can travel during your summers..."

"The world awaits you."

CHAPTER 33

Bill felt free as he drove under the covered bridge that crossed the river that divided Waterview and its neighboring communities from the more rural areas with small farms and century old windmills contrasting against streamlined wind turbines erected within the last few years. Logandale was not only a reasonable commute timewise but a pleasant one visually. Somehow, the old and the new did not stress the eye or disturb the landscape, but instead, made the story, the history, more interesting by bringing the past and the future together like one multi-generational family getting together for Sunday dinner. Dark clouds on the horizon were typical of the sky here, Bill remembered, often making themselves irrelevant by drifting off and dumping their rain on places uninhabited by people and watering the few crops that dwindled off where the farmland ended and the rolling hills began. Bill came to the fork in the road and took the left road. Dr. Swan's office would be a few miles after it as the Hamlet of Logandale appeared. On first view, Logandale reminded him of his old hometown, but a block more past the sign identifying it, it seemed to burst into a busy commercial zone of small department stores, independent ice cream and candy shops and small restaurants offering diverse cuisine. Bill's mind drifted to thoughts of where he would eat lunch and how this place could become his daily routine. No, he was thinking too far ahead and assuming too much. This was an interview, just an interview. The female voice on his GPS softly said, "You have reached your destination." He pulled his car into the spot near the door, Logandale Surgery: Dr, Michael Swan and a space where another name had been scraped off the glass door. He got out, straightened his clothes and went in.

"Good morning, you must be Dr. Victor, "a middle aged attractive blonde receptionist said with a welcoming voice. "Mick is waiting for you. You can go right in." She stood up and opened the door for him. "Mick? Dr. Victor is here."

Dr. Swan looked just like his photo on his website, slender dark-skinned face with a sharp jaw and friendly brown eyes. According to his bio, he was 54 years old, but he looked younger. He extended his hand and gave Bill a hearty handshake. "This is my receptionist and better half, Nancy Swan RN.

"Nice to meet you, Mrs Swan."

"Call me Nancy, we are not that formal here."

"And you can call me Mick if I may call you Bill?"

"Of course."

"Come into my office and I will tell you all about our practice here."

"Thank you."

"Would you like some coffee?" Nancy asked?

"That would be great." Anticipating the next

question, Bill added, "No sugar please. Just a drop of milk would be fine."

"You've got it!"

***

At home, Dora was nervous and full of hope that Bill would get the job in Logandale. So far, things had been going pretty well considering the abrupt life change her husband was having to deal with. She knew he had nightmares connected to his service in the Middle East, but that was to be expected. Wouldn't it be great if life normalized and didn't throw any unexpected trauma at her at least for a while. She didn't know when to expect Bill to come home or what she thought he might tell her when he did, so she called her mother for a quick chat. Her mom was usually at home watching The Price is Right on TV at this time but with the wonders of modern technology, she could pause the show and get back to it after a short phone call. The sound of the ringing phone was soft so Dora turned up the volume a little. Elizabeth usually kept her phone by her on the table next to the couch and picked up on the third ring but this time, the phone continued to ring, five, six, seven …. No answer. Maybe Mom was in the bathroom. She usually didn't take her phone in the bathroom for fear of dropping it in the toilet. She had told Dora that so, she must be there. Dora ended the call. Her mother would see she had missed a call and probably call back when she came out.

Bill was hired on the spot. He spent a half hour just

relaxing and getting to know his soon to be colleague. Dr. Swan gave Bill a tour of the office, his own space, full of plaques from Cornell Medical School and hospitals, the space that would be Bill's office, the examining rooms, a small conference room and a very calm and green patio and meditation area in the back inside an atrium. If anything was the antithesis of an army field hospital, this was it.

"In the fall, of course, it is more colorful, and winter, it is warm, but you can watch the snow fall. I need that just to unwind and, do you meditate?" Dr. Swan asked.

"I do, only thing that helped me through the trauma."

"I learned TM when I was in my twenties. "

"I started with that and found it helpful even before I got into the really horrible stuff over there, but then I kind of devised my own approach. This place is amazing, not what I expected in a surgeon's office."

"It's my baby so to speak. I had an unused storage room over at the hospital made into something like this. No atrium but lots of plants and comfortable seating for the staff. Not just your normal lounge. We have that, too but wait till you see what I designed."

"So, Dr. Victor, you will need to fill out some papers but you can take them home if you want and fax them to me tomorrow?" Nancy said as she joined Bill and her husband in the short hallway.

"That would be fine."

"Or if you prefer, you can drop them off here when you are done. Feel free to bring your wife. I can give you the key and show you how to turn off the alarm. Or if you come during office hours, you can come right in and show her around." Dr. Swan was already feeling relieved that he found the right person to be his partner. Why bother interviewing multiple candidates when the feel with Bill was just right. And he came highly recommended.

"That would be great. Dolly will be so happy. I can't wait to tell her. After all this time of waiting, this is going to make her really happy."

"There's a nice restaurant around the corner, The Greener Palm. Maybe your wife would enjoy lunch there when you come," Nancy suggested. "I can't wait to meet her."

Bill thanked the couple, took the papers and said he would call about stopping by. He wasn't sure how to tell Dolly. Should he call her right away or buy her some flowers or something and tell her when he got home? Oh why wait. He got into the car, rolled down the window and called her. He was surprised when he didn't reach her. Maybe he thought she would have been sitting on the couch, her phone in hand, waiting breathlessly. Well, why wasn't she? This was a great day, a red letter day, a day of all days and he was going to be a civilian doctor, a surgeon in a private practice in a nice office and a meditation atrium at that! The vibrating of his phone broke into his thoughts. It was a text.

Mom fell. Ambulance took her to Good Samaritan. I am here. Hope things went well. Bill immediately replied. "I am on my way. "This was not the time to mention the job. He would save that. Hopefully, the fall was not serious and Elizabeth would recover quickly. Yet, he knew that falls for an older woman could be the beginning of a series of events that could lead to something more. Dolly hadn't mentioned how bad the fall had been or if there were any fractures. In the best case scenario, his mother-in-law would soon be out of the hospital and recovering at home and they would be able to celebrate. He drove a little faster on the return trip and spent less time thinking about the scenery. There would be plenty of time for that.

CHAPTER 34

Before Bill could get to the desk to inquire about Elizabeth, he saw Dora sitting in the waiting room alone and she appeared to be crying as she hung over the side of the chair a coffee cup in her hand. His heart sank, but then she looked up.

"What is happening?" he asked his wife, rushing to her side. |Are you crying? What ...".

"Oh no, they took her for x-rays and I needed to sit down. Not enough chairs in the ER."

"Oh, so how is she?" He sat down in the chair next to her and put his arm around her.

"She was on the floor in the kitchen, I don't know how long, but when I found her, it was awful. There was blood on the floor because she broke a cup and cut herself, but I didn't know that at first. They had to stitch up her hand. I had called her and she didn't answer and I waited. I shouldn't have waited..."

"Okay, it's not your fault and she is in good hands now."

"I have to go back in. I just want to finish my coffee. She should be back soon and I don't want her to come back and not see me there."

"Of course. Finish your coffee and we'll go in. It will be okay."

"I don't even know how long she was on the floor

and neither does she. She was conscious when I found her so at least I was able to talk to her as we waited for the ambulance. I don't know why she fell. "

"Well, we will figure it all out. "

"The doctor who examined her when we came in said she thinks Mom broke her shoulder but wouldn't be sure until she had the x-ray. She told us not to worry. That is what always makes me worry, when someone tells me not to." Dora sipped the last drops of her coffee. Okay, let's go back in."

Bill took the coffee cup from her and threw it away. Then he took her arm and they went back through the heavy double doors.

Dr. Phillips had a mild manner that offset the sense of panic and worry that filled the ER.. She was honest and direct, yet compassionate. She didn't beat around the bush, but neither did she beat the bush looking for the worst case scenario. She was coming toward the ER as Bill and Dora approached from the other direction.

"Mrs. Victor, your mother will be back soon," she said in a reassuring voice.

"This is my husband, Dr. Victor. He is a surgeon," Dora told her with a sense of pride."

The doctor immediately turned her focus to Bill. "She has a broken shoulder and will need surgery. Dr. Aiken can do it first thing in the morning. If you want to talk to him, I can have him get in touch with you. It is routine surgery and Mrs. Black will be able to go home, probably the day after tomorrow. The social worker will explain the services that are covered by her insurance." Dr. Phillips shifted her words to Dora. "Does she live alone?"

"Yes, she does, but we are close by. I can stay with her for a few..."

"This may be more than a few days or even weeks. We need to find out why she passed out."

"I don't think she passed out. "Dora was shocked by the idea. "She fell. She just slipped and fell. That is what she told me."

"Well we will check and find out what happened, but as for the surgery, that should be straight forward and if she doesn't have any additional issues, and she heals well, then that should be fine."

"She didn't pass out. Why would they even think that?" Dora mumbled.

"Don't let them upset you. She probably slipped and fell, maybe on a wet floor or something. She'll be fine. And don't worry about the surgery," Bill said, putting his arm around her shoulder.

As they wheeled Elizabeth back into the room. She was sitting up.

" Bill, can you do my surgery? They said I need surgery."

"No Mom, not this time. I am sure your surgeon will

be the best." Bill thought it might be a good idea to give Mick a call and see if he knew the surgeon, this Dr. Aiken. He looked at his watch. "Maybe a text a little later. Too close to dinner time."

"Good name for a doctor," Elizabeth commented. Aiken. "Almost as good as that one we used to know. Dr. Payne. Or Dr. Hertz." mumbling to herself, amusing herself.

"So Mom, How did you fall?" Bill asked.

" I woke up early and my throat was dry so I made myself some tea. It was really early, the sun was not even up, but I wanted some tea. I think there is something wrong with the whistle on the tea kettle. I didn't hear it. I grabbed it but it was so hot, I dropped it. I don't know. I ended up on the floor. "

"Did you feel dizzy or anything?" Dora didn't want to think that there was anything more than a slip and fall in this.

"Dizzy? No, I was a little sleepy. I just wanted a hot drink, but not that hot. Broke one of my good cups. One of the ones with the flowers on them. The lilac one smashed. Made me sad. I loved that cup."

"It's okay, Mom. It's just a cup and I can get you another."

"So you were on the floor a long time?" Bill asked.

"Oh yeah, a long time. I can tell you, you get a whole different perspective of a room from down on the floor."

A nurse with a clipboard came over to the bed.

"So, Elizabeth, you are scheduled for your surgery at 8 am tomorrow. Dr. Aiken will speak to you before the surgery to explain everything you need or want to know. So will the anesthesiologist. You will be asleep for the procedure and will not feel anything. They will give you pain meds before the operation so you have a head start on not being in pain when you are fully awake. I am not sure who the anesthesiologist will be, but they are all good and we will make sure you are taken care of. Your family will be called as soon as you are out of the OR."

"We will be waiting in the waiting room, "Bill added placing his hand on Elizabeth's."

"I understand you are a doctor," the nurse turned her attention to Bill. "I can get Dr. Aiken to talk with you if you want. I can have him call you?"

Bill gave her his cell number and thanked her.

"But Dr. Aiken looked at the x-rays and said it is a simple operation, a clean break with no complications. So Elizabeth, you don't have to worry about anything. Sometimes we let the patients go home the same day, but we would like to have one extra day to make sure you can deal with being home and we have to talk to you about services, help and therapy you can get at home, things like that."

:Well, thanks, we appreciate your encouraging words." Dora strained to see the name tag.

"I'm Barbara. I will be with her tomorrow. Okay, Elizabeth, I will be with you so you have nothing to worry about."

"Thanks, Barbara," Elizabeth said with a sigh. If only I had gotten that whistle fixed on the tea kettle, I would be home getting ready for afternoon tea."

"We will be admitting your pretty soon, but I can get you some tea. "I'll look and see if we have some cookies."

"Tea would be great, "Dora replied, I can run down to the coffee shop to get us all a snack. "

"Sure, I'll stay with your mom to keep her company. Can you get me coffee?"

"Sure. Ill pass since I have already had way too much."

When dinner time rolled around, Elizabeth was in her room and being served a light meal of bland chicken and some peas along with some consomme and a cookie. There would be no more food or water after that. Elizabeth urged Dora and Bill to go home as she felt she was in safe hands and wasn't worried about the upcoming operation. They were reluctant at first, but also very tired and decided to grab dinner at the diner on the way home. Dora took a deep breath, got into her car and they drove a few blocks to the diner. Dora had been so occupied by her mother's fall and hospitalization that she had forgotten about her husband's interview. It suddenly dawned on her as she turned off the engine and got out of the car. She was looking forward to a simple dinner and a conversation that she hoped would have good news. Yet, since Bill had said nothing, she was not sure it was going to be good news or perhaps any news at all.

"So, what happened in Logandale?" Dora asked while glancing at the menu. She held her breath a little, hoping this would be a celebration and not a disappointment. She surveyed his face wondering if his slow response was to tease her or if he didn't know how to break the bad news or if there was just nothing to tell her, yet.

"Oh yes, Logandale, very lovely community," he teased.

"Yes, I know., I have been there," Dora said impatiently.

"We should have lunch there someday. I hear there is a really good restaurant not far from my soon-to-be office."

"Wait, what? You got the job?"

"I did indeed and I think we should go there, I was going to say tomorrow, but with your mom having surgery..."

"You got the job? You got the job. Oh my God, you actually got the job!."

"Yes, my love. On the spot. Sat and talked to Dr. Swan, drank coffee and they said I should take you to the restaurant around the corner when I come in to turn in some paperwork."

"I am so happy!"

"Babe, it is going to be a nice life now. You would like his wife, Nancy. She is a registered nurse, but she is also his receptionist. They are both into photography and I think you would, I mean, will like them.

"I can't believe it. I expected you might have to go to many interviews before you found the right position. But you think this is just what you want?"

"Oh, it was one of those things where you walk in the door and you feel like this is where you belong. I can't wait to take you there and show you."

"Well, if everything goes okay with Mom, we could go after visiting hours and make a shot back to the hospital in the evening."

Maybe, if you don't think it is too much in one day."

"We will see mom when she comes out of surgery and visit with her and then go to lunch. It will be a long day, but if we go back in the evening, we can get updated and visit with her. She is supposed to come home day after tomorrow so maybe this will be the best time, when we know she is in the hospital getting the care she needs."

"That sounds right. "

"So, let's enjoy our dinner and maybe turn in early tonight."

"Great, what are you going to order?"

"Onion rings. I love their onions rings."

"Okay no, really, what else?"

"Oh, okay, I'll have a veggie burger and one order of onion rings. This is how I celebrate. How about you? Oh look, Bill, they have a special stuffed cabbage. When was the last time you had that? Used to be your favorite."

"Maybe ten years ago. Okay. Sounds good."

Dora reached for Bill's hand and gave it a squeeze. "I love you, she said, feeling like they were both newly married again.

"Oh Babe, there aren't enough words to tell you how much I love you. I feel like this is the beginning of the rest of our lives."

"Well, it really is, isn't it?

CHAPTER 35

Dora slept in peaceful calm, unlike any night she could remember. If she had ever been unsure whether her marriage would come back, she now knew that it was stronger than ever and that Bill truly was the love of her life. The sun made lines on his body through the cracks in the blinds. She watched him breathe, remembering the many nights she wondered if she would ever watch him breathe again or feel his heartbeat or wrap her arms and legs around him. And there had been a nightmare, perhaps, a brief one where he seemed in a state of terror and then went back to sleep. But it came and went leaving him sleeping calmly and peacefully.

Oh, God, how he had made her feel when they got back from the diner! How she had shuddered in anticipation as he came up behind her as she brushed her teeth and ran his hands over her breasts seeking out the most pleasurable places through the thin fabric of her nightgown, planting increasingly intense kisses on her neck. She had surprised herself by letting out a soft sound of desire she hadn't heard herself make in years. His fingers caressed her erect nipples as she felt him pressing against the bottom of her spine. He was hard. Her body responded, as she felt her insides begin the churn, her own hardness begging to be released. He picked her up and carried her to the bed where all the years of longing exploded into unrestricted passion and expressions of love, not just once, but over and over until they fell into a deep sleep. Now when Dora looked at him, it was different. It was not with fear of what was to come, but of hope of all that could be.

"Dolly, Dolly, Dolly,: Bill whispered.

"Good morning." she said softly with a devilish smile on her face." How are you feeling?'

He took her hand and pulled her to him but said nothing.

"If my mom weren't in the hospital..."

"I would ask you to stay here in bed with me all day." He finished her sentence with a sigh. "But later, we will have more time later."

Dora looked at the clock. It was only 6:45 am and there was still plenty of time to get to the hospital before the surgery. Still she hurried to get dressed as Bill sat on the bed dressed from the waist down but shirtless.

"I sent a text to Mickey Swan last night to see if he knew your mom's surgeon."

"Dr. Aiken?"

"Yes, he said he did and we should not be worried at all. I meant to tell you, but, well, we sort of got distracted."

"Indeed we did."

Dora was looking for her shoes. "Want to get breakfast at the hospital?" she asked as she slid her feet into her sneakers. She had considered wearing heels but then thought better of it as she knew that she would be standing for a long time.

"Sure, I think we will feel better if we are there even though we won't see her before her surgery."

"I agree. At least we will be nearby."

As Bill reached for his shirt, and pulled it over his head, his phone rang. The display told him that the call was from Charles Aiken.

"Hello"

"Good morning Dr. Victor. Charlie Aiken. I will be doing your mother's surgery this morning. I spoke to Dr. Swan last night and decided to call you first thing today just to touch base and answer any questions you may have."

"Thank you. My wife is concerned, but I assured her all will go well."

"So Mickey told me you are a surgeon yourself, just out of the military."

"Yes."

"Well, thank you for your service and welcome home. Oh and congratulations on being chosen to work with my friend, Dr. Swan.   He is a great guy. So, we seem to be just about 15 minutes behind schedule, which is about normal, so I expect to be getting your mom prepped and ready to go soon. She already has the IV in so the rest should be painless for her."

"That's good to hear. I will share that with my wife."

Dora stood in the doorway. "What? What is happening?"

"It's Doctor Aiken. Everything is fine. Do you want to talk to him?"

"No, that's okay. I'll talk to him later. You can tell me what he said."

"We are about to leave so thanks for calling."

"You are giving yourself plenty of time. Don't have to rush."

"We decided to have breakfast at the hospital so we're good."

"Good idea. They have some good choices in the coffee shop there. Oh and I wanted to tell you that I ordered 600 mg of Gabapentin to be given to her before the surgery so she will be ahead on pain medication."

"Sounds good. We will talk to you later, then."

"So, they are only running 15 minutes behind and the doctor has already given her pain medication so that she will be comfortable when she wakes up. So we don't have to rush and can enjoy a leisurely breakfast,"Bill relayed the message."

They got into the car and drove to the hospital, about 15 minutes away. The hospital lobby was quiet and the coffee shop was nearly empty except for some staff and an elderly couples at the far end with bags full of pink gifts.

Dora and Bill went up to the counter and ordered two full breakfasts with eggs, pancakes, bacon and sausage.

"Who knows when we will eat again?" Dora quipped.

"The food looks pretty good. Not sure if what they feed the patients is good, but your mom isn't picky about her food, is she?"

"Nope, as long as nothing on her plate comes from inside any animal."

"Not a fan of liver, then."

"Absolutely not."

"I never heard of any hospital to serve liver."

"I think my mom told me once that when she gave birth to me, she told the hospital staff she was a vegetarian just in case. She calls herself a vegeprefarian, but she is fine with meat."

They chose a table by the window with a view of the garden by the entrance. Bill went back up to fill their paper cups with coffee. Black for him and light for her.

"Nice hospital, at least it looks nice, "Dora said.

"Well, that's a start. I will be affiliated with Valley University Hospital."

"Where is that?"

"You probably remember it as Logandale General."

"Oh yes, I was born there.

Bill watched his wife sip of her coffee. A feeling of

deja vu passed over him, only it was Brenda he saw for a split second. He remembered the last thing said to him.

"Don't worry. When you are back home with your wife, everything will get back to normal. You are probably the strongest person I ever met. Have a good life. You deserve it." Then she got up and left him. He blinked his eyes and Dolly was still sitting there eating her breakfast, drinking her coffee and worrying about her mother. Brenda had been right. After last night he knew what she said was true.

It was a beautiful day. Summer lingered, but let a cool breeze announce the coming of fall in a few weeks. They decided to go for a walk around the grounds. Dora looked at her phone. It was almost 9:23.

'The surgery should take another hour or so. We should have brought a deck of cards."

"I don't think I am in the mood for cards."

"Then, we can just relax."

Dora's phone buzzed.

"Looks like I have a text… from the social worker here. She wants me to call when I can. Maybe I should call her. Name's Lorraine..."

"Sure, go ahead."

Dora's fingers moved quickly on the keypad.

"Hi, this is Lorraine. I am away from my desk..." the recorded message quickly shut off as a real live person with the same voice interrupted. "This is Lorraine, is this Ms. Victor?"

"Yes, I got your message to contact you.|"

"Your mom's in surgery, are you free to stop by the office now. My office is on the second floor, same building. I need to go over some services she will need when she gets home."

"Okay. I can be there in a few minutes. We are out in the garden."

"Great, see you in a few, then, Just take the elevator to the second floor and turn right. You will see the office on your left. The sign says Patient Home Care Services. The door will be open. You can walk right in. My desk is on the left by the door."

Dora, relayed the message to Bill and they both got up and headed inside.

"I think she can get home help and a physical therapist," Dora said. "My teaching schedule allows for me to be with her a few hours a day and I could sleep over there until… well, we'll work it all out."

"Don't worry, one day at a time. She should recover quickly."

"Yeah but I am worried that she could fall again."

"You should call your brother."

"Of course. After we see Lorraine and I have answers to his questions." Bill opened the door and they headed down the hallway to the elevator.

When they came out of the elevator, Lorraine was waiting for them outside the door of the office.

"And you are Mr. and Mrs. Victor?

That would be Doctor Victor and Doctor Victor," Bill said with a smile.

"Oh, I am sorry, I didn't know." Lorraine motioned for them to come in to her office. "I thought I should tell you about what will happen after Elizabeth is discharged. I will go over all of it with her later, but this will make it all easier. "

"Of course, "Dora replied as they sat down.

CHAPTER 36

"Elisabeth, Elisabeth, you are all done," a woman's voice said."You are in recovery and it is all over. You can wake up now."

Elisabeth felt a quick pang of annoyance at having been disturbed, but it took her a few seconds to remember what exactly was over and why she was in recovery. She had felt nothing and was not in pain, but still foggy. She started to feel some mild nausea and then the doctor came over.

"Good morning again Elizabeth. How are you feeling?

"A bit queasy," she mumbled as the doctor bent over to hear her.

"That should wear off soon, but if it doesn't go away, we can give you something for it."

"I'm hungry."

"Well, you will have to wait for food, but you will be having lunch in an n hour or so and your family is here so you will see them as soon as you are a little more awake."

"Thirsty."

"Well we will get you something to drink in a bit. Right now we will just take it slow and when you are ready, we will take you back to your room so you can see your family."

"Elizabeth let out a sigh," as a nurse came over. "Breathe Baby Girl, take some deep breaths."

"Baby Girl? Who's a baby girl? Are you talking to me?"

"Okay, breathe, you need a little more oxygen, sweetheart."

Elizabeth took another deep breath.

"That's right. Keep breathing. "

Dora and Bill were back in the coffee shop, drinking another cup of coffee and sharing a giant blueberry muffin. Dora was trying to call Taylor, but he didn't answer so she left him a voicemail.

"Taylor, it is Dora. I sent you a text yesterday. I hope you got it. Mom fell and is in surgery for a broken shoulder. Give me a call when you can. I haven't seen her yet, but I think she must be out of surgery by now. I want to update you. So call asap. "

As soon as she finished, her phone showed an incoming call and was vibrating in her hand. She answered and as she expected, it was Dr. Aiken telling her that Mom was done and all had gone well. She would be ready to see them in an hour.

"If everything is okay with your mom, do you still want to take a quick trip over to Loganville and grab some late lunch after we see her?" Bill asked.

"I would. If she is being discharged tomorrow, I don't think we will get any chance to go in the near future and you have to hand in that paperwork, so yes."

After meeting with the social worker, Dora had so many things to think about. People would be coming and going at the house but Elizabeth would need someone to stay with her and she knew she would have to get it all organized. Waiting to hear from her brother, wasn't helping. A trip to see Bill's new office and have lunch would be a welcomed break in all of it.

"We will make sure we are back for visiting hours at 6 pm."

"And I will need to get clothes ready for her and bring whatever else she needs to go home in. And then there are the things the social worker mentioned, a wheelchair..."

"I wrote it down. I have no place to go tomorrow. We'll get it all done. It always seems more complicated than it is."

"I hope you are right."

Back in her room. Elizabeth was almost fully awake. A nurse was asking her questions. Did this hurt? How did she feel? All sorts of questions. She put a little white thing that looked like a stapler on her finger and took her temperature on her forehead. She examined the IV and smiled when Elizabeth asked when she would get some food.

"Not too long now. Lunch is in an hour or so."

"Because I am getting hungry now."

"Are you still feeling nauseous? I can't give you food if you are nauseous."

"Not nauseous, just a little queasy because I need some food in my stomach."

"Oh, okay. We will get you a little snack for you soon, then."

Dora and Bill walked into the room.

"Good morning, Mom. How are you doing?"

"Hungry. I didn't have breakfast."

"That's because you were in surgery. Doctor told me that it went well."

I don't know, I was asleep.

"You did great," the nurse said. "She did great."

"What does that even mean?" Elizabeth asked."

"You dealt with the pain well and there were no complications."

"Well, I was asleep, so there was no pain."

"How about now?" Bill asked.

"No pain, just hungry"

"We'll get her something," the nurse said as she scurried out the door."

"Well, I guess you are glad that it is all over," Dora said, half a question, half a statement.

"I guess. "

"Well it should be smooth sailing from here."

"How long do I have to stay here.?"

"They said you might go home tomorrow," Bill said, leaving just a little room for the unexpected.

"Does Taylor know?" Elizabeth asked.

"I am waiting for him to call. I left a message. He should get it soon."

Her mother groaned. "Well, whatever. There is not much I can do about anything now."

Just then a woman in blue brought in a tray and set it down on the table by the bed. She removed the top of the cloche and gently swung the arm of the table over Elizabeth.

"There you go."

"That's it?" Elizabeth asked in disappointment. She was hungry and all she saw was a white blob on a white plate and some tea, that was familiar, and what was the other thing? Applesauce?

"Well, there is a cup of tea, no milk for now. Then you have applesauce and a scrambled egg white."

"A scrambled egg white? How do you scramble an egg white?"

Dora took paper off the tray and read it.

"It says it is egg souffle."

Bill tried to stop a laugh. It didn't look appetizing, but the description was creative.

"Souffle," Dora repeated, "You know, Mom, an egg

with lots of air whipped into it."

"Egg white, not egg."

"Sorry, Mrs Black. That's all you can have right now. As much tea as you want and I can get you apple juice. There is supposed to be apple juice."

"Yes, I want the apple juice."

"Liquids, clear liquids are fine."

"Can I get up to pee?"

"Do you have to pee now?'

"No, but I will. Can I get up or..."

"I am afraid you will have to sit on the bedpan for now."

Elizabeth took a spoonful of the apple sauce, a sip of her tea, turned the egg with her fork, and then pushed her plate away from her." "I am not using a bed pan. I will just wait until I can get up and go to the bathroom."

"Well, Mom, you will be having lunch in a bit. "

"And I know what it will be. Jello and broth."

"I think...," Bill was interrupted as Dora's ring tone sounded. It was Taylor.

"Doreen," for some odd reason Taylor never called her by her right name. At some point in her teenage years he had decided to call her Doreen, and he drew it out like Doreeeeen, and it annoyed the hell out of her. Still, she was glad he finally called. "How's Mom? Why didn't you tell me she was sick?"

"She's not sick. She fell and I found her on the floor yesterday. I left as message as soon as I could."

"And she's in the hospital?"

"Yes, she just came out of surgery for a broken shoulder, but that"s all. She should heal and be fine after a few weeks."

"Is she awake? Can she talk?"

"Sure. Mom, you want to talk to your son? "

"Of course I do." Dora, Dolly, Doreen, whatever her name was handed the phone to her mother.

"Sorry to hear about your fall..." Taylor and his mother spoke for several minutes and then Elizabeth returned the phone to Dora.

Her brother asked her to keep him updated and said he would come down the next weekend. Dora was relieved that her brother would be down. The guest room at her mother's house would only need a dusting and vacuuming and she could order some food to be delivered.

After the social worker came in to advise Elizabeth on the services she would receive in her home after her discharge, Dora and Bill assured her that they would be with her as much as possible and that Taylor would be down in a few days to set up a temporary office in the small room where his dad used to develop pictures so he could work from his mother's house. Just as the lunch cart arrived, they kissed Mom good-bye and told her they would be back in the evening. As they left the room, they could hear her mumbling about the lemon jello and broth. The woman in the bed next to her assured her that she would get solid food for dinner.

When they got home, Bill brought in the mail. There was a letter from the college so he gave it to Dora as soon as he saw it. Dora opened it, and read the letter. "Congratulations, you have been awarded a full year sabbatical for the next year. Please contact the office of the dean to formalize your acceptance...

"Bill, I got the sabbatical. I am going to be off for a whole year." She would show him her plan for her research later, but for now, this was the third of good things happening in threes.

CHAPTER 37

It was a pleasant drive to Logandale. Dora hadn't remembered just how pleasant that ride was, but it delighted her to think that she would be making this trip from time to time with Bill working there. When they stopped by the office, there was a different receptionist there and Bill introduced himself to her. She was a younger woman named Stephanie. She handed Bill a manila envelope.

"A few more papers. I will be here until 3 pm. But if you need more time, Monday morning will be fine."

"Okay, I have a key..."

"Well if you want to, you can put the papers on the desk, but no one will get to them until Monday so whatever you do will be the same."

"Okay, thanks, Stephanie. "

"You having lunch at The Greener Palm?"

"Yes, we are."

"Oh enjoy. Nice place. Very nice ambiance and the food is good, too. If you like paella, theirs is the best. Lots of vegetarian dishes but also a few meat dishes. Very earth friendly."

"Thank you,""Bill said as Dora squeezed his hand.

As they walked around the corner to the Greener Palm, Dora gave a little giggle. "I am so psyched that you will be working here. After all you have been through, this is your reward, our reward."

"Welcome to The Greener Palm," a tall man dressed in a tan suit said as he took two menus out of a slot by the cashier. "Having lunch with us today?"

"Yes please," Dora replied as she looked around the room. It was simply decorated with an understated tropical theme. "Very tasteful," she commented in a whisper.

"And our food is good, too." the tall man replied. "And if you would like, we have a view of the pond over there."

"Oh, Bill., they have a pond. Please a view of the pond."

After being seated and handed the menus, Bill exclaimed, "Wow I can hardly believe I am here and what a change this is. I thought I'd never get back to civilian life and end up in such a nice place."

"Quite a contrast, isn't it? And it is so great for me, not just having you home, but it's like a shot in the arm for me." She giggled and placed her hand on his. "No pun intended."

"Let;'s see what we are going to eat."

"South American picadillo. beef, almonds, raisins … sounds yummy," Dora was feeling truly happy.

"You know, I am feeling really hungry and we will be eating late tonight so..."

"Go for it Billy," she giggled again. "What do you really really want?"

He turned the menu around and pointed discretely at a table a few feet away. There was a young man being served a large platter of seafood and steak with fries and onion rings.

"That must be the East Coast grilled surf and turf," Dora said, pointing to it on the menu.

"Wait, it comes in two sizes. That doesn't look like the lunch size. I don't need all that, I 'll get the lunch size and a clam chowder."

"Sounds like a great choice. I am going to have the Greener Palm Salad. And the soup of the day…."

"That's tomato bisque," the waiter said as he waited for confirmation and the drink order."

"Two waters for now," Bill said as Dora nodded in agreement.

The waiter set down a basket of various types of freshly baked bread. Dora took a piece of the pumpernickle and buttered it. Bill chose a piece of raisin bread.

"I am a little worried about Mom," Dora said, reaching her free hand out to touch Bill's wrist. After she comes home tomorrow, I hope things go well.

"Well, Taylor will be down tomorrow night so, or the following morning so I am sure it will all go smoothly."

"Yes, but I feel like this could be the beginning of the end. It is inevitable."

"Why don't we just take it a day at a time. Soon as she is improves enough, we can bring her here for lunch"

"Or dinner and maybe we could bring Taylor. "I think Taylor said his wife and the kids could be here for Labor Day Weekend. I don't know how long he plans to stay, but he is bringing all his computer stuff so he can work from Mom's house."

"Lucky guy to have a job where he can work from home. "

"Can't do surgery from home but Logandale is close enough."

"Oh, I am not complaining at all."

"The building where Taylor used to work burned down six months ago and thankfully no one was there at the time. But everyone started working from home and the company realized that they didn't even need the building."

"That's pretty good. "

"But I am still worried about Mom. I didn't really let myself think about what could happen to her, but I guess it was always in the back of my mind."

"She's not that old, Dolly. What is she now, seventy five? She is in good health. I wouldn't worry too much. It will all work out, just take it slow and don't stress yourself out, Look at that crane over there. What a natural pond with such wildlife.!"

"Was there no beauty at all where you were? I mean, to distract you from all the bad stuff?

"There were beautiful sunrises and sunsets. There were some beautiful people, but most was beyond horrible. "

"Can you forget that now that you are here?" She knew her words were trite and shallow, but they came out anyway."

"Forget? Not really, not right away. But it is a process and little by little, maybe the flashbacks and nightmares will slow down and finally disappear.'"

I hope so, "Dora squeezed his hand,

"Look," Bill pointed to the bird as it spread its wings and slowly rose up just above the water and then over the trees.

"Rising up like a Phoenix from the ashes. Maybe it is a sign"

"It's an egret" the waiter corrected them as he served them their lunch. This one shows up fairly regularly. It is a beautiful thing to see."

"It is." Bill opened his napkin and placed it on his lap.

"Is there anything else I can get you?"

"No, I don't think so," Dora gave Bill a nod and he nodded back .

"Then enjoy your lunch and call me if you need anything else."

They enjoyed their lunch leisurely, savoring every minute and every taste, sound and movement of the birds and animals at the pond. It was the most exquisite afternoon.

On the drive back, they took a little detour around the pond and down the wooded back roads they remembered from when they first married. They stopped and walked down a dirt path to the place where Bill had proposed to Dora. There was a new bench near the exact spot, but the bench they sat on that day was gone. They sat, silently, holding hands and gazing at the trees as a bright red cardinal perched above them made happy little sounds. Dora gave a little shiver, although it was not cold, but Bill wrapped her light jacket around her tighter and then wrapped his arm around her, sharing the warmth of his body. Dora leaned into him and let her head drop onto his shoulder. They sat silently for a few minutes, absorbing the peace and the promise of a new life.

"Bill, I have been thinking."

"About what?"

"About the next step forward."

"Oh, okay."

"Maybe," she hesitated feeling suddenly shy about what was to come next. "Well, maybe it is time to think about," She started to giggle.

Bill turned towards her and cocked his head like a robin listening to the ground for worms.

"Maybe it is time for us to start a family."

"You mean..."

"Yes, with kids. I am ready to have a baby now. I am in good health. I should be able to do it."

"Did you ever doubt that you could?"

"No, I was just not ready, but now I am."

"You know I always wanted kids. And now? Oh baby, I would like nothing more." He pulled her close and held her as she slid her arms around him. When they kissed, Bill felt something he had never felt before, a new kind of passion and desire.

"What time is it? she mumbled as their lips moved against

each other."

"Time enough to stop home before we go see your mother."

"Let's go, then. Take the shortcut."

CHAPTER 38

"We'd like to keep her in the hospital for a few more days. Just to do some tests, rule out ant neurological problems. She seemed confused today and had some trouble forming words." the doctor said as they stood in the hallway near Elizabeth's room.

"But she is expecting to go home tomorrow, "Dora responded, worrying that any delay would make her mother very stressed.

"Well, it would only be two or three more days. I could tell her we just want to make sure she doesn't fall again before she is healed enough."

Dora took a deep breath and turned to Bill who had put his arm around her in support while the doctor was speaking to them.

"She might be willing to stay if you make it clear exactly when she will be going home," Bill said calmly. "I will tell her it is for the best and we will make sure we are here when we can be."

Dora let out an audible sigh. "Okay, I guess so."

Dora felt her phone vibrating in her pocket and pulled it our quickly, hoping it was her brother.

"The phone lit up and she saw his name. She quickly pressed Accept. "Hey Taylor, what's up?"

"How's Mom?"

"They want to keep her in the hospital for

observation a few more days, but she seems to be doing okay. I guess."

"Well, I can head down tomorrow morning. I should be there around 7 pm."

"Take your time. Drive carefully." She knew that Taylor tended to drive a lot faster than she did and regarded speed limits as mere suggestions for the old and weak. He actually said that once and she didn't know if he was kidding or not.

"Oh, don't worry. I am bringing my work gear, my computer stuff. Do you know if there is a table in that little room where Dad used to do his photography? "

"I don't think so. When he died, we pretty much cleaned it out but I have a table, a folding dining table that seats 6, would that work for you?"

"That sounds perfect. Are you with Mom?"

"We are in the hallway. We have been talking to the doctor and I am worried that she will be upset when we tell her she has to stay."

"Well, when you get in, I can talk to her if you want. Try to tell her it is best and let her know I will be there when she gets home."

"Okay, well that should help. We'll go in now. Not sure how long it will take to tell her if they are bringing breakfast, how about I call you back in about ten minutes or so. I just saw the social worker go in."

"Sure."

Elizabeth was in good spirits when her dinner arrived. When Dora took the lid off the plate, there was a full dinner of macaroni and cheese, green beans that looked like they came from a garden and not a can, and small piece of chocolate cake. Elizabeth beamed with joy. And a cup of tea sat beside the plate on the tray with two sugar packets (which she would not use) and some milk in a small silver pitcher.

Well this is more like it! If they are going to feed me like this, maybe I will stay a few more days."

Dora looked at Lorraine as if to ask…

"We haven't had that discussion yet, but we would like you to stay two more days, until you are strong and we are sure you won't fall again."

Elizabeth's eyes shot from the social worker to Bill and then to her daughter."What exactly are you not telling me? What are you hiding?"

"Not hiding anything," Dora replied. "But it would be best for you to take it slowly so when you get home, you will be safer and more comfortable."

"Okay, if you say so. But I refuse to stay here more than two more days. They can't keep me against my will, can they?"

"No," Lorraine answered, and when you get home on Friday, you will be visited by a home health aide, a visiting nurse and a physical therapist."

"You think I need all those people?"

"For the time being, until you are better able to get around and take care of yourself," Bill added as Dora called Taylor.

"After Elizabeth talked to her son, she was much more at ease. Knowing he would be at her home when she left the hospital made her more secure and even joyful."

"We will be a real family and we can have dinner together and it will be wonderful. I am sad he didn't come down when the lilacs were still in bloom, but a least he is coming."

"How long is he coming for?" Bill asked Dora.

"He said at least two weeks. Maybe more."

"He told me, his wife might be able to come down and bring Ellie. I would love to see my granddaughter," she began to cry. "I have not seen my baby in years and now she is going to college..."

Dora didn't say anything, but there would be a surprise in store for her mom. Ellie had been planning on coming down for a visit before she went to wherever she was planning to go for her gap year, but now that Elizabeth had been hospitalized, Ellie decided she would stay for a few months, if her grandma would have her. What a blessing it was that things fell into place as they did. Dora was so tempted to tell her mom all about it, but she bit her lip and resisted. Since everything seemed to be going well, at least for the time being, Dora felt less stressed and more hopeful. The next two days would fly by and her mom would be home. Taylor had assured her that he would be there. Time to take a deep breath and let it out slowly.

CHAPTER 39

Elizabeth's release from the hospital went without any delays as all her tests came back good "for a woman her age" and she was in good spirits. Any confusion she may have had at night was gone and one of the nurses told Dora and Bill, that that was not an issue. Both Dora and Bill nodded in acceptance that nothing serious was going on and that she could safely return home where she would be comfortable, well-cared for, and happy. Elizabeth's last hospital lunch had arrived and although she was officially discharged, she got to eat it as the nurses aid brought the wheelchair. Taylor had called to tell them he was less than 30 miles away and would be there before they could get their coats off.

"Coats off?" Bill laughed. "It's 80 degrees outside."

"I don't think he meant it literally. It is something we used to say."

"No, I think it was, 'I will be there before you can wipe your feet," Elizabeth responded. "At least that is what my mother used to say."

"Well anyway, he will be here very soon."

"Do we have coffee in the house? I know how he loves his coffee all day long. "

"Yes, Mom, we are all set."

"Something to have with..."

"Yes, Mom, I shopped, there is everything you need.

No one will go hungry."

Reassured that everything was under control, Elizabeth eagerly got into the wheelchair and was pushed toward the elevator. Bill drove his car around to the main entrance so when he arrived at the door, it was easy for them to help her into the car. Buckled in and ready to go, they headed for home. Elizabeth was in good spirits but kept mentioning how she hoped Taylor would get to the house safely, but as they turned the corner onto her street, she saw a black pickup truck in the driveway.

"Is that Taylor's truck? He didn't tell me he had a truck."

"I think he always had trucks, although this one seems new," Dora replied.

The tall and slender man who emerged from the truck had salt and pepper hair that covered his ears and an angled jaw with a chin full of stubble. It appeared that he was starting a beard.

"Yeah, that's Taylor."

"He looks older," Elizabeth observed, realizing how much time had passed since she last saw him.

Taylor stopped and watched from the back of the truck as they pulled into the driveway next to it. Elizabeth was anxious to get out, but Bill jumped out of the car to make sure she didn't get out by herself, with her arm in a cast and all.

"Just wait a second, Mom.," Bill cautioned. "Let me help you."

Taylor rushed over to the car shouting hello and waving. He joined Bill at the car door, to help. With both men helping her, she felt more secure than ever. Dora got out of the car and followed behind the three after closing the door of the car.

"Good timing," Taylor said.

"Couldn't have been better,|" Dora added.

"You must have been driving very fast." Elizabeth said in a familiar scolding voice.

"Not too fast, Mom. You don't need to worry about me."

"Moms always worry," Elizabeth murmured as she entered the house.

As Dora got her mother seated and made her some tea, Taylor and Bill started to bring in the office supplies, computer and accessories into the house, setting some by the door and others directly into the spare room where there was already a table set up so that Taylor could create a temporary office for what turned out to be the month he would be there.

"Yes, I managed to get someone to take care of things back home, and the lady said she wouldn't miss me, so I can stay for a few weeks, maybe a month, make up for all he time I missed."

"Oh my God, am I dying?" Elizabeth said, half

joking, but feeling that it was odd her long-lost son would come down to be with her for a whole month, unless someone told him she was on her last legs.

"No, Mom, we are here to help you recover and it is about time, I know, I know, that we spent some time together.

"Because I am old and probably closer to death than you realized."

"No, Mom, but so much work can be done online these days, that I can run my business from anywhere, so why not here?"

"You just missed the lilacs. They are gone now, dead. There weren't many. "

"Yeah, Mom, I am sorry about that."

"I wish you could have seen them, Tails. I wish I could have saved some for you. Maybe put them in the freezer or something."

"That's okay, Mom. I came to be with you, not the lilacs."

Taylor and Bill continues moving things into the room that was being transformed.

"Oh I almost forgot," Taylor picked up a brown bag that had been set on the table. "Bagels from the Bagel Bin," He set them on the table and Dora took them out and plated them along with four containers of assorted cream cheese.

"Well thanks, Son. Very thoughtful of you."

"What can I get you, Mom,"Dora said as she took a plate from the cabinet."

"Egg with veggie?"

"You've got it."

"How did you know to get veggie cream cheese, Tails?"

"I would never forget what you like, Mom.":

"What if I changed what I like, after all this time, "There was a little dig in her words,

"Then I would go back and get whatever you wanted,"

"Right answer. Good son."

CHAPTER 40

Taylor's wife, Miriam and Ellie arrived in time for the Fourth of July celebration, the same day Elizabeth learned that Angela Bookman had died. It was not long after the end of the cruise. It was Rita who called her and related the whole story.

Angela had enjoyed much of the cruise, even though her health had been deteriorating rapidly. By the time they had disembarked, an ambulance was already on its way to the dock. Members of the ship's medical staff brought Angela down to the waiting ambulance on a stretcher causing a pause in the routine of calling passengers group by group to disembark. It was orderly and it was sad. Angela's daughter was inconsolable, tears running down her face while her wife tried to comfort her.

"She was happy and we will always have the memories of the cruise. You did the right thing for her."

"But I just wanted to bring her home and sit with her..."

"I know. We can stay in the city nearby and do that here."

"It's okay, Mom," she said as she ran alongside the stretcher. "I am here."

"Are you going to ride in the ambulance with us or meet us at the hospital" the ambulance driver asked.

"You go and I will meet you there," Rita said.

"I will go with you," Rachel said as they helped her into the back of the ambulance. She quickly pulled herself in beside her mother, taking her mother's hand in hers and saying it again. "It's okay, Mom. I am here, even though she knew her mother didn't hear her. And yet, she hoped that maybe she did, somehow. You never really can tell.

Rita hailed a cab and frantically made phone calls so she could get a hotel nearby and drop off their luggage. She was in luck, it all worked out quickly as she found a hotel that was within walking distance of the hospital and handed the cab driver a chunk of *money to cover the trip to the hotel and a big tip. He thanked her and placed the luggage on the sidewalk where the bell hop came and took it into the lobby. She checked in, but was told that it was too early and the room wouldn't be ready until 3 pm.

"No problem, can I leave the luggage someplace. I need to get to the hospital.

"Sure, just give it to Henry", the lady behind the desk pointed to the same man who had brought it in. He handed her some tickets as he attached their mates to the suitcases. "I will put them min the closet and you can get them later."

"Thanks." Rita was off to the hospital where Angela had already been admitted and was being brought to her room as Rachael stood in the hall crying.

"Oh Baby," Rita gave her a hug and kissed her on her forehead. "We will get through this. I was able to get a hotel nearby so we don't have to worry about anything. We can stay with your mom and everything will be taken care of. Just focus on your mom. I know this is a tough time."

Rachel watched the bed as it moved into its space in the otherwise empty room. There was no one else in the room even though it was a room meant for two patients. When everything was in place and the nurse motioned for them to come in, Rachael pulled a chair over next to her mom and Rita took the chair from the other side of the room and placed it a small distance away so she could give her wife a little privacy while still being there for her,.

They spent the next days running between the hotel and the hospital and grabbing food in nearby restaurants or delis, hoping Angela would wake up one more time to say good-bye, but Angela never regained consciousness. Three days later, she died. The hospital called at 2 am to tell Rachael, and they sat in the dark room staring at the window and the New York City skyline, not saying much. There was not a lot to say and the cold numbness enveloped them both.

Other than the little family they had left, Elizabeth was one of the first people they called to tell them that she had passed. Elizabeth had received the call just before Taylor's wife and her granddaughter arrived and it was the first thing she old them. They offered their condolences, but then went on to ask about Elizabeth's health.

"My shoulder is healing well," she told them."It aches a bit and I am still getting therapy to move it, but I think I have come a long way. They said 8 weeks and it is only three. I only use the wheel chair when I go places and that is more for protection than necessity."

"We don't want you to fall again." Taylor added. "Your balance is a little off because of the shoulder. But I think she is doing well." He turned his words and his attention to the rest of the family. "So we are finally all here together."

"I thought this day would never come. "Dora said. "How long are you staying?" she asked Miriam.

"Well I can stay for about two weeks. We thought Taylor could go back home with me, and we could take the truck and we would leave Ellie with the car and she could stay at least to the middle of September. That way she could help you all out while enjoying Waterview and spending time with her grandma."

"That would be great." Elizabeth started to tear up. Nothing would make her happier than getting to spend time with her beautiful granddaughter. She was overjoyed that the girl wanted to be with her and that they had some quality time to look forward to.

Dora was excited as well. She had not seen her niece for several years and her mind was filled with all the great things the three of them could do. There would be quilt exhibits, farmers' markets, concerts on the village green, things Dora did with her mom when she was a kid. But then, maybe Ellie had her own ideas. Anyway, it would be good to have her there. The people sent by the hospital to help around the house, were no longer needed, but Elizabeth couldn't do the things she used to do without help, although she thought that time would bring her back to where she was before the fall. She looked forward to the day she would be able to be independent again, driving herself to church on Sundays and having coffee across the street with... oh no, she took a deep breath when she realized there would be no more coffee after church with her friend. Well, maybe she and Ellie? Maybe not. Young people these days were not so keen on going to church. Perhaps there would be new rituals to replace the old. Elizabeth could deal with that. Change was a good thing. Right?

CHAPTER 41

Bill found it easy to fall into the routine and demands of his new job, sharing a practice with Mick Swan. He saw patients that needed minor surgery and even no surgery at all. He performed the routine procedures on the former and reassured the latter. Now and then, a patient required something more complicated, but his military service had prepared him well, and his relationship with his partner grew as they became friends. They sometimes played golf together, but their real passion outside the office was fishing. Bill's dream about spending time in a nearby river up to his thighs in boots and listening to the water rushing buy, or maybe going out into larger waterways on his friend's boat came true and he didn't have to wait to retire to enjoy it. Mick sometimes talked about his family, especially his elderly mother, who at 85 could still remember in detail, her work in the Civil Rights Movement where she met her husband, Joseph, Mick's father and got married in Rev. Adam Clayton Powell's Abyssinian Baptist Church in Harlem.

Bill shared his stories about his early life and how he was the sole survivor of his birth family, his parents having died when he was in his twenties and his only sibling, his sister, dying in a multi-vehicle accident just after getting her master's degree in psychology from Columbia. It had affected his view of life, his sense of security and his years in the military didn't help. Yet, being home was starting to calm him and make him less pessimistic.

A pull on the line made Mick sink in his heels and pull back. Bill looked at him in anticipation as his friend tugged and pulled in one direction and an unseen fish was tugging and pulling in the other. As the water ran over the rocks, the fish jumped over a large one nearby and got stuck briefly between its crevices. Then the current and the pulling of the line jarred it free as he reeled it in, a trout, a decent sized trout. Life was good.

Dora and Ellie helped Elizabeth into the car, putting her walker in the trunk. Elizabeth was happy that she had made a step up out of the wheelchair and could go out and enjoy the summer before it was over. It was a day they had decided to head up to Logansville to meet Bill and have brunch at The Greener Palm. Elizabeth had never been there and was excited that she was not stuck so near home when she should have been dining on the French Riviera or riding in a gondola in Venice. She chuckled. Well, time had a way of creating obstacles to what we dream will be our futures. For now, this was more than enough. Times like these were precious.

One Sunday when Ellie asked her grandmother if she wanted to go to church, Elizabeth was pleasantly surprised. Ellie had been baptized in the Catholic Church, but Elizabeth was pretty sure she didn't attend mass anymore. While Ellie confirmed that this was true, she added that she had been to a Catholic wedding and knew enough about the mass not to make a fool of herself and that she really wanted to take her grandmother. So they went, missing the earlier mass but making it to the noon service. Things just seemed to take longer these days. When Elizabeth asked to go to the coffee shop after mass, Ellen suggested they have lunch there. So they did. And they had a folk group that reminded Elizabeth of the Kingston Trio performing folk songs that they used to sing at the hootenannies of her youth. Ellie laughed when she heard that word and later looked it up and enjoyed some of the old music on You tube. She enjoyed the lunch and the music, and mass hadn't been bad at all. A young priest gave an interesting homily about looking at the world with love instead of fear and she found it relevant in the examples he gave. Elizabeth told her that she didn't normally go to church every Sunday and that there was no reason to start now. Ellie was relieved. There were things she would rather be doing on Sundays.

Dora had plenty of time to spend with her mom and Ellie. Sometimes when Dora visited, Ellie would go hiking on the trails of the nearby woods. She pretty much had no social life, because at 16, the teen activities weren't even close to her level of maturity or intellect, and she couldn't get involved in the singles' scene even though Waterview didn't offer much of that anyway. So she visited the library often and read books in the soft chairs in the Reading Room or under trees on the Village Green, or in her grandma's backyard and swam in the nearby lake. Her life was free of stress, but not exciting. She truly loved being with her grandmother, though, and didn't regret her decision to come down and spend time with her. She had already learned the simple truth that life was short and unpredictable. Her gap year would bring her all the excitement, social life and travel she needed before she settled down to more formal studies at Harvard.

As August drew to an end, and Labor day passed with its community picnic that they all attended, the weather showed only a hint that cooler weather was on its way. Elizabeth seemed to have less energy, so they kept the outings to a minimum and spent most of the time reading and listening to music at home. Elizabeth was accustomed to a nap after lunch that was lasting longer and longer. A half hour had stretched into an hour and sometimes she even slept two hours and never seemed to wake up refreshed. But she had blood tests that didn't show anything to be concerned about. Those were the exact words the doctor used, "Nothing to be concerned about."

Dora's schedule was flexible as she was not teaching, but spending her time doing the preliminary background research for her study of the *Needs of Veteran College Students with PTSD*. She could spend time online and in the library as needed. Later, she would be visiting college campuses and would have less freedom with her time.

September flew by and as October arrived, it brought cooler weather, an almost sudden changing of the color of the trees, and a brief burst of energy for Elizabeth. One Saturday, Dora and Ellie took her to a park and helped her do a little walking on the path by the lake with her new all-terrain walker. She struggled a bit, but was able to sit from time to time to catch her breath and enjoy the scenery. The ducks were floating on the ripples in the lake, and some man was fishing from a rock that jutted out next to the bridge where two bicycles were crossing.

Ellie handed her grandmother a bottle of water. Ever since Ellie had arrived, she made sure Elizabeth stayed hydrated. Elizabeth drank a few ounces and handed it back. She didn't have much of an appetite these days. and when they had tea together, hot or iced, Elizabeth was never able to finish her scone. She had stopped baking and making meals, and let others do that for her. When Ellie didn't cook, Dora did, or they ordered from a local deli or restaurant. At night, after dinner, the family gathered around Elizabeth's television to watch Jeopardy. Sometimes Bill was there, but often he had to stay late at the office. Especially on Thursday nights when they had late hours. Ellie was impressed by how many answers, well questions, her grandmother got right. Many times Ellie thought how nice it would have been if she had known her grandmother better before.

It was late one Saturday night when everyone had gone, leaving Ellie and Elizabeth alone. Ellie tried to get her grandmother to play a game of cards with her or maybe a board game. Elizabeth said she was too tired and would be turning in early. It was 8:30 so Ellie got her some water and helped her into the bathroom, watched her brush her teeth and then helped her into bed. She kissed her grandmother like a mother would a child, tucked her in and adjusted the lights.

"Could you open the curtains a bit/" Elizabeth asked. "I like to see the moonlight and the moon is so bright tonight."

"Sure. I hope you sleep well."

"You, too. I love you, Ellie."

"Love you, too, Grandma."

Around 1 am, just as Ellie was about to put her book down and turn off her light to go to sleep, she heard a noise in the bathroom, like a glass shattering. She went to look and found the door partly open and her grandmother on the floor unconscious. She quickly got her phone and called Dora and asked her to call 911. Her heart beating heavily, she knelt down by her grandmother and cried out her name. Nothing, but she felt her pulse and she still had one. She touched her pale face and it was warm. But Ellie was terrified and it seemed like forever before Bill and Dora arrived a few minutes before the ambulance.

CHAPTER 42

The ER was almost empty. The nurse on duty said that would probably change, but for the time being, Dora found a comfortable chairs to sit in while Elizabeth was taken to various rooms for tests. She was going in and out of consciousness, but for the most part was not lucid enough to communicate. Only at one point, on the way to the hospital in the ambulance, had she opened her eyes, stared at Dora and then uttered an incomprehensible chain of sounds and then went back into unconsciousness again. *Aphasia*, Dora whispered to herself, remembering that this trouble speaking had happened once before when she overdosed on meds due to a poorly organized weekly pill box and a less than perfect memory, but that it had gone away quickly. Ellie had had the presence of mind to round up every bottle and every pill Elizabeth was taking on a regular basis and put them in a bag for Dora to take with her. She knew exactly what her grandmother had taken. There was no overdose this time.

Dora had rushed out to get to her ride in the ambulance, but she asked Bill to check in her top desk drawer for a folder with the papers that named her as her mother's healthcare proxy and contained a DNR and her mother's signature certifying that her mother did not wish to be kept alive by artificial means if she had no chance to recover. Bill texted her that he had found it and was on his way to the hospital with it.

When Bill arrived they showed the papers to the nurse on duty who had them copied and handed the originals back to Dora. Bill sat beside her and held her hand until a doctor came in without Elizabeth.

"She has had a stroke. She is unconscious. We are doing what we can."

"How bad is it? Will she recover?" Dora asked while Bill tightened his hand on her shoulder trying to sooth her.

"We can't be sure yet. I wish I could tell you more, but we will know more in the morning. You should go home and get some sleep. We will be able to tell you much more in the morning during visiting hours. I will make sure someone comes to sit with you and give you all the details and the prognosis."

"Thank you, doctor," Bill said softly. "We will be here."

"I wish I could give you a guarantee that she will be better, but on the other hand, now is not the time to assume the worst. We most certainly will give her the best we have and we have the best right here."

"Thank you, "Dora added as she stood up trembling."

Ellie was uncomfortable being alone in her grandmother's house and didn't sleep much. She had come down to help take care off this woman she barely knew, and during the few months she had been there, had gotten to know her and love her deeply. All the birthday cards and Christmas presents Elizabeth had sent her over the years had been carefully selected, and sent with much love, but barely scratched the surface of the warmth Ellie had come to feel since she had arrived. Between childhood and the teen years and a future promising so much adventure, learning and achievement, there was this little place in time that she would always remember and cherish. Grandma, Grandma's house, Grandma's community, and even Grandma's favorite coffee shop. Now Grandma was in the hospital and it didn't look good or feel good to Ellie. Would Grandma survive? Could she even recover? Either way, the time with her grandmother would soon come to an end as she prepared for a gap year experience she anticipated as being life changing.

In the morning, Dora showed up at the hospital early and went up to see her mom as soon as they let her. Entering the room, she realized that Elizabeth was asleep so she sat down quietly and watched her, a tear running down her face. She took a deep breath and waited for someone to come in and update her on her mom's condition. She had called the hospital, but couldn't get any information. Bill had called the doctor Elizabeth went to regularly, but there was only voicemail. Dora slid her hand through the bars on the bed and held her mother's hand gently.

"I love you Mom. I am here for you. I will always be here."

There was no response at all from Elizabeth.

When breakfast arrived, it was wheeled next to Elizabeth's bed and left there. Within minutes a man entered the room.

"Good morning, I am Nurse Ed, the doctor will be in soon. He has an update on Mrs. Black's condition. Are you her daughter?"

"Yes, I am."

"Nurse Ed hesitated, as if he wanted to do something more, and then repeated, "Well, the doctor is on his way. Can I get you anything while you wait?"

"No thank you, I am fine."

Fine, she thought., She was not fine, but thank God, the doctor was on his way.

Dora let out an audible sigh, hoping it might wake her mother up, but, nothing. Her mother didn't even move, but her vitals seemed normal, blood pressure and heartbeat. The doctor appeared in the doorway. She had not met this doctor before.

"Good morning, I am doctor Abrams, the neurologist. Are you Mrs. Black's daughter?"

"Yes, I am, Dolores Victor."

The doctor pulled up a chair and looked into Dora's eyes. "Your mother has had a massive stroke. There was a lot of bleeding in her brain. She is not in a coma, but she hasn't opened her eyes. Right now, we can't tell what will happen during the next few days,.

Some degree of recovery is possible, but we just don't know yet.

"Is there anything that can be done..."

"Right now we will keep monitoring her, give her meds to prevent another stroke and wait."

"Her breakfast is here, but how can she eat?"

"You can try to feed her. Maybe she will respond to that, but she is getting nutrition through the IV right now. What you can do is talk to her. Maybe she will hear something. We will need several days to know what is happening, but we will have the physical therapist come in and get her legs and arms moving. The good news is that the brain has an innate ability to heal itself after injury, even large injuries like a massive stroke. The ability of the healthy areas of the brain to take over the functions damaged by stroke can certainly allow for recovery over time. While the recovery process takes time and a wide range of therapies, there is the possibility of recovery. But, we can't tell just yet what the prognosis is. Talk to her and tell anyone else who visits her to do that as well."

"I will do that," Dora responded. She reached out and stroked her mother's forehead whispering, "I am here mom. I love you. "

CHAPTER 43

In the days that followed, Bill, Dora, and Ellie visited the hospital together and separately. Taylor kept up with what was happening by phone. One day while sitting and holding her mother's hand, Dora was sure Elizabeth opened her eyes and the next day she was sure she heard her mother whisper," I saw your father," but no one was around to witness either and when she told Nurse Ed, he smiled and got close to Elizabeth's face and spoke to her.

"Elizabeth, good morning, can you open your eyes for me?" He tried several times. "Well, we will just keep trying. If she opens her eyes again, write it down and we can talk to the doctor. Patience is what we need now."

One bright Tuesday morning, Ellie decided to walk the two miles to the hospital. Dora was at the college library and told Ellie she would meet her in her mother's room. Bill would come at lunchtime when he had a two hour break between office hours. Ellie dressed in her comfortable jeans, a tee shirt and a light plaid shirt with a single button buttoned. She put some lip gloss on and touch of blush and it made her lips look a little pink, not like makeup, but just some healthy color. She filled her thermos with some lemon ice water, and put it and her purse in a lunchbox sized back pack. It was a gorgeous day. A few small clouds broke up the sunshine but it was a perfect fall day. As she headed through the park, where she often liked to sit and relax, she noticed that the leaves on the trees were in full color now, the reds like fire and the yellows like the sun. She walked fast because it invigorated her, and strolling was not her style. The birds were unusually loud, but their songs made her feel that this was their world and people were pretty much irrelevant to them except when they filled up the bird feeder on Grandma's front lawn.. That was okay with Ellie. She quickened her pace heading up the hill to the street where the hospital parking lot was. A bright red cardinal seemed to be flying with her, flitting from tree to tree along the way. She stopped and he stopped. She pulled out her thermos and took a swig of cold water, and he chirped at her. Then she put the water away and continued the last leg of her journey and then entered the familiar hallway, headed for the elevator and up to Room 111. When she reached the room and looked in the door, she saw nothing. There was no bed, no people, nothing. She stood still, trying to collect her thoughts, checked the number beside the door again and then turned to a nurses aid who was walking by.

"Where is my grandmother?"

The woman in the blue scrubs didn't seem to understand.

"I am looking for my grandmother, Elizabeth Black, she was in this room yesterday."

Quickly a woman at the nurses station came out from behind the counter and said, "You are her granddaughter?"

"Yes, "Ellie replied, "Has she been moved?"

"I am so sorry." The woman put her arm around Ellie and Nurse Ed came over.

"Didn't anyone tell you? I am so sorry, but your grandmother passed away this morning. Early at about 4 am. Someone should have called your family. Why don't you sit down," he pointed to a nearby chair in the hallway. "Can we get you some coffee or tea."

Ellie sat down, feeling weak and faint. "Coffee please."

"Can we call someone in your family?" the woman in the scrubs asked.

"No, I'll call."

As she took out her phone, she saw a message from Dora," Grandma passed away. I was hoping to reach you before you got to the hospital? Did I?"

Ellie texted back. "No, I am at the hospital. They just told me." Then she burst into tears.

Dora texted back. "Stay there. I will be right there."

***

Bill and Dora gathered up Ellie's things and took her to their house to stay until her mom and dad arrived for the funeral. Dora made the arrangements and the funeral was scheduled for the Friday after one night of visitation on Thursday. Taylor and Miriam arrived early Thursday morning and stayed at Elizabeth's house. It felt oddly empty and yet, they gathered there for tea and to share memories. The laughter mixed with tears. She was too young to die so soon. People were living into the 90s and she had only made it to 74, just short of her 75th birthday. Yet she had had another stroke during the night and… well, they didn't need to talk about what caused it, she had died and they had to deal with that. They had gotten in touch with Father Kelly and Mom would have a nice mass. When the day came, more people showed up than they ever expected, showing that she was known and loved by more people than they knew. After the funeral, the cortege proceeded to the cemetery where most of Elizabeth's family were buried. It was an old cemetery but well-kept. After they got back, Dora picked up some food from the deli and invited anyone who had made it to the burial to come back to Elizabeth's house. Besides the family, there were a few neighbors who also joined them. People brought food, much of it was homemade.

Tyler parked his car in the side driveway, next to the lilac bush.

"Oh my God, do you see this?" he said. Look at that!"

Dora looked as she got out of the car, and then she saw it. On the bush was one bright lilac bloom fully open and in full splendor.

"Do they normally bloom in October?" Miriam asked.

"Never," Dora answered with tears in her eyes. "I think she did this for you, Taylor, she told her brother.

"I love you, Mom," Taylor said as he looked up at the sky. "Let;s get a vase and bring it inside.

CHAPTER 44

Dora sat in her living room chair looking at the small twig with the lilac on it, the one she had brought home from her mother's garden outside the kitchen door. Her first thought was to go and place it on her mother's grave, but her brother stopped her saying, "It is her gift to you. I don't think she wants it back. Think about what you really want to do with it. I'll take a picture. We can each cherish that for the rest of our lives. Have it put on a canvas like real art. This will only give you a few days in a vase. It was enough for me to see it, to know she loved us both so very much."

The weather was getting cooler now and she searched for her favorite sweater, and found it in the back of the closet. She took it off the hanger and slipped it on before she took the lilac out of the vase. She couldn't believe this small, but whole bloom, had emerged just before cold winter weather would begin to set in. She had never seen flowers blooming on her mother's lilac bush or any other bush in mid fall. Then she put her hand in her sweater pocket and found a small card. It was the one Mrs. Bookman had given her at Paul's funeral, the one she had thought must be a Bible verse. She read it and recognized that it was from a poem by Walt Whitman.

In the dooryard fronting an old farm-house near the white-wash'd palings,

Stands the lilac-bush tall-growing with heart-

It was all so puzzling, the tree, the bush, the timely finding of this card with these selected verses of Whitman's poem. So random, so out of season like the lilac, and yet so seemingly coordinated. Staring at the small card, Dora noticed the dedication on the bottom…

In loving memory of Sol Bookman, lover of poetry, family, and life.

The sun was warming the afternoon sky and the wind had died down. Dora knew she would have only an hour or two more of daylight. She took her warm green coat out of the closet, put it on, dropping her house keys into the pocket and then, she gently took the lilac from the vase, blotting the water dripping from the stem with her sleeve. She locked the door and walked past her car, heading up the street toward All Saint's Cemetery. Unlike her mother's resting place, this was small and just beyond Waterview's main street at the end of the village about three blocks past the village square. She pulled her coat tight around as the wind swooped past her and walked, almost as if she were part of a procession, a procession of one, past the firehouse, the bakery and the garden store. A neighbor, coming out of the store with some plants in a wagon, called after her.

"Dora, I am so sorry to hear about your mom. You are in my prayers."

Dora mumbled a thank you, although she was not really aware of who the woman was. Her thoughts were focused on other things. Down past the children's playground and onto the path that led up the slight hill to All Saints. Acouple of times, she had the feeling that someone was following her but when she looked around, she saw no one. Imagination can get the best of you in times like these.

The wrought iron gates of the cemetery were open as the path widened, welcoming visitors. There was a small guardhouse and office, but Dora didn't need to go in. She knew where to go. She had known since that time Paul made her go with him on Halloween to show her the family plot and pretend the place was haunted and that they were in a horror movie.

Up the right fork, past the big oak tree and the bench beside the towering statue of the angel. Count three rows and then…there it was. Paul's grave. The marker, a small bronze plaque instead of a tombstone, had just had his name added. She stood looking at it for a few moments, tears welling up in her eyes, her throat feeling tight, the lilac dangling at her side. She let the tears fall silently. Then she knelt down beside the grave and whispered softly, "I am so sorry, Paul. There are so many things I should have said. So many…" then she stopped, not really having any more words, and feeling a little lost. She took the lilac in both hands, like a child offering a flower to its mother, and laid it on the grave just below his name, Again she felt someone's presence. An intense warmth enveloped her and she trembled just a bit. Afraid to look up, she continued to gaze through blurry eyes at Paul's name and the light purple lilac.

The feeling that someone was watching her grew stronger. She froze for a moment, becoming like the statue down the path. Her eyes fixed themselves on the grass next to the grave. Her breathing quickened. When she let her eyes slowly move to the side, she knew there was someone there. Still kneeling on the ground, she saw two feet in a pair of white sneakers, two legs in faded blue jeans and then the figure of the boy. The sun was behind him, back lighting his form in a silhouette. Still, she recognized him. She looked at him for a second and was about to speak, when she heard his voice.

"I saw him," he paused. "I saw him, Paul Hicks, him." He pointed down at the grave. "That day in the street. The day of the accident, I saw him right there and then when I blinked, he was gone."

Dora took a deep breath allowing her eyes to meet his as her body leaned back on her heels.

"I saw him." The boy's voice was barely louder than a whisper. "He was there."

"I saw him, too, right there in the street and I also blinked. He was there, with us.

"I don't think anyone would ever believe us,," the boy said sadly.

"Well, I believe you. I saw him because he was there."

"Were you his friend?" The boy crouched down next to her.

"Yes, I was his friend."

"Are you okay now?"

"Yes, I am. Are you?"

"I'm okay and I am glad you saw him, too."

" He will never be forgotten, Dora said softly."

"I won't forget him," he paused, "or you." He stood up and offered his hand to help Dora. "See you around."

Dora, just nodded and Devin nodded back and then he turned to go back down the hill. Dora watched him as he walked away, growing smaller and smaller as he left the cemetery and headed home…on foot. She took a deep breath and the crisp air made her cough a little. She looked at her watch. Time to start dinner. Bill would be home soon.

www.ingramcontent.com/pod-product-compliance
Lightning Source LLC
Chambersburg PA
CBHW061115100726
47911CB00013B/554